the
Candidate

MARGARET BOHANNON-KAPLAN

the Candidate

TATE PUBLISHING
AND ENTERPRISES, LLC

The Candidate
Copyright © 2012 by Margaret Bohannon-Kaplan. All rights reserved.

No part of this publication may be reproduced, stored in a retrieval system or transmitted in any way by any means, electronic, mechanical, photocopy, recording or otherwise without the prior permission of the author except as provided by USA copyright law.

This novel is a work of fiction. Names, descriptions, entities, and incidents included in the story are products of the author's imagination. Any resemblance to actual persons, events, and entities is entirely coincidental.

The opinions expressed by the author are not necessarily those of Tate Publishing, LLC.

Published by Tate Publishing & Enterprises, LLC
127 E. Trade Center Terrace | Mustang, Oklahoma 73064 USA
1.888.361.9473 | www.tatepublishing.com

Tate Publishing is committed to excellence in the publishing industry. The company reflects the philosophy established by the founders, based on Psalm 68:11,
"The Lord gave the word and great was the company of those who published it."

Book design copyright © 2012 by Tate Publishing, LLC. All rights reserved.
Cover design by Kenna Davis
Interior design by Jomel Pepito

Published in the United States of America
ISBN: 978-1-61862-743-8
1. Fiction / Political
2. Fiction / General
12.10.31

Prologue

I wrote five financial and public policy books in the mid-1980s and another thirteen books in the same category in the 1990s. In 2010 I couldn't stand the fact that we were discussing the same issues despite the numerous men and women that had poured thousands of hours and millions of dollars into solving, or at least warning of the problems we face today. When I was doing my share of writing about the dangers of government debt in the 1980s, Peter Grace and Milton Friedman were two of my favorite correspondents. I mention them here since neither was mentioned by Loren Dutton below.

Loren Dutton is the acknowledged Father of Financial Planning. In the foreword to *Doesn't Anyone Care About the Children?*, a Harry Singer Foundation book, Mr. Dunton showed the same frustration that I'm experiencing now:

Why Weren't We Told?

"But we were," will be my answer to the thousands of people, maybe millions who will be asking that question by the year 2000.

At the end of this century, the disgraceful and precarious fiscal situation this country is in will be too obvious for any congress or administration to ignore or cover up. It is then we'll hear the above question. Too few are asking it now!

We are told that twenty-six percent of government's income goes to pay interest on the national debt; not paying the gigantic principal—just the interest. The principal is what we're leaving to our children and grandchildren.

"Why weren't we told?" will be the question of the next decade.

I may not be around at age eighty-four, so I want to answer it now! And in just three words..."but we *were!*"

Told, that is, by those concerned and willing to speak out. Men, and one woman I know of, trying their best to alert us to the situation we were getting into and the changes it represented. *Paul Reveres* is what Gary Bauer, former Under Secretary of Education and later a policy advisor to President Reagan, called these people trying to warn us. The *Paul Reveres* of today. One might have been enough in 1776, but now it takes a number of them to alert us to the dangers and call us to action. Unfortunately, no action of any note has taken place.

The ones I have been listening to might not have a horse among them, but they have been sounding a similar clarion call of danger approaching.

First, for me there was William Simon, one time Secretary of the Treasury. His two books, *A Time for Truth* (1978) and later, *A Time for Action* (1980), galloped off the pages and into my consciousness. Simon was writing about deficits and the dangers of the growing government debt more than 15 years ago. Was it because he didn't shout it from horseback that not enough people paid serious attention to what Bill Simon was saying in his books and speeches well over 15 years ago?

Peter G. Peterson, former Secretary of Commerce wrote and talked about the danger. His first book, *Social Security: The Looming Crash,* inspired five former U.S.Treasury Secretaries to join forces. William Simon, John Connaly, Douglas Dillon and Henry Fowler showed us, and Congress, what financial irresponsibility was doing to the future of our children and grandchildren.

Still nothing happened.

In a second book, *On Borrowed Time,* written with Neil Howe, Pete Peterson tried once again to warn us. Its subtitle, *How the Growth in Government Spending Threatens America's Future,* should have roused the nation. After he got through no one could legitimately ask, "Why weren't we told?"

In 1988 I reviewed *The Coming Revolution in Social Security,* written by Haeworth Robertson, another insider. Robertson, as a former chief actuary of our Social Security system, was not someone who had looked critically at a distant department. It was his depart-ment's own inside projections which he viewed with alarm. He didn't need a horse or a clarion cry. He got our attention by letting us know if Social Security is not changed significantly it will eventually cost more than taxpayers will be willing to pay. He warned that thirteen percent of payroll in 1980 would become forty to fifty percent during the working lives of the students whose words you'll read here. We were told, but did not act.

About this time, the very articulate Governor of Colorado and now head of the *Center for Public Policy* at the University of Denver burst on the national scene saying things about the future which nobody wanted to hear.

His book, *Megatraumas... In the Year Two Thousand* bellowed warnings about where we were headed and pleaded for tough decisions. Too few listened—but we *were* told.

Finally, a courageous woman! Helen P. Rogers, a fourth generation Californian, stopped counting on politicians to solve the problems and decided to take matters into her own hands. She ran for the United States Senate as an independent and wrote an insightful book titled *Alternatives*. It was her campaign platform and proved that there were intelligent and logical alternatives to the government policies that were leading to a disappointing future for her five children—and ours too!

But with no real power behind her, the Senate was not to benefit from this brilliant woman's solutions to some of the problems this country was facing. Those were problems my generation had created by sending many undisciplined financial spendthrifts to Washington.

Paul Volker, Chairman of the Federal Reserve added his voice and said, "We are in a real sense living on borrowed money and borrowed time."

Martin L. Gross took a different approach. He followed his New York Times best seller, *The Government Racket: Washington from A-Z* with a Ballantine best seller, *A Call for Revolution*.

Oh yes, you who in ten years or less, will be asking, "Why weren't we told?" must now admit that we were told. We just weren't listening.

Maybe the tellers weren't shouting from horseback, but they deserved a far greater and more concerned audience than they received. Tell that to the children.

Loren Dunton
San Francisco, California
August 9, 1994

I used the pen name Helen P. Rogers in those days to avoid the embarrassment books such as *Social Security: An Idea Whose Time Has Passed* might generate for my husband and our sons. Helen was chosen as an inspiration. I was terrible when it came to public speaking; but if Helen Keller could lecture despite being deaf and blind, who was I to shy away from it? P stood for foot-in-the-mouth General George Patton as a warning against being too blunt. Rogers (Will Rogers) was a reminder that politics must be approached with a bit of humor and a down-to-earth attitude.

As I write in 2012, it is obvious that my efforts resulted in no more reforms than did those of my more illustrious collaborators. My hope is that there are more readers of fiction than non-fiction so a smaller percentage of a larger number of informed citizens may make the difference. Some of the then non-existent grandchildren that I referred to in the 1980s are today on the brink of adulthood. I tried in vain to rescue them from the effect of failing to take action. I implore you, the reader, to take the discussions in this series of books seriously. The Thirteen are ordinary people who discuss ideas and come up with solutions. If there are enough of you who contribute solutions your grandchildren will be the beneficiaries and you, along with those of us who earlier saw the inevitable consequence of ignorance and apathy, will be vindicated.

The first two chapters of *The Candidate* is the fiction I used in 1996 to describe a Harry Singer Foundation program to a high school class to solicit their feed back. Some students thought the program was real and asked how and where they could sign up, while others wanted to know what happened to such and such a character.

I hope you, the reader, will have the same curiosity and find these original thirteen characters worth following though the six books planned for the series, and, in the process, learn something new that may lead to fruitful discussions between you and your elected representatives, family and friends.

Margaret Bohannon-Kaplan
Carmel, California
September 17, 2012

1996
Mapleton High School

As Mr. Hoffer ushered his students up the mahogany staircase, he wondered if he had done the right thing by suggesting this meeting at Mapleton High. He loved his town and was earnest in his desire to find a way to help it solve its problems, but he dreaded what a comparison between Mapleton and Bloomfield might do to the self-esteem of his students.

He had used the self-esteem curriculum in his social studies 101A class for two semesters, before it was integrated into the self-awareness program. He knew about identity. Country, town, family, religion, race, and occupation were ingredients of self-esteem. He figured the course was initially included in the history and social studies curriculum because of the humiliation suffered by Americans of German and Japanese descent during World War II. He never really bought into the self-esteem craze, probably due to the healthy self-image of the Catholic, Jewish, Black, Hispanic, and Japanese friends with whom he had grown up. The self-awareness program at Bloomfield High had been studied over the years by other school districts, but never copied. Statistics showed an increase in vandalism and juvenile crime in Bloomfield over the same time period. As far as Mr. Hoffer was concerned it was just one more example of good intentions gone awry. Laws and programs that don't work are rarely eliminated. The education bureaucracy was no exception.

Personally, Mr. Hoffer thought self-awareness—getting in touch with one's feelings—was something society needed more of. Everything had become so impersonal—people didn't seem to care about each another, and if they did, he wondered, how would they know it? Feelings were experienced second hand. Television, movies, and the exaggeration of the tabloids allowed emotions to be exercised vicariously and nearly risk-free. Minimization of risk had become an American obsession at the end of the twentieth century.

Well, at least his students came out on top in a comparison of school buildings, he concluded as he surveyed his surroundings. He had worked hard to help pass the Bloomfield school bonds, which had built a thirty-six million dollar structure, whose clean cathedral-like lines soared as a monument to learning. It housed the finest pool, gymnasium, science, and computer labs. The huge auditorium was equipped with the latest technology. As he looked down at Mapleton High's main entrance, he felt like he was climbing the stairs of the high school he had attended twenty-five—no—it was twenty-seven years ago. His own mother had graduated from the same school in 1950, and it hadn't been new at the time. It was clear that Mapleton High was of the same era—constructed before the Second World War—maybe before the First World War. Unbelievable! Didn't the citizens of Mapleton care about their kids?

Of course they did. Mr. Hoffer mentally answered his own question. There—he had done it again—been distracted by appearances. This weakness of his had led Mr. Hoffer to expand the senior government curricula to include consumer skills. He felt intensely about the evils resulting from merchants conning consumers, and politicians conning constituents because he was so vulnerable himself. He constantly switched sides on the debate about whether growing up watching TV made young people more sophisticated or more naive. You would think it would be especially clear to him, a person dedicated to the study of the social sciences and a product of the first generation to have grown up with television. Mr. Hoffer was certain there was something different about the generation that saw birth and death in hundreds of sometimes bizarre situations, simply by switching channels, and the generations who had experienced, firsthand, the birth of farm animals and siblings and had huddled around the death bed of loved ones. How do the former distinguish reality from illusion? How do they determine the essential from what is extraneous? He had been drawn into the trap; he had judged the concern of the community and the quality of what went on at the school by observing the age of the Mapleton structure.

The uncertainty that had assailed him at the bottom of the staircase returned as he recalled why he was chaperoning five Bloomfield High School students to a meeting at Mapleton High. Mapleton students consistently were accepted at the best colleges and universities in the country. They were in demand by employers in surrounding states and openly preferred to graduates of many colleges. Mapleton High always ranked among the top in academic and sporting decathlons. Although there was no doubt Mapleton's building was old, it and the surrounding grounds were well kept, and the town itself had the lowest taxes coupled with the lowest crime rate in the nation. But the main reason he and his students had come to Mapleton today was to find out about a program they called Another Way.

As Mr. Hoffer shepherded his five students down the third floor hallway toward the assigned meeting room, he spotted his counterpart, the chair of the Mapleton High School Social Studies Department, hurrying down the hall to greet him.

"John! It's great to see you again. We're so excited about having you and your students join us for the day."

Funny how Mr. Hoffer always thought of himself as Mr. Hoffer. It was a bit strange, but nice, to hear John coming from the small, dynamic, gray-haired lady in jeans. He had known Phyllis Clarry for almost fifteen years now. She had inspired him to become a teacher. She must have given over twenty years to the profession and most of it at Mapleton. The community was lucky to have her. He had seldom encountered a teacher with so much energy. Her enthusiasm was boundless and it affected her students.

Phyllis touched his shoulder as she escorted Mr. Hoffer and his brood into the conference room. With a broad sweep of her arm she said, "We've got doughnuts and power bars, juice, milk, and coffee, of course, to keep a couple of us on our toes. Please help yourselves and then find a seat at our large, but friendly, round table. Then I'm going to have you introduce yourselves. Name tags are useful, but too impersonal."

As she poured herself a cup of coffee, Phyllis looked fondly at the Mapleton students, already spaced around the table, leaving room for the guests from Bloomfield to fill in. She kicked herself for suggesting Mapleton students not group at the table. She should have known Janet would have organized the proper set up without coaching. There I go, she thought, it must be instinctive for adults to down play the capabilities of teens. Janet was a natural organizer. It was she who had decided who would comprise the Mapleton panel. The two teachers had tentatively agreed on one student from each grade, in order to keep the group small, but representative. Phyllis had thought the class presidents would be logical choices, but Janet had argued that kids who really wanted to sell the concept of Another Way would provide the best selection pool. Just what the students had to go through to prove their salesmanship was hazy to Phyllis, but she knew only twenty names per grade were allowed in the final drawing to determine the final competitors. All of those around the table had run the gauntlet; written submittals detailing what Another Way meant to them, and orally given explanations to a series of specific questions. The Mapleton representatives knew their stuff, she acknowledged with pride.

There were thirteen places at the table—the two teachers and a representative from grades eight through twelve from each school, plus Janet, who was officially billed as Phyllis' assistant. Janet was the first person Phyllis had thought of when she agreed to John Hoffer's request for in depth information about Another Way. But Janet insisted that twelfth grade students be given the same opportunity to serve on the panel as interested students in other grades. She refused to be the only appointed representative, and so her nametag read Assistant, with no indication that she was the senior class president at Mapleton High.

As the last visiting student slipped into his seat, with a large glass of milk and three chocolate covered doughnuts, Janet began speaking, as she and Phyllis had agreed she should.

"Good morning, and welcome to Mapleton High. I'm Janet Norwood, a fellow student, and I'm here to help coordinate things and be generally helpful. Commitment is what Another Way is all about, and it's clear that everyone around this table is committed. Why else would we be gathered in a classroom on a Monday morning a full hour and a half before the school day officially begins?" Janet paused and smiled. "We have a lot to accomplish in a short time, so, even though we can read your name and grade on your tags, we'd like you to quickly introduce yourselves, and then Phyllis will take it from there."

She nodded to the small blond girl on her right.

"I'm Megan Goodwin, and I'm in the eighth grade here at Mapleton High School," she said, simply and sweetly.

"Hi. I'm Amanda Miller and I'm an eight grader too, and I'm really excited about being here. My mom is really happy because I've been driving her crazy for days and now she's expecting some relief."

Everyone laughed at the friendly, outspoken, dark girl with the lively eyes. She was thin and all legs, like a colt or young fawn. But her height and self-assurance gave a contrary impression.

She appeared to be much older than her fragile eighth-grade counterpart, who had spoken a moment earlier.

"All right! I want to wish you all a good morning and terrific day," boomed a young man, who not only made Amanda look dainty, but the six-foot-one Mr. Hoffer, who was seated to his right, appeared to be a relatively small man in comparison. "I'm Lincoln Williams, a senior here at Mapleton."

"Wow! Lincoln Williams!" exclaimed a Bloomfield boy seated at the other end of the table. He blushed and looked confused as all eyes turned to him out of turn.

"I'm sorry, I'm just crazy about basketball," he offered by way of explanation.

"No problem." John Hoffer, who was next in line, laughed. He had to admit that Lincoln was a dead ringer for the legendary Magic Johnson. One sports caster had suggested that Lincoln had the potential for a similarly illustrious career. "I'm impressed that Lincoln Williams is in the room and I'm lucky enough to be sitting next to him. I'm Mr. Hoffer, chair of Bloomfield High School's Social Studies Department, and the one whose curiosity bears the responsibility for whatever happens here today. I'm delighted that so many people wanted to participate and I congratulate those who made it." He turned, pleasantly, to his right.

"Good morning. I'm Dorothy Avila, a member of the sophomore class and I, too, want to welcome you all to Mapleton High."

Dorothy was a very attractive girl whose large violet eyes and long dark hair was reminiscent of a young Elizabeth Taylor. She had charisma and a 4.0 GPA. Her class, no doubt, would have chosen her as their representative, if they had been allowed to do so, therefore it was fitting that hers was the name that was drawn from the twenty sophomore names that were submitted. On the other hand, all of the students in the room were the cream of the crop. Only top students made it to Mapleton's final selection process.

Heads around the table nodded in Dorothy's direction and then all eyes focused, once again, on the boy who had identified himself earlier as a basketball fan. He was surprised to be included, and not altogether happy to find himself in Mapleton's conference room this morning.

"I'm Mario Lee," he said quickly, "and I'm a freshman at Bloomfield High."

Phyllis Clarry sat next to Mario, but she indicated that the attractive red head on her right should speak next.

"Good morning. I'm Lisa Wainright and delighted to have been chosen to represent the seniors at Bloomfield High at this conference today."

"Welcome," chimed a melodious voice, the more lovely because it was unexpected, since it came from the least attractive person at the table—a heavy girl with a noticeably scarred face, who had appeared plain until she spoke. Phyllis was amazed. This was one of the fifteen hundred students that attended Mapleton High School that she had never seen before.

"I'm Raeann Cotton, a relatively new-comer to Mapleton and a member of the junior class."

"I'm Harrison Davis, a sophomore at Bloomfield," offered the handsome young man seated at Raeann's right. He had closely cropped, brown hair, and glasses that accented his steel-gray eyes. Mapleton's freshman representative was next to Harrison.

"Paul Egan. I'm a ninth grader here at Mapleton High and I hope that this meeting will exceed everyone's expectations."

Bill Adams was to the right of Paul. Bill was a junior at Bloomfield High, and probably the most charismatic member of that contingent.

"Well it comes down to me then—last-at-last. Since, as students, we are constantly subjected to alphabetized lines, you'll know what I mean when I introduce myself. I'm Bill Adams and I'm honored to represent the Juniors of Bloomfield High and I expect to learn a lot here today."

"Almost last Bill. I'm Phyllis Clarry and I head the Social Studies Department here at Mapleton High School. Please call me Phyllis. I add my voice to the welcomes," she said warmly. "I sense that we are all anxious to get started, but first, I have a few introductory remarks.

"When Another Way was first proposed to the faculty at this school, the speaker was introduced as a representative from a private foundation who was trying to increase volunteerism. It was like introducing an expert on transportation, as someone who was here to give tips on bicycle riding. Volunteers are a vital part of Another Way, but not the whole. Another Way is more accurately about human energy. Not energy used by humans, but a unique form of energy.

"The human energy which concerns Another Way is tied up with the inalienable rights referenced in our U.S. Constitution. Those rights are rights to control our human energy. No outside force can make individuals love, hate, talk, or think, unless they agree. A person may be kidnapped, imprisoned, and tortured, but he still has control over his own human energy, and with control comes responsibility. Humans have the power to reason, to imagine, to learn from the past, and to change themselves and their environment. They can do more than adapt, and when they are able to freely exercise their human energy they progress—at least materially. We call it, Mempner Hext."

"What?" Amanda blurted.

Janet quickly came to Amanda's rescue: "Memp equals MMP, which stands for man's material progress, which is attributable to NR, it stands for natural resources but sounds like ner; plus Hext. The HE stands for human energy and the XT stands for times tools. Put it all together and you get Mempner Hext" Janet typed as she spoke and the words were projected on the wall behind Mario.

Man's material progress is attributed to natural resources, plus human energy, times tools.

"I don't get it. Like, what do you mean by 'natural resources'?" Amanda wore a puzzled frown.

"Natural resources are useful items occurring naturally in a locality, as opposed to being man-made," Lincoln improvised.

"But there are no natural resources without human discovery. Oil wasn't a natural resource in ancient Egypt anymore than atoms were in the 19th century, before the concept of atomic energy was developed." This time it was Paul who chimed in.

"Hold it everyone." Phyllis laughed. "Janet, Lincoln, and Paul are sharing some of the information they gleaned from the course on responsibility that Mapleton requires of all freshman. But, since we only have one day, we can't wander too far in that direction, so let me continue with my introduction so we can get to the business at hand.

"Another Way is about freeing and directing human energy. Americans have always made effective use of human energy; more than any other people, in any other place, at any other time in history. You might wonder why and how. Why? Because, as I said earlier, they were guaranteed by our Constitution, the right to exercise greater control over their lives. How? By understanding how human energy works and then by promoting those things that make it work better—more efficiently, more effectively—and restricting those things that prevent it from working.

"The point I want to get across to you, so you will have it as a back drop for everything else that you hear here today, is that human energy thrives in a free society and freedom is always accompanied by responsibility. When people act irresponsibly, freedom is diminished. In our own country, when private individuals and groups acted irresponsibly, government picked up the slack. When some families failed to care for their members, government stepped in to cover for their irresponsibility. When jobs were scarce, many employers failed to treat employees with dignity and justice, and the market couldn't compensate. The market cannot be responsible for all the value in a society.

Our Constitution expected the free market to be balanced by volunteerism, based most often on religious conviction. When that didn't work, the fall back was law. And so, laws expanded to protect the workers. When people began operating motor vehicles at dangerous speeds, or while under the influence of alcohol, society responded with more laws. Always, laws were enacted to compensate for lack of responsibility. People failed to use their human energy responsibly, failed to voluntarily abide by inner laws I like to think of as soft power. You have probably heard the expression that if men (meaning mankind, of course) were angels they would need no laws."

"So, increasing responsibility is the primary purpose of Another Way and volunteerism is a by-product?" Harrison ventured.

"Responsibility is not so much the goal," Phyllis continued, "but a necessary ingredient. The goal of Another Way is to preserve freedom, so that human energy can thrive."

"So, the ultimate goal is to nurture human energy. Right?" This line of reasoning was not alien to Harrison, and he was genuinely interested. Harrison had one brother and came from one of those rare homes with a stay-at-home mother. Religion played a large part in his home life, and those who must label would probably call him conservative. "Could we say responsibility is a secondary goal, and one which involves volunteers? And isn't it true that both responsibility and volunteerism are needed to ensure that human energy thrives?"

"That's it. I think you've got it," Phyllis laughed. "Okay then. Let's get down to business. Here's the plan. The Mapleton students sitting around the table are all involved in Another Way, in the community. You're going to get a chance to ask them whatever you want. Each student has prepared a brief presentation, with maybe a few excerpts from the paper that gained him or her entrance to this select group. We have all agreed that you may interrupt to comment, or ask questions, any time something perks your interest. Think of the presentations as icebreakers. We may not even get to them all depending on how the discussion goes. You can turn the conversation to satisfy your curiosity. However, I suggest you write down specific questions that we will answer after lunch if they fail to get addressed during the course of this morning's free-for-all." Phyllis looked around the table. "Okay? Any questions? Everybody understand?"

"Got it," said Bill cheerfully, and the other Bloomfield students murmured assent.

"All right," Phyllis addressed the Mapleton contingent. "Who wants to go first?" A few of the Mapleton students had squirmed down in their chairs, hoping to avoid eye contact with Phyllis. "Anyone?" Lincoln cleared his throat and caught her eye. With a broad smile, Phyllis nodded in his direction, and Lincoln began speaking.

"I couldn't believe it when my paper won me a place on today's panel. When I turned it in I knew it was sentimental and thought it was too personal, but it must have struck a chord. I mean, Another Way has really meant a lot to me; it has changed my life and I guess the same thing has happened to others. See," he paused. "Another Way gets you thinking about what you really value. It redefines success and wealth. Right now, in Mapleton, success comes from helping others, and wealth is meaningful work. Another Way encourages people to stand up and declare, this is who we are, and we have something to give to our country. It's not our money, but our intellect, our will, our character. I've been connected with the TVC for four years."

"What's that?" Amanda broke in. "I mean what's the TVC?"

"I was about to explain," Lincoln answered defensively. "TVC is what we call the Truly Volunteer Corp. It is a group of volunteers of all ages and abilities, individuals and organizations, working together in the community. The truly signifies that no one receives wages or salaries. Another Way is not subsidized by taxpayers like 'Points of Light' and a lot of other so-called volunteer groups in the country. Another Way depends on trade. The Another Way logo says it all."

Lincoln paused and pointed to the small ceramic lapel pin he and all of the Mapleton students were wearing. It was a white circle with a red dollar sign in the middle, with a black line across its face. "The Another Way logo has a double meaning. The dollar sign with a line through it means it is possible to do things without waiting for dollars—without waiting for grants and subsidies. We trade. It has taught me, and I think everyone that has been connected with Another Way for any length of time, to become resourceful."

"In fact, a main purpose of Another Way is to locate existing resources, in your community, your group, and even yourself, and use them more efficiently. Another Way causes everyone to become more creative," Megan added with enthusiasm.

Phyllis was impressed. Lincoln was giving his presentation, and without any self-consciousness; Megan was right in there, setting the conversational tone Phyllis had hoped to achieve. As the middle child of seven, it was not surprising that Megan got along so well with others. In fact, she was rumored to be just about every eight grader's best friend—boy and girl.

"Right." Lincoln didn't miss a beat. "The logo also signifies that there are things in life that matter more than dollars."

Amanda interrupted a second time: "Can you prove anything matters more than dollars? People I know are cynical—especially kids. They assume adults only do things for money. They don't believe anyone cares enough about anything to give selflessly."

Paul piped up: "Lots of people assume nobody will do anything without getting paid and, yet, we polled Mapleton residents and discovered that most people didn't want anything for themselves from volunteering, besides the knowledge that they were making a positive difference in the community."

"Okay. Here's my problem." Harrison was intrigued. "If grants are available, then why would anyone want to participate in new programs without funding? Why pass up free money?" Actually, Harrison was playing the Devil's Advocate. He didn't believe there was such a thing as free money.

Mario entered the conversation for the first time: "I agree with Harrison's point. First of all, I don't think it's possible to do anything without money, and if you could, what's the point?"

"Yeah," Harrison added. "Why make do without money? At the very least, money makes everything easier."

"Almost everything. Except, like Amanda was saying, it's hard to gain the trust and the cooperation of the people social programs are intended to reach if they think the only reason you are helping is for the money. We're talking 'community values' here." Lisa was hooked.

Mario picked up where he had left off: "Yeah, but if a community were to turn down federal and state subsidies, those subsidies would just be distributed to other communities."

"No way!" Amanda was incensed. "That's not fair. Why would any community scrimp and save unless they could keep the savings and use them for something it really wants and couldn't afford otherwise? The volunteers would be crazy to do the work and have another community capitalize on their efforts. No way!"

"Yes, way! And it may not be fair, but it's true," Mario countered. Mario lived in a crime-ridden section of Chinatown and commuted to Bloomfield High, where gangs exercised less control than they did in his own neighborhood. He was a dedicated student, but the commute, coupled with an after school job in his family's restaurant, afforded him little time to socialize with his peers.

"Well, if you're right and it's true," Amanda said cautiously. "Then it would be stupid to turn down money, even for the sake of values, while another community gets the stuff done easily, and probably better, using dollars. Anyway, what's the big deal? If no dollars is what Another Way is about, I really can't see it."

"I don't think you have to worry about anyone turning down subsidies or trying to get along without grants," said Mr. Hoffer. "Just imagine how many people have a vested interest in keeping grant money flowing? There are thousands of consultants, and people who hold seminars, write books, and advise active nonprofits where and how to get money to run their programs. There are even more government employees and employees of grant-making institutions whose livelihoods depends on reading and evaluating proposals. There's no way that's going to change; at least no easy way. There's got to be a darn good reason to change, and if you come up with one, it won't be easy to sell."

"We can't continue business, as usual, just because it's easier," Lincoln responded. "The result would be three things we don't want. One, less successful programs because participants don't respond. Why don't they respond? Because they don't believe that paid volunteers really care. Two, an increase in the national debt. Why? Because dollars needed to pay down the debt are diverted to pay for costly social programs. The more than three hundred and sixty-five billion dollars in annual interest on past spending, buys nothing. Cutting annual deficits doesn't begin to solve the financial calamity awaiting our generation. Three, a good reason not to change our value system. How's that? Because those who care enough to give freely would be chumps not to take money offered by the government—just what Harrison and Mario said. The chump factor is a darn good reason not to change."

Lisa had declared math as her probable major on her college applications. She always paid strict attention to numbers. "I hate to say this," she reluctantly volunteered, "But I think your figures concerning the deficit are wrong."

"I'm talking about debt, not deficit. A deficit is the difference between outgo and income, and the government is still spending more than it brings in. Years of deficit spending has resulted in interest payments of over a billion dollars a day on our national debt," Lincoln countered.

"Can you imagine what three hundred and sixty-five, separate, American communities could do with a billion dollars every year? Just think; for what it costs to carry our national debt, we could give a billion dollars to a different community every single day, without raising taxes. Or a million dollars to a thousand communities every day, or to 365,000 communities a year." Lisa was excited.

"There are fewer than twenty thousand incorporated communities in the entire country," Janet interjected. She had recently uncovered that fact in the 1996 Statistical Abstract of the United States, when researching her term paper for history.

"Okay, then," Lisa retorted. She was having such a good time manipulating figures in her head that she had forgotten her mistake had started this turn in the discussion. "Every single community in the United States, would get just under twenty million a year, or better, than one and a half million dollars a month. Incredible!"

"So what can we do to make changes?" Amanda asked.

"We can reverse the three outcomes we don't want by focusing on incentives and disincentives. We have started doing that here in Mapleton," Dorothy offered.

"So, you are trying to reverse the three things you don't want by concentrating on the third: the chump factor—the disincentive to turning down subsidies," Bill began slowly. "And I assume you mean subsidies from outside your community, because they would be called resources if they came from within the community—right?"

"Right!" Lincoln felt like progress was being made. "When I became involved with AW my freshman year, we weren't actually turning down subsidies, but we stretched them so we could sometimes launch five or six community projects, with the subsidy meant for one." Lincoln looked straight at Bill as he said, "We think the people in a community should use their own resources. Right now, Mapleton residents fund projects in other communities via federal taxes, and many of those projects in other communities are wasteful. Some communities are better than others at budgeting and get more bang for the buck. We can't control that. The goal is to keep more of our paychecks in Mapleton where, if we become more resourceful and more efficient, we will reap the benefits. We would like all Americans to have the same opportunity. Consequences are the best incentives and disincentives. Before our efforts were worthless or were, at best, diluted."

"Before what?" Bill asked.

"Before our state started giving refunds to local communities without strings," Lincoln explained.

"Refunding what?" Bill came back.

"Refunding the actual percentage earmarked for social programs, of the dollars paid by Mapleton residents in both federal and states taxes," Lincoln answered.

"I don't think states can refund the tax dollars you pay to the federal government," Lisa said.

"Oh, but they can if they want to. When the federal government sends dollars back to the states, as it has been doing lately, some states keep tight rein on their local governments, controlling them by disbursing those dollars on the state's terms, while others, like our state, continue the power meltdown by parceling dollars, without mandates and stipulations; no strings" Lincoln said. "If federal and state governments want to solve problems they have to step aside, they have to untangle the web of regulations, waiver-by-waiver; one small step at a time. The time is right for Regflex."

"What is Regflex?" This time it was Harrison who couldn't control his curiosity.

"The Labor Department has Workflex and the Department of Education has Edflex— programs that give states the ability to focus federal money where they think the dollars can do the most good. Regflex is flexibility, when it comes to government regulations. It is a product of a growing trend to bypass the lengthy legislative process of reform and use executive power to give localities increased authority and flexibility. The Clinton Administration was willing to approve all reasonable waiver requests. Regflex is simply an attempt to extend waivers. The National Performance Review (started by the Bush administration) believes the federal government should keep out of the way of anyone who is working hard and honestly to accomplish a job. The idea is to give local agencies the authority to put aside rules and regulations that can be shown as counterproductive to public goals," Lincoln finished.

"That's right," said Mr. Hoffer. "For instance, the Environmental Protection Agency wants to establish performance partnership agreements that offer states freedom to mingle money and duck red tape in return for agreements on performance, with respect to a state's overall environmental quality."

"The point," Lincoln stressed, "is when a community regains control of its own resources, any stretching of those resources will result in tangible—" Lincoln was cut off in mid-sentence this time.

"The people achieving the savings get to keep the savings!" Amanda sang out. Amanda was boisterous and free of inhibitions. She was genuinely interested in just about everyone and everything and was as comfortable in the school setting as she was in her own home. Little wonder, since both her parents were teachers and crazy about children. They had planned a large family, but, unfortunately, Amanda was their only child.

Amanda irritated Lincoln. Mapleton's coach was working with him to increase his patience on the basketball court and he could see the flaw was spilling over into other facets of his life. Good grief, he reminded himself, she is only in the eighth grade. He should have been so bright at her age!

"Exactly." He attempted a smile in Amanda's direction.

"Okay," said Harrison. "But why take dollars from local communities in the first place? If the best of all possible worlds is to have those dollars come back without strings, why not simplify the process and not have local governments pay federal taxes in the first place."

"Excuse Me! Is anybody home?" Amanda was on a roll. "You can't run the country without taxes. Who is paying for the interstate highways, the military, the court system—all those things that benefit the entire country?"

"So, don't take me so literally," Harrison retorted. "Let me rephrase. Why should local communities pay that portion of their federal tax obligation that is earmarked for social programs when it is returned to them eventually?" He turned toward Amanda. "Is that better?"

"Sorry. I guess I came on pretty strong. I just got excited," Amanda apologized.

"It is confusing," Dorothy said in a conciliatory tone. "What you're suggesting is that the federal government reduce our taxes. That is suggested in every presidential election. It is the goal, but it won't happen until local governments can show they can, and will, take care of their citizens, using local resources. That just proves what we have been saying about values. Americans value people and are, for the most part, compassionate. They will never stand for hungry and sick people sleeping in doorways and on park benches. Taxes will continue to rise in an effort to curtail social problems until communities prove there is another way—a better, more cost effective, and compassionate way to handle the problems."

"Yeah, another way. Another way that doesn't depend on the dollars of people who reside outside the local community. Another Way. I got it! Pretty good. I see where the name comes from," murmured Amanda. "*Another Way.*"

"Under our Constitution the federal government is responsible for the general welfare of all its citizens—plain and simple! I remember the president saying, recently, that if Congress really cares about social problems they should prove it by giving him the money needed to enforce the regulations already on the books, and to fund programs that could make a difference." Lisa said.

Lisa, as a senior, felt embarrassed to ask—especially when Amanda, an eighth grader who had just declared she got it—but she wanted to understand, and she didn't.

"My understanding is that tax dollars from all communities throughout the nation had to be pooled precisely because not all local communities treated their needy residents with compassion. I thought we all agreed that that was the reason the federal government took over the role. Federal programs were a response to need and a reflection of American values—American caring. It seems to me Another Way takes a step backwards by leaving social problems solely to local residents."

"Yeah. That's what Phyllis was telling us earlier. Government mandates are a reflection of the irresponsibility of the past," Bill added.

"That's why a track record has to be established; a track record of compassion and competence before taxes can be reduced. That's what Another Way is about," Dorothy said earnestly.

"It's a matter of understanding human nature," said Paul. "*We're all in this together*, doesn't work, if forced. If people are given no choice, they resent it. Such an approach fosters a *why should I bother* attitude. No one wants to be prudent so someone else can waste the fruits of their endeavors."

"You're basically saying people are selfish," Mario declared. "So what else is new?"

"No, No, No—not at all! In fact, Paul's point is exactly the opposite. Polls conducted as part of the Another Way project have shown that if ordinary people stop and ask themselves what they truly value, many find out it is community, human relationships, and the feeling of helping someone else. Those things are valued as a close second to family relationships and religion. So the point is that it's not so much that our values need to change, but they need an environment that encourages their expression." Lincoln wished he could make them understand.

Lincoln was an all-star basketball player, a local celebrity. Everyone, especially his mother, expected him to become a pro—that's how kids from the project made it. But he loved to debate; the art of persuasion was the skill he wanted to master. A keen mind resided inside his handsome seven-foot frame. He believed he had a vocation to use law as a vehicle to effect social change. His broad smile and warm personality made political office a viable option sometime in the future.

"Under our present mandated system, people aren't allowed to respond to those values because they don't even get a chance to acknowledge their existence. They are supplanted by anger and resentment at being forced to help someone else."

"People feel they are being taken advantage of," said Harrison.

That's better, Lincoln thought. "Exactly," he said. "When dollars are wrenched from people who have worked hard, have been frugal, and have their own lives together, and those dollars are given to those who have squandered their assets, or not yet mastered the art of living, and those dollars are, in turn, squandered on things their original owners would consider extravagant and wasteful; that is a definite disincentive."

"Okay. Okay," Harrison confidently launched into a summation: "It's not values that need to change, it's just that people need to ask themselves a few questions to discover, maybe rediscover, them. The problem is our political structure stifles the expression of those values."

Lisa still looked confused. "I had a question when Mr. Hoffer was talking about grant making institutions," she said. "Last year I worked on a grant proposal seeking funds to start up a shelter for runaways in Bloomfield. During my research I learned that by law, billions of dollars have to be distributed by nonprofit, public and private agencies every year. I'm not clear how grantmakers fit into the Another Way concept of trade."

"Janet, why don't you take this one?" Phyllis nodded to the girl at the other end of the table, who alternately shifted her attention between a small tape recorder on her right and the laptop in front of her. She was purposely trying to stay out of the discussion. After all, Lincoln was the twelfth grade representative from Mapleton; her role was administrative aid. But she knew Phyllis was right to draw her into the conversation at this point because she had worked hard the past two years developing Mapleton's fledgling Another Way trading program.

"Are you familiar with trading stamps?" When Lisa shook her head, Janet appealed to Mr. Hoffer, "Probably Mr. Hoffer knows what I'm talking about," and Mr. Hoffer responded.

"There still might be a few around, but they were extremely popular twenty or thirty years ago. Grocery and other retail stores gave stamps with your receipt at the check-out counter, based on the amount of your purchase. These stamps were pasted in books and redeemed for merchandise, trips, and all sorts of things. The greater the number of stamps collected, the better the choices. Blue Chip and S & H green stamps were two companies that printed the stamps, sold them to merchants, and administered the programs," Mr. Hoffer concluded.

"Airlines do stuff like that now. You get redeemable points for so many miles flown," Bill said.

"And credit and bank cards offer premiums for purchases charged to their cards, and you redeem tickets won in arcades for prizes," Paul added.

"Well, we have the Another Way Dream Machine in Mapleton—it is administered by students in a classroom situation with oversight by the volunteer center. I worked on getting local grantmakers to translate grant dollars into merchandise and services, which we listed on our Dream Machine. Others worked to attract national grantmakers. Still others looked for brand new resources in our business community and asked them, and individuals who would normally give dollars to charities, to list goods and services on the Another Way Dream Machine. Money is about the only thing that cannot be listed as a reward on the Dream Machine.

"Paul mentioned the polls we took in Mapleton that found that more than half those polled didn't want anything tangible for their volunteer efforts. They were anxious to trade their time and effort just for the opportunity to make a difference. People who don't want anything for themselves can always choose something for other family members, their school, church, neighborhood, or a nonprofit. They can combine credits. In fact, recently, a church ended up pooling the credits of their parishioners and redeemed enough material and professional carpenter skills for an addition to their Sunday school. Before the Dream Machine they would have spent hours in vain searching for a grant, or taking out a loan, and spending their time raising the money to pay back the loan with rummage and bake sales. Now, they can spend that energy improving the community. The building materials and craftsman were listed on the Dream Machine and funded by a grantmaker who, in the old days, would have written a check for far more than the cost of materials and what little professional labor was needed."

Bill was confused. "Why would the grantmaker have written a check for more than was needed?"

"Grant seekers inevitably request more than is needed to cover administrative costs and the unexpected. It's the way it's done. You add a little here and there just to make sure you don't have the added stress of pinching dollars. It's a different story when you have a job to do and a finite amount of your own money. In that case, you might end up supplementing the money you have with your own labor, the labor of your friends, and maybe substituting some used, or less expensive, material, in order to stretch your resources. The church got most of its labor from its own members and even the professionals were members of the congregation. You save a lot when you only need a few professionals to guide the amateurs. And by the way, if you don't believe that people pad requests, just ask those people who depend on annual grants to keep their programs going."

"I can attest to that," Harrison volunteered. "My father counts on annual research grants to fund his work at the university. He often talks about the waste that goes on in the department. Everyone knows they can get along with far less money, but nobody would ever dream of asking for less. In fact, a couple of years ago they threw a gigantic party just to use up all the funds before the end of the year. Their budget would have been cut if they hadn't spent all that was allocated. There's no incentive to save."

"I think I'm hearing the chump factor again," said Paul

"That's right," Janet agreed. "One more thing. In the old days, the grantmaker would have made its funding choice from the hundreds of proposals submitted, on the basis of a well written business plan."

"In other words, grants went to the best presenters—those who were skilled at writing proposals," Lisa surmised.

"Exactly," Janet said. "Grantmakers are getting tired of funding what doesn't work. They are ready for results. They want more bang for their bucks and that's what we get when we leverage our resources and use trades instead of dollar subsidies. By acting as a redeemer of credits, the grantmaker is funding programs based on the proven support of people who cared enough to contribute upfront—their time, labor, and materials—whatever it took to gather enough redeemable credits. In effect, they earn the project."

"You said something about Problem Solvers a couple of minutes ago. Could you explain what that is?" Mario requested.

"It's a school-based club that attempts to solve problems in the community. High school kids make recommendations based on research. At Mapleton High, the Problem Solvers cooperate and coordinate with the teachers involved in community-based learning, which is something somebody else will tell you about before the day is over, I'm sure. But I'll give you a brief rundown on a couple of last year's Problem Solver projects.

"Problem Solvers discovered that with the same money it cost to post temporary signs and to knock on doors to inform residents of an annual cleaning, street sweepers in Mapleton could put a regular schedule on permanent signs and provide regular monthly cleanings.

"One of our elementary schools wanted an all-day kindergarten but there was no room at the school and no money to pay a full-day kindergarten teacher in their budget. Parents and teachers at the school met, and the best they could come up with was applying for federal funds. That pot had already been emptied, so they decided to let the Problem Solvers have a go at it. We did a lot of interviewing and discovered a fixable. Working mothers of kindergartners had to leave work in the middle of the day to pick up children at noon and schlep them to daycare across town. We got input from all the people affected: neighbors, parents, employers, and groups that care about giving kids a good start in education. We came up with several recommendations."

"Like what?" Mario pressed.

"Like having the affected employers donate to the redemption catalog and recruiting volunteer drivers; or getting volunteers to remodel extra space in a retirement complex in the neighborhood for a daycare so the morning kindergartners wouldn't need to be driven across town, but could interact with the older people in the neighborhood." Janet paused to catch her breath. "We discovered many of these older residents were eager to assume grandparent roles to assist the graduate students. Others jumped at the hands-on educational experience involved in working with kids near their own facility."

"What happened?" asked Bill.

"The recommendations were made last year and long range plans are being worked out, involving the university, the business community, and the retirement complex, and, of course, the school. Meanwhile, mothers do not have to leave their jobs because the various employers rented a van and the kids are being chauffeured to their multiple afternoon destinations by volunteers from Mapleton Cares, an Another Way organization."

Janet realized she had wandered from her subject, trading, but decided to add one more thing. "Problem Solvers has a talk show on Mapleton's most popular radio station. There just happens to be five schools involved in Problem Solvers, this year, so each school hosts a show one day a week, Monday through Friday. Callers suggest problems and the students choose which to work on for the following the week. Depending on the quality of the problems and number of students available to research, several problems may be acquiring solutions at the same time. Students suggest possible solutions on the air with their friends, family and neighbors glued to the radio. We have a virtual media blitz solving community problems here in Mapleton."

"Fantastic!" Lisa was impressed, and a little envious. She didn't realize it, but she was really helping Janet get back on track when she said, "But I would really like some examples of actual trades."

Janet took a moment to reflect and said, "Okay. Probably in Bloomfield, when people want to get an operation for a sick child, or send kids to camp, they solicit through the mail, use the media, or go door to door making compassionate appeals. In Mapleton, instead of solicitors, traders might offer to perform bookkeeping or other office tasks, gardening, hauling, providing entertainment, or even operate a daycare center in exchange for something for a group of kids."

"If you go door to door, some people might let you cut their lawn, but they won't have an operation to hand you in return." Bill laughed. "You must collect checks, or points, or something, in order to pay for the operation. Unless, of course, a surgeon answers the door and you offer to build him a garage in exchange for an operation," he joked.

Janet agreed. "As Bill says, if you and your friends cut enough lawns, you'd eventually collect enough community currency to choose an operation via the Dream Machine. You would look under health care and find a list of grantmaking nonprofits whose mission includes health-related projects. You would work out the details of a trade with the grantmaker before starting any grass-cutting campaign."

"In the final analysis," Bill said, "the grantmaker would foot the bill instead of cutting you a check."

"Something like that," Janet replied. "It's a mind, or should I say a value-setting exercise, with economic considerations. In this example, the grantmaker might be able to make a better deal with the hospital and surgeon, than the patient could and, thereby, stretch resources."

"Now what about the homeowner who had his lawn cut; I thought he was supposed to trade something of value," Lisa persisted. "The way I see it there are no recipients, but everyone is a giver. Could this be true?"

"Well, you're right that there are no recipients, or rather, everyone is both a recipient and a giver. We prefer to call everybody a trader. You may think being so picky about words is silly, but there is proof that words change minds. Traders are equals; givers and recipients aren't. There is a difference between being entitled to something through no personal effort and earning. The person who agreed to have his lawn mowed could trade, on the spot, or make a future commitment." Janet paused. "Everyone in a community has something to contribute. That belief is a cornerstone of Another Way. Volunteers are encouraged to seek out ways to help others discover and share their talents, to encourage those who benefit from good deeds, to pass a good deed on to the next guy."

"Habitat for Humanity does that right now in Bloomfield," Mario interjected. "People who get help building their house, then help other people build theirs."

"That's the idea," Janet said. "I was in a group my sophomore year that kept a wish list of the good deeds that needed doing in the community. As members of our group became aware of new needs, the list was updated. All volunteers are expected to act as matchmakers—matchmakers, not grantmakers. We don't just identify 'need,' we all keep a sharp eye out for potential solutions and volunteers. For instance, the person whose lawn you cut might be a lonely older person who loves to bake. You tell her about a harried young mother in another house down the street who barely has time to breathe. Can you see the possibilities?"

"You match the two. And her 'pass it on' might not be just bread or cookies," she said looking at Paul and Mario who were licking their lips and massaging their tummies, "She might read or play games with the children so the mother can keep a doctor's appointment or shop in peace or something," Megan added.

"Fine," Lisa said, "but matches like that are already going on in Bloomfield and all over the country."

"But, in fewer numbers and without the cost efficiencies," Janet replied. "Remember, Another Way, is a mobilization of existing resources. It's a way to enhance the good things already going on."

"Good job, Janet. We have to talk about existing resources before we go any further. I know one of you has that presentation." Phyllis looked around the table expectantly.

Raeann cleared her throat as Janet began projecting the charts she had called up on her laptop while Phyllis was speaking. Raeann had composed them using PowerPoint software.

Raeann had recently arrived in Mapleton from Texas. She lived with her mother and younger brother. Her mother ran a desktop publishing and web creation and management business from her home. Raeann knew just about everything there was to know about computers. When her peers were playing with blocks, she was pounding on outdated computers that were relatively worthless, even as trade-ins. In the six months she had been at Mapleton High she had upgraded the school's home page and added all kinds of useful and highly technical features to Another Way's computer databases. She practically lived at the computer lab where she was highly respected. Two years ago, she had been critically injured in the automobile accident that accounted for her scarred face. Despite her best efforts, she was unable to withdraw from people. She was in constant demand, due to her ability as a computer programmer and expertise with the Internet. She soon came to realize that people looked beyond her appearance to what she did, and who she was. She knew she had learned a valuable lesson, despite herself. She felt sorry for all the people she knew who spent far too much time working on, and worrying about, their physical appearance, and too little time and energy developing their character and abilities.

"You will each have a more detailed copy of the organization charts to take with you. I'll go through my personal experience as a newcomer, and then let you ask questions. How's that?" Raeann asked.

"Sounds great," Mr. Hoffer answered for the Bloomfield contingent.

"I've been at Mapleton two semesters. I belong to Helping Hands through my church, and also to Problem Solvers through school." She held up her jacket where two lapel pins were displayed in addition to the Another Way, logo every Mapleton student wore. One lapel pin was a school house, with Mapleton HS in black letters, and the other was a green hand with gold trim, and Helping Hands in white letters.

"Helping Hands affiliates with organizations that work with the elderly, and because there are, occasionally, young kids at its shelters, it exchanges ideas with those organizations that work with young children and teens, as well as the poverty groups.

"Anyone can belong to an organization by donating only a small amount of time on only one occasion. For example, you might have an hour of time and want to make good use of it for no particular reason, or maybe to honor something or someone. Nonprofits in Mapleton offer what they call celebration opportunities—one-shot good deeds that can be done on your birthday, anniversary, or as a thanksgiving for recovery from illness, for a new job, birth of a baby, and so forth," Raeann concluded.

"In Bloomfield," Mario said, "community service is thought of as a punishment. If kids—and even adults sometimes—get into trouble, they can work it off. Community service is not exactly prestigious."

"Mapleton encountered the same problem, so courts no longer offer community service as an option for juveniles or adults guilty of misdemeanors," Dorothy said. "To make community service prestigious, Mapleton annually offers hundreds of awards at an elaborate ceremony. And that's in addition to community currency."

"Community currency? What's that?" Lisa asked.

"Janet. Could you give me one of those handouts? The community currency one, please. I don't think we used them all for the Bloomfield take-home folders. Try the third shelf." Raeann pointed to the rear of the room. "Thanks," she said as Janet passed her the handout.[2]

Addressing the group, Raeann smiled and said, "You'll each have your own copy to go over later at your leisure. I don't expect you to get it all the first time you read it. You'll find a couple illustrations there. The first is a family that spends five hours volunteering together. The mother is over twenty so her basic per hour rate is ten community dollars, so she makes fifty community dollars. The basic rate for her sixteen year old daughter is eight community dollars so she makes forty community dollars. The son who is not quite eleven, is stuck making the basic rate of five community dollars so he makes twenty-five community dollars. These three are all outside working in the garden. The father has twenty-two years experience as a tax attorney. He is inside going over the books in order to advise the accountant about an unusual situation. His basic hourly rate as an adult over twenty is the same as his wife's basic rate; that is ten community dollars, and that would be it if he were doing gardening. However, he is working in his professional capacity with twenty plus years of experience and so adds forty community dollars to the basic rate of ten and he earns fifty community dollars per hour times five hours equals two hundred fifty community dollars."

"That's not fair," Amanda and Paul announced at the same time and were ignored.

"We got it," Lisa volunteered for the Bloomfield group, although a couple of the contingent looked a little confused.

"Good. Just remember, not all volunteer hours are equal, so that's why there's an exchange rate." Raeann addressed Amanda and Paul, "Professionals are too expensive for most non-profits because they are in short supply. That's why hefty incentives are needed.

"The second illustration is a lot easier. It's about a fourth grade class that brought pets to visit elderly people and explains that there are a lot of things they could have traded with these people. The main point is that when a class performs or participates in the same project, they don't receive community dollars as individuals. Also the exchange rate for community dollars differs per grade."

Amanda pointed to Megan, then herself, and asked, "How many community dollars for a visit from kids like us?"

Raeann directed an uncomfortable look in Phyllis' direction, and Phyllis understood Raeann's hesitation and took over. "It's apparent that the schools Marta was working with started high school in the ninth grade so I'm afraid you and Megan would fall into the 5th through 8th grades category in the illustration. However, the beauty of the Another Way program is that it can be adapted in numerous ways to any community. We changed it in Mapleton and if you adopted the program you would probably want the 8th grade included with the rest of the students at

Bloomfield high. In that case your class would be credited with one hundred twenty dollars."

Phyllis sat down and Amanda beamed and immediately posed a second question.

"What if only part of the class wants to do something together. Does it matter how many volunteer?"

"Good question, Amanda. I almost forgot to point out that any group of at least twelve –any age—can acquire community dollars by doing something as a group." Raeann smiled. "It can be a church group or men or women's group."

Amanda pressed. "No special number then,"

"One group can have more, but no less than twelve individuals of any age and must include at least one adult".

"A lot of people could probably acquire more community dollars volunteering as individuals, like the family illustration," Harrison observed.

"That's right. If they agreed ahead they could put more community dollars toward the same reward. But remember it won't work if the individuals are cast members in a play or any performance. There are more guidelines in the handout. As Phyllis explained, every community can add and subtract from the general outline proposed by Another Way."

"Reminds me of a franchise. McDonalds restaurants are pretty much standardized but we know which one is better than another in Bloomfield." Everyone laughed at Mario's illustration, but he had more to say. "Our restaurant could have joined the China World franchise but my dad wanted more flexibility. We have a much larger selection on our menu and are free to experiment with new recipes."

Raeann was impressed and made up her mind to take the family to Mario's restaurant. "Sounds good, Mario. What's the name of your restaurant?"

"Lee's Exceptional Chinese." Mario was blushing now, his shyness was back but didn't prevent him from adding, "It's in the Bloomfield-Mapleton phonebook and we have 'take out' too."

Raeann smiled and noted several people making notes as she glanced around the table before asking, "Any questions about something other than community dollars and Chinese restaurants?"

"How do you know which group to join?" Bill wondered aloud.

"I've never been in a sorority," Raeann began, "but when I described the biannual Mapleton Rush to my mom, she said it sounded just like the rush sororities and fraternities stage to recruit members on college campuses. For two weeks, nonprofits are allowed to state their case for fifteen minutes at the end of each class. There are displays in the lunchroom with handouts and kiosks showing videos. Speakers are featured in the gym, where a free lunch can be picked up at the door. It's a lot like a fair with lots of exhibits on display, Monday through Friday, for two weeks; actually ten days. The idea is to get students to commit. There are sign up sheets and trial volunteer packages. Last semester, some nonprofits offered variety packs, complete with a party, or fun activity after each event."

"I can understand Red Cross, Habitat for Humanity, Salvation Army, Big Brothers and all of those, but do churches and public agencies like social service, park, and police departments also recruit at rushes?" Bill asked.

"Churches don't recruit, but programs which originate in churches might recruit volunteers. For instance, Red Brick Road is a program sponsored by Mapleton Presbyterian Church. Members do all kinds of things to make the lives of sick children a little happier. They display material during rushes and people who want to help can join without belonging to the church. Helping Hands originated at St. John's Episcopal Church. Now, if you happen to be an acolyte, or sing in the church choir, that's great, but it's not Another Way."

"A large component of Another Way is the concept of leverage, which I don't think we've discussed yet," Raeann addressed Phyllis. "Is it okay to bring it up now?"

"Absolutely," Phyllis answered encouragingly.

"Well," Raeann began, "leverage means stretching existing resources. Social workers know which families need assistance but simply don't have the time, or resources, to do what they would like to do. A harried social worker willing to supervise five college students, each in charge of ten high school volunteers, who, in turn, might channel the enthusiasm and optimism of a few elementary school volunteers, would leverage the time and energy of one by fifty, and that's not even counting the youngest group.

"Another example of leverage is sharing computer resources. In Mapleton, for example, we have older TVC members using computer rooms at Boys and Girls Clubs in the mornings, when the kids are in school; and, as a trade, they act as tutors in the afternoons, familiarizing kids with a variety of software programs. Sixteen computers used to sit idle until two o'clock, and then they were used only for games. Now, the kids are learning skills and are able to gain experience for job resumes by volunteering in the Boys and Girls Club office, or doing projects for other local nonprofits."

"That's great!" Bill enthused.

"Okay, here's something I still don't understand," Amanda began. "What could anyone possibly trade if they're sick and old? Or, how about the homeless? I guess I still don't get this trade idea."

Raeann plunged in. "The trade possibilities are limitless! For example, one bedridden patient in a nursing home traded a story from his past to my brother. My brother's fourth grade class put on a show at a nursing home and, in trade, they interviewed the patients as part of a research paper. In the classroom, each student had thought of three questions to ask in trade."

"Great idea!" said Mario. "I bet they learned a lot more than they would have just reading about recent history in a book."

"Not only that, the older people loved the attention. The kids were so enthusiastic that the older residents felt they had really made a contribution."

"Sounds like win-win!" observed Harrison.

"Some of the options depend on the health of the older person," Raeann continued. "Kids, especially the young ones, often need chaperones. Sometimes retired people take a young person fishing, or to a golf course; they teach skills like carpentry, electrical work, plumbing, painting or share hobbies like the fishing and golf I just mentioned."

"The police say that just having older people sitting on park benches has kept drug dealers out of Mapleton's Kennedy Park," Paul interjected.

"Just being there—just sitting in a recreation or common room, providing a friendly lap in a rocking chair. A consistent presence is valuable when both parents are working," Raeann added. "It's nice but not necessary to be able to read stories, play cards and board games."

Phyllis entered the conversation. "Just keep in mind that it is possible to be affiliated with Another Way, even though you were initially the recipient, not the instigator, of a good deed. Remember that Janet was explaining earlier that everyone is a trader. Recipient, beneficiary, giver, donor—in a trade situation those terms are meaningless. Young people might go into a nursing home to distribute fruit baskets and end up hearing stories and being treated to an old fashioned musical performed by the residents.

"Also, remember Janet told us that finding the potential in other people is part of what TVC members are encouraged to do. It's really true that everyone has something to give."

"I just wanted to add one more thing to the list of trades. The Problem Solvers at Mapleton High compiled a list of questions

Paul was ecstatic, from what he chose to interpret as praise from Raeann, but he thought he managed to reply coolly: "I don't have time for scouting this year, what with computer projects and all, but last year? Yeah. Some of us decided what community projects we were going to do at the beginning of the school year. We basically planned activities so that we would participate in three organizations and get the flavor of a variety of programs. We ended up winning awards in three categories."

"Is there a purpose for all the awards and lapel pins, beyond appearances? I mean suppose you're the kind of person who doesn't get excited over wearing symbols? I know lots of people like that; in fact I'm one of them," Lisa admitted.

Phyllis responded: "I suppose awards and pins are a matter of taste. There's no reason you have to wear them, although they are a witness of your commitment, and seeing them might inspire others.

"The badges, you haven't heard about, are earned, like scouting badges, by fulfilling a set of requirements. These badges signify an objective competency. In Mapleton we have access to software, which uses artificial intelligence to evaluate the performance required to qualify for some Another Way awards. It provides help where needed until a score signifying an objective level of mastery is achieved. In addition to the computer evaluation, Volunteer Corps members must have participated in activities and submit written recommendations from beneficiaries, co-workers, and nonprofit leaders.

"Badges may be earned for business skills, child-care, health-care, art, tutoring, construction and all sorts of things. We've made our Volunteer Corps' badges prestigious in Mapleton and they have recently gained national recognition from some employers and institutions of higher learning. The recognition will grow as more communities become involved with Another Way and understand the effort required to earn a badge. Before long the awards will inspire admiration around the globe, as symbols of exemplary achievement."

Phyllis gave what might have been a nostalgic sigh and continued. "There used to be a connection between school and the marketplace. Students knew they were being prepared to face the normal ups and downs of life and to cope and make a living. In recent years, a lot of kids failed to understand that what is learned in school—work habits, analytical ability, math, science, and even things like grammar, punctuation, and spelling—should transfer to the work place. Service in the TVC helps students make that connection between school and the real world."

Now it was Mr. Hoffer's turn to reminisce: "At one time, an employer could assume an applicant with a high school diploma could at least read, write and follow instructions. I understand that Minnesota's governor increased funding for that state's reading readiness programs, after forty-two percent of the employers in his state reported that high school graduates lacked basic reading, writing, and math skills. Both high school and college diplomas have such diverse and, generally, little significance today, that many businesses are forced to administer their own examinations in order to determine the competency of a potential employee. Training is expensive for business, and is commonplace. Business spends eighty-two billion dollars a year to train employees, graduates and non-graduates, of both college and high school."

"The Problem Solvers at Mapleton High tackled the welfare-to-work issue this year," Janet informed the group. "We learned a lot. For instance, what is the market for elementary and secondary education?" She answered her own question, "Post secondary education, and the workplace. Of three thousand institutions of higher learning, only six hundred exercise any selection in admission. There is no need for students to qualify; they will be accepted no matter how inadequate their preparation. Labor is obviously dissatisfied with the job the schools are doing, but they never say what they want. Labor hires college graduates to get skills that should have been learned in high school. It's easier for business to produce abroad and sell in the United States, than to tell local communities they have lousy schools.

Lincoln waited until the train of thought had been played out, and then he said, "I'd like to tell our visitors about a real situation in Mapleton, prior to Another Way, but it's an example of the type of thing Another Way inspires."

Phyllis again nodded, and Lincoln began: "My uncle used to work for the Jeremiah-Hilde Company when it was having a hard time attracting good employees. The company considered moving because of that, and also because of criminal activity in the area. But relocation turned out to be so costly that Jeremiah-Hilde opted to improve the neighborhood and develop a local, ethical and competent work force instead.

"The company agreed to sponsor twenty local Boys and Girls Club members between the ages of ten and twelve. It provided a team of mentors—one for each child. The mentors got advice from the local Big Brothers and Big Sisters staff. Jeremiah-Hilde employees were expected to volunteer five hours a week for a three-month period, annually. This schedule resulted in four separate mentors year-round for each child, and the sixty hours a year commitment was not an undue hardship for employees. The mentors encouraged the children, even helping with homework, keeping in touch with their schools, and planning trips to expand and enrich the children's lives. The company arranged for some paid time for an employee to work on projects, which would slowly introduce each child to the company. One project was decorating for an office party; another was a landscape project. One mentor and his child built shelves and others painted recreation areas or cleaned up files or moved books around in the company library.

"As the children became teenagers they were offered after-school apprentice jobs where they acquired useful skills and were exposed to career options ranging from relatively low level technician slots, to professional positions requiring graduate degrees. The company entered into a work-study contract with any child who managed to sustain good grades. The child decided how much education would be enough, not his financial and family circumstances. The company was able to build its own inventory of topnotch employees this way. Just as it had hoped training homegrown employees reduced costly turn-over and produced loyal long-term team members. Neighborhood kids in the program developed leadership skills and were able to influence other kids; so, in addition, crime decreased in the area." Lincoln sensed he was losing his audience.

"Okay," Lincoln's voice rose and he quickened his pace, "forget what the kids got—hope, a stake in the future, the esteem that comes from being a constructive human being. We all saved tax dollars that weren't needed to train these low-income kids for jobs. We all saved the unemployment checks that might have been necessary, had the Jeremiah-Hilde Company been forced off-shore."

Mario had been taking this all in and was coveting a piece of the action. If only Jeremiah-Hilde was in Bloomfield. "What is a work-study contract?" he asked enviously.

"The contract was similar to the agreements the military has with recruits—so many years of service for so many years of education. Escape clauses were built into the agreements that allowed other means to pay back Jeremiah-Hilde. I'm sure not everyone returned to work there."

It made sense to Mario.

Bill seemed lost in his own thoughts during the Jeremiah-Hilde discussion. Now, he said quietly, "What bothers me is how people figure out what to do so quickly. I know about the rushes twice a year, but…" He paused. "Take Paul and his friends. How could they know what they wanted to do without spending a lot of time doing research?"

Lincoln felt vindicated. They had been paying attention after all. He beamed at Bill and said: "They used Troop Forty-Seven's computer. They had immediate access to all the nonprofits in Mapleton. That's thanks to City Links and that's the subject of Paul's presentation coming up."

Paul was pleasantly surprised to learn that Lincoln knew about his presentation. He was also surprised at the turn the discussion had suddenly taken. How could anyone possibly think a few scouts could discover what needed doing in three separate categories, figure out what to do, how to do it, collect the resources, and not duplicate any other efforts in the community—all in a few short months? The programs were not scout programs; they were programs, possibly funded and well thought out, in response to already identified, pressing, community needs—and just waiting for volunteers to make them happen.

Two of the programs he and his friends had chosen had been operating for the past two years. The other was a great idea, which was estimated to take two hundred man-hours. The six scouts had pooled their energy and taken the project from beginning to end. Actually, that one was the most satisfying. Paul decided on the spot to use the three scout projects as examples in his City Links presentation.

"Let's take a short break and then we'll get Paul's description of City Links. After that we've been invited to the Center for lunch," Phyllis said. The girls traipsed down the hall to the rest room while most of the guys headed for the snacks. People mingled, stretched their legs—and the boys took good natured jabs at one another. Phyllis noted the little pairing that occurred was based on age. The seniors—Lincoln, Janet, and Lisa—found one another, probably to talk about colleges and the future and the youngest students; Amanda, Megan, Mario, and Paul, gravitated to one another as well, that is, until Paul discovered Raeann had reemerged.

"Okay, let's get this show on the road people," Phyllis said as she watched Paul abruptly leave Mario and rush to Raeann's side. For a split second Phyllis questioned her own motives and timing and wondered if she was trying to help out Raeann. No, she reassured herself, there was still a lot to cover before lunch. It was time, anyway, to get back to the table.

"Okay Paul," Phyllis said. "Take it away!"

Paul obliged: "It was recently estimated that it would cost eleven billion dollars to connect every school in the nation to the Internet. This estimate assumed installing about twenty-five computers, per school, in a special classroom, or lab, where teachers would bring their classes at an assigned time each day. We found that parents with technical knowledge were Mapleton's best resource.. By using private trades, in a matter of months, we had Internet access at every library, school, public building, and most nonprofit agencies. It is now possible for every resident of Mapleton to have access to the information on the Another Way home page. It only takes a modem and local toll free phone call to connect."

Lisa wasn't so sure. "What do you mean by private trades? Exactly who would trade what for what? Computers aren't cheap and wiring networks isn't either."

"Do you think I'm lying?"

"Paul!" Phyllis came to the rescue. "Where are your manners?" Turning to Lisa, she explained, "We followed the example set by San Carlos, California."

"Isn't that in Silicon Valley? Those parents aren't only skilled they are CEOs and founders of high tech hardware and software firms. I bet they contributed money and equipment too."

"You're probably right, Lisa, but Paul mentioned that the parents here in Mapleton were our greatest asset when it came to technology. Technology, whether it is making silicon chips, wiring, programming—it isn't new to northern California. We have people who work right here in system programming and application software and others who commute the two hours plus into Silicon Valley. These skilled people are among the private trades for donations on the Dream Machine. Many postings–requests and offers are for computers, hardware and software plus skilled labor. Sometimes companies donate new products just off assembly lines and ready to be consumer tested and other times the products are older but still useable

Bill was anxious to get Bloomfield connected. "I bet we have lots of the same technical people in Bloomfield."

"Probably more," Phyllis agreed. "Bloomfield is more than double the size of Mapleton and just as close to Silicon Valley."

Lisa still wasn't convinced. "What about the ongoing fees for maintaining the connections to the Internet and the computers and other equipment?"

"The local community pays the ISP bills for service to all public buildings."

"What's ISP?" Amanda wasn't phased even though Paul looked at here with surprise. "I suppose the I stands for Internet but the SP—special people, social product? What?"

"Internet Service Provider," Harrison said matter of factly.

Phyllis apologized. "I think using abbreviations common to a single trade is rude and I apologize. Every occupation has its own insider language—especially government. Some Internet Service Providers can and some cannot donate their services. They need to pay their overhead with money so sometimes other donors offer to pay the monthly bills for service to several or one or two buildings or groups of users over a period of time running from one month to annual.

Bill was surprised to learn that taxpayers who traded their services were treated differently by the government than taxpayers who contributed money to pay the bills for someone else to perform the same service. "I think people who donate labor should get the same tax deductions as the people who donate money. By supporting a tax code that distinguishes between the two makes it clear that the government irrationally favors one type of donor over another."

"Is he right?" Dorothy had been silent for awhile but the disbelief that showed on her face was obviously strong enough

53

to overcome any shyness or hesitancy she may have had to speak earlier. "People get tax deductions for gifts of money but not for gifts of time or labor? That does reflect on the nation's values."

"That may be," said Phyllis, "but time's running. Can you get us back on track, Paul?"

"The Chamber of Commerce, in most communities, publishes cursory information regarding local organizations and there are often other publications, including numerous pages on the web, which do the same. Our polls showed us that these summaries provided too little information to be truly useful to potential donors of time, goods, and services—"

Paul was interrupted by Amanda. "What do donors want to know?"

"Our polls showed us they want to know where to go and what to do." Paul was animated. "Let me give you some real life examples that occurred before we had Another Way in Mapleton.

"My mother heard that the local YWCA got five thousand dollars from a foundation. She knew that half of the money went to three schools—to fund a program designed to offer solutions to domestic violence—and the other half went to the Y's career education and independent living and skills training program. She thought she might volunteer and want to get more detailed information to pass on to her women's group, so she made a phone call and was told to call back in two days. With Internet access, she could have downloaded the information on the spot. Instead, she did what comes naturally—procrastinated, and nothing came of the inclinations.

"A lawyer friend of my dad's attempted to donate legal services to children's causes. He registered at the local volunteer center and called various agencies. No one knew what to do with his offer and, again, nothing came of it.

"My uncle wanted to give speeches to promote a cause he believed in and was not allowed to do so because he was not on the board of the organization that provided research for the advocacy agency.

"Our family came up with an extra turkey one Thanksgiving morning and started calling, while the bird was still in the oven. Fourteen calls resulted in taped messages on machines; even hot lines were not manned, so if anyone was looking to refer a homeless person to a meal, they wouldn't know where to send him or her. The telephone operator and her supervisor tried to come up with ideas regarding where meals were being served to the needy, or where a large turkey might be welcome, with no results.

"The outcomes might have been different if needs and resources were constantly updated and available for viewing on the Internet. Not that having access means using access," Paul laughed, "but, in the last example, if the telephone operator had access, she could have consulted her computer and told someone without a computer looking for a meal, or willing to provide a meal, where to go, even on Thanksgiving.

"As for the grantmakers—those who donate anything, other than time…" Paul was interrupted by Amanda once again.

"You mean, those who provide the funds to operate a project in Bloomfield; those who give checks." Amanda thought she was helping Paul.

"Yes," Paul acknowledged, "Grantmakers want to know how much is spent on a program, how many units are being served."

"Units?" Bill questioned.

"Sometimes, programs serve people," Paul explained. "Sometimes they work with animals, or plant trees, or work to save the environment…"

"Okay, I got it," said Bill.

"Even the traditional grantmakers were dissatisfied with the inadequate information, and individuals often solved the problem by writing large checks to their Alma Maters, or already well-endowed, distinguished institutions," Mr. Hoffer added.

"Grantmakers need to be able to compare programs so they can put their resources to work, doing what they think is most important in the most cost-efficient manner. We post the tax returns of every nonprofit on the Another Way home page, with general instructions for analysis. In addition to the information posted for grantmakers, volunteers need to know about mentors and apprenticeships, training opportunities, the hours they can perform each job, who they would work with, and everything they can about the programs so they can make informed choices."

"Annual reports provide that information," Lisa volunteered.

"Annual reports are vague and generalized," Paul countered. "The information we feed into the computer for our programmed search is much more detailed." Paul was anxious to explain how to access the information via the Internet, from Another Way's Volunteer Opportunities page, which he had helped Raeann construct. Now, he decided, was the time and place to describe the scout projects. "I think it might be easier to grasp if I give you some actual examples, so I'm going to tell you how we came up with the organizations we decided to join last year in scouts. I think the best way would be to first tell you the outcome of our searches and then take you through the steps to show you how we got there."

"Sounds good, Paul," said Phyllis.

Paul began: "Troop Forty-Seven has twenty-two members. We each choose a community service project every year. We all try to earn in the neighborhood of twenty stamps to add to the Mapleton Scout Summer Camp fund. But last year I decided I wanted a computer. When I consulted the Dream Machine I discovered I could get a pretty decent reconditioned computer with the software I wanted for about a hundred hours, so I decided to make that my trade proposal, plus twenty more to contribute to the camp fund.

"Six of us—Jim, Neil, Robert, Sam, Jason, and I—joined the Giraffe Project and chose to renovate a small park, which had a bathroom with peeling paint, a couple of sagging benches, a non-operating drinking fountain, a boarded up slide, and three swings—two with dangerously worn seats. We had a blast and transformed that disaster into a little kid's fantasyland—and it only took us two months, once we got started! We worked seven Saturdays and a few Sunday afternoons. I personally put fifty-five hours into the project, and Neil put in about fifty hours. He's the artist in the group. He did a lot of the design work at home, in the evening, and transferred his creations to plywood, which some of us painted. Sam and Jason worked on the playground equipment. They did most of the more skilled work, whereas Robert and Jim did most of the heavy work; you know, carrying stuff, constructing paths, and landscaping, according to Neil's design.

"Jim and Robert joined Mapleton Cares with me too. We each donated thirty hours of labor to get a combination, vegetable and flower, garden started at this homeless shelter. Jim and I also joined Break Away, which is an organization that recruits retired people, mostly for mentoring positions. Break Away was mostly Jim's choice because his grandfather was heavily involved in that organization. We became kid recruiters. Supposedly, it is harder for older people to turn down a kid's plea than a plea from one of their peers. Anyway, Jim and I got pretty good at the art of persuasion and, together, brought about sixty new mentors into the program."

"Wonderful!" Phyllis couldn't restrain herself. This was what Another Way was all about.

"But the best thing that happened at Break Away," Paul continued, "was finding Gus and Bill. These guys are retired construction workers. Gus is supposed to be one of the best carpenters of all time. Anyway, since we had decided to start the park renovation at the Giraffe Project, after the snow melted, Jim and I—the great persuaders—were able to get Gus and Bill to help us. We learned so much from those guys! Gus and Bill brought their own equipment to the park and taught Sam and

Jason how to use a jig saw to cut the animals and fire engines and all the neat things Neil had drawn and traced onto plywood.

"Even after the Giraffe Project was finished, they kept finding more projects to work on—always as a team. None of them, except maybe Gus, has much family of their own. Anyway, Sam, Jason, Gus, and Bill are now inseparable; they're like grandfathers and grandsons. I guess the rest of us consider Gus and Bill to be more like uncles. Whatever! For sure, they are definitely family now. Those guys are really funny…"

As Paul rambled on, Bill couldn't help wishing he lived in Mapleton. He wished he could have been one of the six boys he was hearing about. Not that he didn't love and appreciate his grandparents, but his grandfather was rather frail and he missed the athletic workouts with his father. His father had taught him to ski at an early age and they frequently took long trips together. Sometimes his mother came along and made it a family adventure. Bill grew up on the Nevada side of Lake Tahoe where his parents managed a large ski resort. They had been tragically killed in a hold up in Reno and Bill had been sent to live with his paternal grandparents in Bloomfield. Although it snowed in Bloomfield, the surrounding hills couldn't compare with the slopes in the High Sierras. Bill had the option to spend vacations with family friends back at Tahoe. His old coach planned to take him to Mt. Hood in Oregon, where snow remains on the mountain even during August and world class skiers continue their training when their home slopes are bare. His grandmother was always trying to find a younger man to substitute as a father figure, but nothing had clicked. Just think of the possibilities in Mapleton.

Bill turned his focus back to Paul just in time to hear Phyllis tell him to tighten his presentation because time was running out.

"Okay, this is how we made our choices," Paul said in a no nonsense voice. "We logged onto the Another Way home page and called up the Volunteer Opportunities forum where we were offered four options. We could search by name of organization, by subject matter, by category of volunteer, or by specific mission of a project. For the Giraffe Project, we searched by category of volunteer. We were then given a choice of narrowing our search by choosing families, groups, or individuals. We chose groups. We then could narrow our search even further by eliminating those organizations that had age restrictions, that specified a group size larger or smaller than our group, and that required a particular set of skills or time commitment. We decided to eliminate groups with age, skills, and time restrictions from our search and selected the smallest group option, which was the two to six category. We had three more choices: working in administration, working with clients, or working with tools. We chose tools, and between working outside or inside, we chose outside. Each time we made a choice, we narrowed our search.

"We found Mapleton Cares by first choosing the specific mission option. There was a pull down menu with fifteen to twenty options, featuring the types of people or goals served. We chose homeless. When given the options I just described for the Giraffe Project, we made the same choices. I forgot to mention we were also offered a time line for each search; under short term goals one could choose one day, one week, one month, three months, six months, nine months. We selected one month. The long-term goal options started with one week and ran through five years.

"We were able to use the name of organization search option for Break Away because Jim wanted to work with his grandfather's program. This obviously shortened our search, although we still had the time options and choice of specific jobs within Break Away."

"Could you expand your explanation of the time line search? I don't understand the short term and long term goals," Lisa said.

"Sure," Paul agreed. "Let's take the Giraffe Project again. Suppose you wanted to do something that could be completed in a day. Your options might include things like: paint a bench or repair the drinking fountain or weed the north end of the lot. Say you chose the one-week option. You might have a list of things like painting all play equipment, weeding the entire garden, and fixing the sprinkling system, as well as the drinking fountain (plumbing skills). Click on one month and you might find that you could have all the play equipment repaired; or a design completed for the landscaping and park renovation. The one-day option to further the preliminary goals of a health or environmental organization might include participating in a walk or run to draw attention to an issue, manning booths at a fair or conference, and so forth. Other short term options—a week or a month—might include being a race staff volunteer, setting up computer data bases, preparing for a conference, educating people about heart disease at a specific event, or writing for a specific publication.

"Occasionally, a long-term goal can be completed in a week: writing, for promotional or educational purposes, for example; or a month: planning programs and recruiting activity directors; or three months: launching new programs; six months or more: planning and implementing a neighborhood celebration, theatrical program, and seeing it through to the end."

"What's the reasoning behind the time lines?" Mario asked.

"Some people want to follow a volunteer project through from beginning to end, whether their commitment is one day or one year. They get more personal satisfaction and control. Time line options are for their benefit. Other people feel just fine about lending their hand to an ongoing project; they enter in the middle and withdraw their services before the end," Paul explained. "Break Away and Mapleton Cares were both ongoing projects. But we all got the most satisfaction from the Giraffe Project which we had control of from beginning to end."

"Yeah, I could see that," said Bill. "A person could paint a bench in one day, beginning to end, and take a special pride in that bench. Satisfaction!

"Just one more thing. I'm wondering about the difference between time lines and time restrictions. I understand time lines, but not restrictions."

"If a project has a time restriction, it means it is an option only available to someone who can put in a minimum number of hours or specific hours on already determined days. That's the case with all mentoring opportunities," said Paul.

"At one point you said something about these computer searches being able to pinpoint the most cost-effective programs so donors of time and other resources could avoid the more wasteful agencies if they chose to do so," Lisa reminded Paul. "I wasn't clear on that."

"The most cost-effective, nonprofit programs can be determined by following the instructions to analyze and compare tax returns which are provided on the Another Way site. I can't recall the exact name of the forum but they are in the area, which also lists the cost of past programs, information about endowments, investment returns, donations, government dollars, time and other resources spent soliciting funds. The only things similar on the Volunteer Options forum are the tools provided to estimate the cost of a new program. There are options in the pull down menus for the estimated number of workers, their estimated per hour dollar cost, the cost of administering the project, the estimated time for implementation and the cost of needed supplies and other materials. There are options to find the estimated cost with and without paid workers and with or without paid administrators.

Paul had an inspiration: "Listen, maybe it would help if one of you would think of your ideal volunteer relationship. Tell me what you want to do. Do you want an on-going job or a job with a specific limit? How many hours are you willing to spend? What schedule would you like—days and times? Do you need transportation? We'll use you as an illustration. What do you say?"

Bill filled in the blanks as Paul spoke. "What do you want to do?" He would love to work as an assistant coach with one or two men. They would be dealing with kids; but the best part of it—the part he really wanted—would be a close relationship with a father figure. He mentally rehearsed what he was going to tell Paul: I would like to help clear a trail or do some kind of surveying in the wilderness—maybe tagging endangered birds or animals.

Amanda's excited words brought Bill back from his musings. "I've got it! Let me, let me please," she begged.

"Let's have it," Paul laughed.

"See," Amanda began, "my mother visits her sister every Wednesday evening, from seven to nine p.m., and drags me along because my father, who is a biology teacher, has a second job working in a hospital lab during that time and she doesn't want to leave me alone. She could drop me off at a volunteer job regularly for those two hours."

"Okay, we've got the time criteria: Wednesday, 7:00-9:00 p.m. Now, what subject should we be searching for? What do you want to do?" Paul prodded.

"Hug crack babies!" Everyone laughed at Amanda's passion. She knew exactly what she wanted to do—no doubt about it! She had seen a TV special featuring abandoned, addicted infants.

Paul didn't have access to the Volunteer Opportunities forum but he was so familiar with the structure he thought he could make his audience see what he saw. "First, we search by subject matter. From a long list of options, we click on infants, then choose ongoing job from the time line options, and two hours a week, Wednesday seven to nine p.m., transportation not needed, no age restrictions. Now search. We would probably get a huge number of job options, but mostly baby-sitting to relieve mothers—who would, in turn, do something to help someone else—maybe a couple group situations with adult supervision, where you would hug or play with infants." Paul tried to recall what was in that section of the database. He had chosen infants because he had recently updated that section.

"There may be one or two hospital situations," he added, "but I think we would do better to go back to subject matter and search this time by health care and narrow it down to infants. I'm not sure you would find drug-addicted babies, specifically, but probably you would end up with fewer options, closer to what you are after. I know for a fact that we have at least two hospitals that need people to cuddle newborns, because I added them to the database myself."

"There are more than that," Raeann broke in, "and there is a sub-level *sick*, and another, *drugs*."

Paul beamed. Raeann didn't miss much. "You can try all this out for yourself. You can view the detailed information if you visit the Volunteer Opportunities forum on Mapleton's home page. You don't have to live in Mapleton. Of course, it takes a great deal of labor to acquire and keep such detailed information current. In Mapleton, labor is provided—about eighty percent—by the youngest generation, and twenty percent by retired folks who still have abilities and experience which should not be lost."

"You say kids—young people—provide close to eighty percent of the labor for what you admit is a very time consuming job," Harrison said. "I'm wondering who supplies the other ten percent? What with studies, social life, jobs, and community service, how in the world can kids shoulder the lion's share? It doesn't seem possible or fair."

"Participation in Another Way, and especially City Links, combines all four of the things you mentioned; studies, social life, community service and jobs. It's efficient." Paul responded.

"Why not take them one at a time, Paul, and show us how they fit into Another Way?" Phyllis suggested.

"Sure," Paul agreed. "But I can't just plunge in without giving them some background. What do you say, Phyllis?" Paul loved to talk, but he didn't want to be cut off before he finished describing what he thought was important.

"You're right; it is a good idea," Phyllis answered. "I think it will be worth the time."

Paul plunged in: "The first step in implementing Another Way was to poll residents to discover the incentives and disincentives to their involvement in our community. Among other things, the poll responses revealed the poor communication between groups in Mapleton—people in different occupations and age groups thought the worst of one another."

"What do you mean 'the worst of one another'?" Harrison asked.

"Business people thought teachers were lazy, people in education thought business people were hard-hearted, and everyone thought government workers were uncaring and incompetent and lawyers were total scumbags."

"No kidding. You got that information from polling?"

"That, and a lot more. Our earlier poll responses proved that Mapleton had an enormous amount of goodwill and other resources, which were not being used effectively. The timing was right for Another Way because two ideas that are essential for Another Way were being discussed at the same time; volunteerism and community-based learning."

"What is community-based learning?" Mario interrupted this time.

"Community-based learning is a teaching method that emphasizes the important connection between academics and community service; between theory and practical problem solving," Mr. Hoffer offered. Community-based learning had been the subject of the keynote speech given by an Ivy League professor, at the last teacher's conference he had attended in Bloomfield. The attendees were about evenly divided in the support and distrust of the notion.

"It's changing the way professors teach and students learn," he continued. "A lot of people think that students should be spending more time solving problems that have some relevance to daily life. A college professor I heard recently has students in his sociology course provide some service to the organizations they research. The idea is to enrich classroom learning by having students interpret information through an actual event, occurring in real time."

"What's the point?" Mario pressed.

"It's through these dynamic interactions with the local community that interesting and relevant questions emerge. Almost always, community-based problems are bigger than a single discipline can resolve," Mr. Hoffer replied.

This was a subject near and dear to Phyllis's heart. Even though she was concerned about the time and the amount of material still to cover, she couldn't resist. If hugging crack babies was Amanda's passion, this was hers: "There is a difference between theory and talking to real people and seeing the effect of social policy as it plays out in their lives," she said. "Learning is supposed to make a difference in your life and in the world. Community-based learning is the bridge between the intellectual classroom and real life. It's not so much what you learn in textbooks, it's what you do with the theories outside the classroom."

"Everyone learns better both with studying and with doing, particularly the MTV generation," Mr. Hoffer agreed. "We have a math teacher at Bloomfield High who believes learning is enhanced by teaching. He claims that after a student is exposed to a mathematical idea they've only become acquainted with, it is only after they have explained it to someone else that they've really learned it. He has his students tutor elementary school youngsters. He figures that way his students are not only learning to get their tongue around math ideas, but they are learning how young children think and why they are often puzzled by math problems."

"Unfortunately, some people misunderstand what community-based learning is all about," Phyllis said. "They think we are giving academic credit for straight volunteer work, but that's not the case. There is a serious academic component to working within the community and benefits to the community are incidental.

"Before Another Way got started here in Mapleton, Miss Donaldson, our economics teacher, used to give her students an opportunity to volunteer for six to eight weeks at a local nonprofit of their choice. She had the idea, before it was popular, that going into the community benefited her students. She maintained that early volunteer experience would remind her students later on in life that they have the ability to influence broader social change. She argued also, that the experience gave abstract economic issues a base in reality. She wanted students to see how economic issues affect the lives of real people and how the tools of economics help us understand these issues. I remember the year before Another Way began, her students painted the living room and bedrooms of a homeless shelter, harvested vegetables for the food bank, and weeded gardens for elderly and disabled residents. I remember because we used her success to convince Mapleton officials to give Another Way a shot.

"The citizens' group in Illinois that divided the 1988 tax reform proposal into manageable portions, which it parceled out to its members, was another catalyst for community-based learning in Mapleton. After studying their respective portions, those ordinary citizens reported back to the group. In some strange way, it mattered to a lot of us, that at least a small group of Americans had read every word in that massive bill. The legislators and their staff admitted that they hadn't. Now, reporting on legislation is a community-based learning project coordinated each year with the Problem Solvers. It's something the rest of the nation knows nothing about, but if they did they would, or should be in these young scholars' debt."

This was dry, generally, unintelligible stuff. That teenagers would, and could, do this was amazing. John Hoffer had no doubt about Mapleton deserving its reputation.

Phyllis turned apologetically to Paul and said, "Sorry, I guess we got carried away."

"Hey, thanks. You saved me from explaining community-based learning, and I'm sure that is definitely one of those things that teachers do better," Paul joked. "I started telling you that polling Mapleton residents showed that the main reason people didn't donate more of their time or material wealth was that residents simply didn't know what needed to be done, where, and how. Also, they wanted to make sure their gift, whether of time or materials, would not be wasted. City Links gives Mapleton residents access to information, which solves these problems. The detailed information was gathered by classes, using community-based learning with maybe some supervision or chaperoning from college students or retired volunteers.

"I was told that Mapleton teachers wanted their students to get a feel for how social research is actually conducted and to understand that the ideas and methods they were being taught are valuable. Many English, Speech, Government, Social Science, Business, Computer and Art teachers in Mapleton rearranged their curricula. Currently, in some Mapleton classes, students conduct community surveys. Other classes find out everything there is to know about nonprofit organizations, local and national. In other classes, students work with directors of local nonprofits to come up with at least twenty-five scheduling options and twenty-five volunteer job selections which are fed to the business and computing classes for input for publication on the Internet and local print media, as well as turned into public service announcements on local radio and TV stations and posters for store windows.

"Anyway, Harrison, in answer to your question, 'how can kids handle it all?' I think now you should be able to see that studies, community service, and jobs are combined through community-based learning. Then, there's social life, right?" Harrison nodded and Paul continued. "If you remember all the talk about parties during Mapleton Rush and understand that doing volunteer work with your peers is generally accompanied by a party atmosphere, if not down right parties during, and almost always at the end, of a project, you will agree that social life is integrated."

"Okay to everything but the jobs," Harrison assented. "I mean jobs that earn real money for gas for my car, clothes, entertainment, and social life outside of Another Way. At least half of the kids I know at Bloomfield High have real paying, after school jobs and a lot of them are saving to go to college. My grandfather set up a fund for my college education and with my dad's affiliation with the university I'm lucky in not having to worry about that. But I don't see how students can put all that time into non-paying volunteer work unless they have rich or connected parents."

"Remember how I worked to get grantmaking organizations to translate the dollars they normally would give in grants, into merchandise and services? We have coupons for gasoline, Pizza Palace and Applebees, tickets to rock concerts, theaters, and sporting events all listed on the Dream Machine for your social life. The college scholarships, partial and full, are one of the most popular donations from national and local grantmakers, as well as businesses." Janet paused, and threw up her hands. "What can a money-paying job get Bloomfield students that a volunteer job can't get Mapleton students?"

Mapleton's TVC Center

"Thanks Janet," Paul interrupted before Harrison could answer Janet. He was beginning to get hungry and lunchtime was within his control. With renewed determination he said, "I hope I've managed to convince you that the information we've just gone over is so detailed that if Mario, for instance, wants to work with animals, he can call up information only about nonprofits that work with animals; if he doesn't have transportation, he can narrow his search to only those volunteer opportunities that provide transportation; if he can only work Saturdays, he can narrow the search still further; and if he wants to make sure the organization welcomes volunteers under age eighteen, he can eliminate a few more choices."

"Okay, that's it for this morning," Phyllis intervened. "Nice job, Paul."

Janet had closed her laptop and packed it and the tape recorder in carrying cases. She stood up and almost shouted to make herself heard above the din of scraping chairs and the mounting crescendo of tension-releasing conversation that filled the room. "Please follow Lincoln down the back stairs and into the van. He will drive us across town to lunch at the TVC Center."

As they came within sight of a large, modern building, Phyllis said, "The center used to be housed in office space traded by a commercial real estate developer, in exchange for bookkeeping and other office tasks. Today, it occupies an entire floor of our new community building which was funded by the tax refunds that were discussed this morning."

"Oh yeah. The chump factor conversation!" Amanda exclaimed in her indomitable fashion.

"Each participating organization sends a minimum of one adult and two youths to the center for a three-month rotation where each volunteer commits five hours a week to the project of his or her choice," Phyllis continued. "Some of the rotating volunteers—we call them Kangas—are engaged in research."

Bill beat Amanda to the punch: "Kangas?" he repeated in disbelief. "You've got to be kidding. Where in the world did that name come from?"

"You'd be amazed," Phyllis laughed. "Someone got tired of saying 'rotating volunteers' and started calling them 'Rows'," which no one liked. We couldn't call them Rotarians—those who rotate—because that name already belonged to the Rotary Club members, and so Joyce, the current CEO of the Truly Volunteer Corps. (you'll meet her in a few minutes), got the crazy idea to call them Kangas. She figured they hop around from job to job, from place to place and the Kangaroo made a nice mascot. You'll understand better after you meet Joyce."

Phyllis classified rotation jobs broadly as administration, conducting research, overseeing the Dream Machine, administering awards, and funding the community's nonprofits. This last one took the most TVC volunteers and would be the focus of today's visit. Volunteers were not accepted directly for jobs that were conducted at the Center; they were loaned by their home-base organization. Volunteers joined an organization because they were interested in a particular mission. Some, but not all, TVC members were willing to accept temporary assignments at the Center because they knew work there increased, exponentially, the mission of their home-base organizations, freeing them, as it did, from the perpetual search for funds. Few on their first rotation could foresee the impact working at the Center would have on their own lives. In many ways, volunteers were affected by their rotations as profoundly as their work affected the missions of their home-base entities.

Lincoln parked, and Phyllis shepherded the group into the main entrance. A wall directory advised that they were on the second floor, which housed the community auditorium. Downstairs were: exercise rooms, a gymnasium, swimming pool, and a few arts and crafts studios; the top floor was the home of a two-storied library, which was located directly above the tutoring center. As she pushed the third floor elevator button, which would take them all to the TVC Center, Phyllis allowed her mind to wander to the tutoring center on the fourth floor. It was actually Mapleton's alternative school, which had more than two hundred computers, several small video rooms, and a counseling area manned twenty-four hours a day by retired volunteers. (Lots of older people didn't sleep through the night.) The volunteers were the mentors and the computers were the tutors. Mapleton residents from age eight to eighty could acquire knowledge at their own speed.

Child prodigies had acquired post-graduate degrees, recognized by the finest universities in the nation, and sitting next to formerly illiterate, but motivated dropouts who could unobtrusively continue their education without stigma. The curriculum for residents under age eighteen, without a high school diploma, was the same curriculum required of students in Mapleton's regular schools. The educational software was equipped with a smart tutor, which tested the student's knowledge as a prerequisite for more advanced courses and provided remedial supplements for the areas where test results spotted weakness. Students advanced at their own speed. Two Mapleton students had been accepted for graduate work at Johns Hopkins University at age twelve.

Community celebrations were held twice a year where degrees were awarded and accomplishments acknowledged with great pomp and circumstance. When the elevator stopped, Phyllis was replaying the good food, music, dancing, and joy of the last gathering where she had come with hundreds of others to celebrate. One of her former students—who, ten years earlier, during his sophomore year, had become involved with a gang and drugs and dropped out of Mapleton High—was awarded a B.S. in biology that day. She had been as proud of Mike as she had been of her seventy-seven-year-old mother-in-law who, the same day, had received a master's degree in Chinese history.

The group exited the elevator and followed Phyllis down the hall toward the glass doors on the left. They could see a young man sitting at a large desk joking with an animated middle-aged woman who had just deposited a pile of papers on his desk.

"Good morning, Joyce. How are you doing?" Phyllis said warmly, giving the woman a hug. "This is the Mapleton-Bloomfield group I told you about. I'd like you to meet John Hoffer, head of Bloomfield High's Social Studies Department,"

Phyllis continued as the tall, lean man and the short, plump woman shook hands in a friendly fashion.

"These," Phyllis extended her arm in a large sweeping arc, "are some of Mapleton and Bloomfield's best and brightest; too many, I'm afraid, to introduce individually. We would like to take two or three minutes of your time here in administration, just to give everyone a sense of who does what."

Joyce smiled broadly and said, "We have been expecting you. Welcome!" Various students murmured hellos or glad to meet yous softly, and Joyce grasped Janet's hand firmly for a moment and then continued: "What a splendid group! I'd like you to meet Bruce Hopkins," she said, touching the young man's shoulder. Bruce nodded awkwardly. Then, turning to Phyllis, she asked, "Do you want Bruce to tell you about his home organization or just what he does here, or do you want me to run through the administration jobs? I know what we agreed, but you're running pretty late, Phyllis, and they're keeping lunch for you in the cafeteria," Joyce said with a grin.

Phyllis was glad Joyce was so easy going. She was currently the only salaried staff at the Center and was hired for her understated efficiency and even temperament. Nothing ever fazed her and, with all the people she had to deal with, that quality was gold.

Volunteers of all ages were apprenticed here to retired chefs before putting time in at the restaurants around town, which were affiliated with the center's entrepreneurial projects. Phyllis didn't want to keep lunch waiting. She knew the volunteers had prepared something special. Too bad the student volunteers didn't come until after school so her group could see them in action and ask questions. Phyllis understood how persuasive student to student feedback could be.

"I think you had better give us the job descriptions, Joyce, and maybe we can meet a couple of your current staff and find out their home organization," she said.

"All right." Joyce smiled agreeably. "You've met Bruce."

Turning to the young man, who by this time had gotten up from his desk and was towering over Joyce, she joked, "It's just name and organization and I've already done the name part for you."

Bruce grinned and said, "AWARE, my home organization, provides sober housing for people recovering from chemical dependency."

"Bruce and several others," Joyce nodded toward the now empty desks behind Bruce, "are on an additional merry-go-round. They are on loan from the entrepreneurial projects, which are just down the hall. Volunteers interested in enhancing their office skills are loaned to us a week at a time."

Joyce patted Bruce on the arm and said, "Thanks, Bruce," as she took her leave.

The room in back of the large reception desk was divided in half. Each half had two desks lined up against the center divider and four desks in a line against the wall. There was a separate, glassed-in section at one end of the room, which reminded John Hoffer of the sergeant's office in the old Police Story reruns on TV. That was where Joyce held court.

Joyce made her way to the back of the room, the thirteen visitors trailing behind her like ducklings. She turned and faced the group and said, "We enjoy the services of four to six retired folk and a total of forty young people, between the ages of fourteen and thirty-four in the research and computer areas. The young people donate six hours per week, each, in two, three hour shifts during a five-day period. Four volunteers donate three hours in the afternoon and four others donate three hours in the evening. We make good use of the equipment during school hours, although, what goes on during those hours varies.

"This morning we had six members of the Human Race using the computers to update their mailing lists, and two volunteers from Deer Hollow Farm used the other two computers to compose a flyer. They weren't Kangas, they were volunteers working for their home organizations and following the Another Way precept to stretch resources by sharing."

Amanda and Megan couldn't control their giggles and Joyce started laughing too, as she realized what might have started the girls off.

"Are you laughing because you know what Kangas are, or because you don't?" she asked the embarrassed pair.

Phyllis came to their rescue: "It's the first time they've heard the word in context," she said, laughing herself. "I already filled everyone in."

Smiling broadly, Joyce patted the shoulders of the two older women who occupied desks in the center of the room as she said, "They're running late, so we're down to brief introductions."

"Sure," said the smaller of the two, "I'm Donna Schwarz from Meals on Wheels."

"I'm Jane Miller, Parents Helping Parents," offered a tall, slender lady with closely cropped dark hair.

"Donna and Jane are here in supervisory capacities. Jane is on a regular three-month rotation, but Donna has been with us for over a year and puts in more than forty hours a week. We have rules, schedules, you know, but I have always thought rules were for deviation." Joyce laughed. "In addition to managing twenty new volunteers every three months, with fine help from Jane, and others like her, Donna has become my indispensable right arm.

"Any questions? Any short questions?" she asked.

"Do the volunteers have to commit to certain days and times for the entire three months, or do they have flexible schedules?" Harrison wondered aloud.

"No, I'm afraid, despite my own inclinations to the contrary, that there really isn't much room to maneuver. That's what efficiency is all about. But the three months go fast and almost everyone looks forward to their time here. A basic tenet of Another Way is to make it fun—and we do." Her visitors didn't doubt it for a minute.

Turning back to Donna and Jane, Joyce joked, "Okay, slaves. Back to work."

Facing the group once again, she extended her left arm and said, "Researchers," then, dropping her arm and moving a few steps to the other side of the partition and extending her right arm, she added, "and computer gurus." Joyce excused herself and talked quietly with the two gentlemen on the guru side of the partition.

Raeann wondered if she was the only member of the Mapleton group not to have done a rotation at the center. As if reading her mind, Phyllis asked, "How many of you Mapleton High students have had a rotation?"

To Raeann's surprise, only Janet and Dorothy raised their hands.

Phyllis was determined to get John to bring his students back when they could all spend more time. Mapleton students would benefit too. There was just too much to cover in one day. Her thoughts were interrupted by a deep, masculine voice.

"Arthur Ragsdale from Mapleton Volunteers in public schools. As computer supervisors, Joe and I are here Monday through Friday, eight to five, on a three-month basis. We had options. We could have chosen to volunteer just mornings, just afternoons, or evenings, or only two or three days a week, but we chose the full time option because, speaking for myself only, I was missing the old routine. Retirement is fine, but it makes you feel good to get back in the harness when you know you can do a job that is appreciated and needed."

"Well, you certainly got that last part right," said Joyce, edging up to the big man and giving him a hug.

"I'm Joe Collins," said a smaller, older looking gentleman at the desk behind Arthur's. "My home organization is Plugged In, a group that gets ex-gang members interested in computers and has them making money points, that translate into things that money would buy." He interrupted himself and looked sheepishly at Joyce: "I can't get used to this trade thing—points, stamps—whatever." Joe addressed the visitors and added, "Not that the Dream Machine isn't a great idea. I'm all for it, it's just hard to teach an old dog new tricks."

"Shame on you, Joe!" Joyce chided good-naturedly. "Joe and Arthur are marvelous with the young volunteers, here, and at their respective home organizations, and know absolutely everything to know about computers and the Internet."

Joe told the visitors about all the home pages the young people at the non-profit called Plugged In had created for the business community in Mapleton. He explained that Plugged In helped kids, especially those that had been able to kick their drug habits, acquire new skills. "Businesses donate to the Dream Machine while the youngsters acquire a cutting edge skill along with community currency and have a marvelous time doing it. There is little temptation to return to their old life style."

"Thanks Joe. Take it easy you guys. Now, on to my private domain," she said as she crossed the room and opened the wooden door and allowed her thirteen followers to line up inside.

At one end of Joyce's long, narrow, glassed-in office, was her desk; huge and neat as a pin, revealing the other trait that made her the perfect choice for the important job as CEO of Mapleton's Truly Volunteer Corps Center. Joyce was as organized and efficient as a marine sergeant and had the patience of Job. On top of it all, she loved to clown around. You might say an unusual profile with conflicting characteristics, but all were essential for her job.

Two empty desks occupied the far end of her office where, Joyce explained, two career oriented youths dedicate ten hours each, per week, though not necessarily at the Center. Their job was to monitor all programs and keep in touch with the various nonprofit leaders; solicit or supervise others to obtain donations of goods and services and generally, to do whatever Joyce needed. They were penciled in as the right-hand of the CEO when the Center jobs were conceived; the job that Donna had usurped and made her own. But, as Joyce explained, there was more than enough work for all three and both, Lynn and Jonathan, were out in the field this afternoon. One was on loan from the Salvation Army, and the other was affiliated with the Special Olympics.

Joyce led the group down the hall, introduced them to volunteer extraordinaire, George Simmons—the gentleman in charge of the Center's recycling department that afternoon—and said her good-byes. Mr. Simmons had everyone sit at a round table, not unlike the one they had left behind at Mapleton High, and, in deference to their time limitations, gave them a brief rundown on the recycling program. He said that recycling programs had been around for years and were proven ways to raise funds. Kangas collected, repaired, and resold cast off goods just as Salvation Army, Goodwill, and numerous resale shops used to do in Mapleton, and still did in Bloomfield and most American towns, as adjuncts for nonprofits, especially schools and churches.

When Mario pressed Mr. Simmons for a rundown of the recycling activity, Another Way style, as he put it, Mr. Simmons explained that those volunteers who chose the recycling department for their rotation, solicited neighborhoods and businesses, in person and on the phone, for any unused and unwanted items—from anything as small as a pair of socks to buildings, automobiles and profit-making equipment. Most used the phones at the center, but others spent their hours scavenging on bicycles, or in cars—if they were old enough to drive. Once a donation was identified, volunteers relayed the find to the center, where other volunteers followed up.

At the beginning, Kangas worked with existing recyclers, whenever possible. After all, the purpose of Another Way was to assist the good efforts already underway in the community. Leverage, not competition, was the goal. Goodwill Industries, St. Vincent de Paul Society, and Salvation Army already had trucks and pick up stations, which were expanded as Kangas flooded the community. Many churches and schools already had an infrastructure for their resale shops. Over time, these agencies merged their entire recycling programs with the center, and because their overhead was covered by the Kangas, they were able to focus on their primary missions of counseling, job training, holding seminars, and so forth. For example, the two hundred-year-old Salvation Army had hospitals, clinics, homes for unwed mothers, recreation centers, camps for children, soup kitchens, homeless shelters, and day care programs for seniors and children, all competing for time and resources.

No one was surprised to discover, during the course of the conversation, that Mr. Simmons was a retired teacher. Knowing they were behind schedule, he shortened his prepared talk and called for a young volunteer to escort the group to Mrs. Atkinson's domain. As the group stood up to say their good-byes, Mr. Simmons pulled back from the table and, for the first time, the students were aware of his wheelchair.

May Atkinson, now well into her seventies, had been a beauty in her day. Still tall and slender, she was a fashion plate even in slacks and sneakers. She had been a member of the Million Dollar Roundtable and won every award the insurance industry offered to its top sales people. The community recognized how lucky they were to have this dynamic lady working with young people at the center. It was said, with a great deal of pride, that what May didn't know, wasn't worth knowing. She spent three or four hours a day at the center, mostly supervising about twenty volunteers, mainly professionals from the old days, who were honored when she requested their help.

Shifts were arranged so that those who volunteered in the commission section had an hour a week of sales training from May, who, in her heyday, commanded top dollar for a keynote address at sales conventions around the globe. May was convinced that the average person didn't aim high enough because they imagined that wealth and fame were beyond their reach. She made it a point to give her volunteers a profile of those considered wealthy by American standards at the end of the twentieth century:

"Eighty percent are first generation wealthy; their annual income hovers around $131,000 and they work 45-55 hours per week. They invest approximately twenty percent of their annual income, their average home is valued at $320,000, and their average net worth is about $3.7 million. Most don't report to a boss and two-thirds are self-employed. They are frugal in what they pay for apparel, they drive cars three years old, and clip coupons."

This last item almost always provoked discussion, as it differed dramatically from her listeners' image of the jet-setting heir or heiress, lazily reclining on the world's most beautiful

"Finders' fees, kickbacks, commissions—they are nothing new," she explained. The commission department could be viewed as a clearing-house for services. On the one hand, TVC members (she despised the term Kanga, and didn't mind saying so) developed sales skills by soliciting businesses and getting them to agree to a commission for any new business generated by the efforts of volunteers.

Volunteers might sell wholesale tickets for sport and entertainment events at retail prices, or even at prices openly marked up for a good cause. All sorts of legitimate memberships and subscriptions might be sold on commission. There was enthusiastic talk of issuing discount cards displaying the Another Way logo and the names of merchants who agree to offer discounts to cardholders.

May was against the idea because, although it might bring in more money, it would be based on effective advertising rather than on personal salesmanship.

"Everyone needs to develop salesmanship," she said. "Even if you are a librarian or work alone doing research, you have to be able to sell a potential spouse on marriage, your children on values, your boss on a raise. Everyone needs to learn how to risk. If volunteers are not able to bring new clients to a business, they do not earn commissions. With each phone call or door-to-door solicitation, their time and effort is at risk.

"This," May insisted, "is a powerful lesson in cause and effect and brings home ideas often missing from social transactions today."

It was imperative that everyone who worked with her understood that actions have consequences. She wanted her charges to learn that success depends on individual ability, not on impersonal, promotional campaigns developed by others. She was an ardent advocate of Another Way's tenet that value is given for value received. She firmly believed that trade was the basis of all economic success.

Leonard Denton, the gentleman in charge of the entrepreneurial projects at the Center, knocked gently on the door. "Sorry to interrupt, May, but my first shift has to leave soon and they outdid themselves with today's lunch."

"Marvelous! I went to the cafeteria when I arrived over an hour ago and I got the recipe for that wonderful pasta sauce. When I decide to give up this position, I'm going to apply for a rotation in the entrepreneurial section and request the restaurant project."

May was still a charmer. Everyone left the commission area convinced that they had spent time with a master of sales.

Len, as he preferred to be called, led the group to the far end of the hall and into the cafeteria where the entire party feasted like royalty. As they ate, Len talked: "I am one of the volunteer directors of entrepreneurial projects. As the former CEO of a

Fortune 500 company, I'm used to pursuing vision and mission. I'm an old overseer. The main purpose of the Entrepreneurial Division is to free Mapleton's nonprofits to pursue their individual missions.

"At a recent conference I met the head of a non-profit with connections to the UC Medical School in San Francisco, who claimed that fundraising had occupied twenty percent of his time in 1973, and by 1995, eighty percent of his time was spent writing requests for grants. That left too little time to pursue research, the purpose of his organization. In 1996, he began concentrating on marketing a product, resulting from past research, hoping to use proceeds to fund his mission.

"Paul Newman may be a celebrity, but he doesn't write checks to charities; he sells salad dressing and donates the profits. We don't have to be scientists or celebrities to do the same thing. Before there was an Another Way in Mapleton, some high school students sold vegetables from their own community garden and created a line of bottled salad dressings that they sold in local supermarkets. The money they earned was divided among the graduating high school volunteers to be used toward college expenses. When my kids were in high school, one hundred percent of the seniors who had been involved with that project went on to college."

"This month, we have approximately six hundred volunteers participating in entrepreneurial projects. Some perform odd jobs, mostly in their own neighborhoods, for relatives, friends, and church members; jobs such as: babysitting, house sitting, yard and basement clean ups, pet care, errands, window washing, and repairs. They have the help of at least one adult volunteer, either to work along with them, as the college students often do, or to coordinate things as many of the retired or disabled volunteers do. Kids clean garages, wash windows, scrub floors; they do those things that are sometimes hard for an older person to do.

"We currently have over a hundred youths involved with a sandwich concession at twenty-five Mapleton schools. Five students at each of the twenty-five schools commit to make one hundred sandwiches one night a week. Sometimes two students team up and make fifty sandwiches, each on two separate school nights. The profit is close to a dollar per sandwich because of donated materials. Last month they made $50,000—most of it, profit. Four adult volunteers transport donations from bakeries and delicatessens and secure space in retail outlets for the sandwiches, as well as some student-made baked goods."

Len paused to shuffle some papers. "Only twenty young people are involved this month in baking the cookies, cakes, and pies, as opposed to the hundred and twenty-five students who make sandwiches."

Again, Len consulted his notes: "It looks like we have twenty kids currently washing cars on weekends and twenty more who are caring for lawns. Adult mentors are working with a dozen other kids to teach them bookkeeping skills. While still under supervision, they bill out at ten dollars an hour. Some volunteers run errands for busy workers and the homebound; errands such as grocery shopping and laundry drop-off and pick-up; others operate a flower delivery and singing greeting card service, and still others purchase tickets or retail items as requested.

"Forty students are involved with children's theme parties. They stage about ten parties a week. They provide theme cakes, favors, games, and stage puppet or magic shows." Len adjusted his reading glasses. "It says here they charge one hundred dollars for up to twenty guests and five dollars for each additional guest.

"Performing is another popular rotation. Kangas, in groups of ten to twelve, memorize and recite inspirational documents in front of service club members, business groups, and church gatherings. We had a group of grammar school children recite the Gettysburg Address, and the Preamble to the Declaration of Independence at a Rotary meeting I attended awhile ago, and my wife's prayer meeting was treated to a recitation of Martin Luther King's "I Have A Dream" speech last year. The producers and directors are almost always high school or college students, with an occasional retired adult involved. The children earn fifty dollars a performance and generally have about two paid performances a month. They also perform for free at schools, shopping malls, fairs, etc., as a public relations activity to recruit new TVC members. The kids perform skits and give wholesome performances just about anywhere at the drop of a hat. The TVC even has its own songs and cheers. There's more than dollars here. This and several other projects are geared toward education and publicity.

"Volunteers also have the opportunity to publish calendars, which are sold around Thanksgiving every year. Most feature drawings by school children or their photos or favorite recipes. That activity is always a good moneymaker and lots of fun for everybody involved.

"So is book publishing. Two months ago, an activity book cleared forth thousand dollars in profit." Len flipped some pages in a notebook and read, "A ninety-six page book cost $7,000 for 10,000 copies and each copy sold for a bargain price of five dollars, which netted $40,000 profit. When the printing is donated, the profit is naturally greater. Last year, there were four book projects. Each one can be completed during a three-month rotation. Unfortunately, participants have to be limited to one adult advisor and ten young people or their product would flood the market. As you can imagine, this is a great learning experience, as well as netting quite a bit of money for the Center and the various organizations.

"Phyllis may have explained how the dollars generated by the volunteers during their rotations are distributed."

"Actually, Len," Phyllis laughed, "I'm not sure myself."

Len smiled and said depreciatingly, "One tends to become myopic in a job like this. Anyway, twenty percent of net profits are distributed evenly among the organizations, and eighty percent of net profits are distributed back to the organizations, according to the number of volunteers each organization contributes to the rotation. A small amount comes off the top as needed to keep the center running. But, the truth is, for the past six months Joyce's salary, electrical and phone bills, transportation, and all overhead expenses here at the center have been covered by separate donations, so the entire proceeds of the entrepreneurial projects, the commissions May's volunteers have been collecting and George's recycling profits have gone directly to the volunteers' home organizations.

"I must admit, as a hard nosed businessman, I was skeptical about Another Way at first, but it has changed our community for the better. There's no doubt about it. These volunteers, young and old, are heroes when they bring the bacon home to their respective organizations. Not only do they have proof that they are doing something worthwhile, they are having fun. By working along side older people outside of their families, young people have picked up skills, developed good work habits, assumed responsibility, and absorbed many things about surviving in the adult world. By overcoming obstacles, conquering frustration, and practicing tenacity, things usually come out right, and they develop character and compassion. With self-discipline comes pride. They gain self-respect through achievement, as well as respect and recognition by the community.

"Without special classes, many have become familiar with banking, investments, insurance, learning how to type, keep books, make intelligent phone calls, take legible messages, and how to sell themselves, ideas, services, and products. Others have learned how to care for and respect tools; how to build and repair; how to plant, harvest, cook, garden, and market. I didn't even tell you about our restaurants or office workers. The point is, these kids—I call them kids, but I'm talking about people of all ages—mastered these things in the trenches by participating along side those with experience and expertise and by acting in the real world and not sitting in classes. These experiences will make them better employees, maybe even employers, and better parents. Taxpayers will benefit from their energy and goodwill, instead of paying for less effective lessons in job readiness and parenting skills.

"Older people are ideal mentors and I know firsthand that many are forced to retire before they are ready. Others find they are healthy and active and not as happy with retirement as they had imagined they would be. George and May, who you met, are just two examples of the many retired volunteers who have skills and life experience they would like to pass on. Many have prospered and are anxious to give back to their communities. Some are alone and others feel worthless. Another Way, via service in the Truly Volunteer Corps, provides an outlet for their goodwill, relief for their loneliness, and admiration and love from the community. Most importantly, volunteers become part of something bigger than themselves—they identify with a cause and discover a reason for living. They experience comradeship, love, and acceptance in a society where people often feel alienated. I don't know where I would have been after my wife died without Another Way."

The group could not help being inspired and impressed by Len Denton's passion. As they took their leave, everyone shook Len's hand. The effervescent Amanda gave him a big hug, and Megan followed suit.

There was a great deal of talking among small groups on the way back from the Center, and Phyllis noted some pretty intense discussions still going on as the students regrouped in their conference room at Mapleton High. She decided to let them comment on what they had witnessed, instead of declaring this the Q & A period as she had intended. She would ask for questions during the course of the conversation.

In one, intense day the group had melded and taken on an identity. No sense spoiling that feeling with formalities this late in the day. She would relax and enjoy it.

"I'm absolutely amazed at the talent and energy of the older people we met at the Center," Lisa exclaimed.

"Yeah! I saw some old guy playing basketball when I snuck a peek at the gym, when I was poking around looking for the rest room," Mario confessed.

"Some of those 'old guys' played pro ball," Phyllis said. "Every older person had a full life before retirement and many had illustrious careers. The people you met today were tops in their field, and there are thousands more like them. As Len told you, they don't want to let the knowledge and skill they gained over a period of years, disappear with them if there is some way they can pass it on."

"Some way," Amanda repeated with a grin, "you mean Another Way, don't you Phyllis?" Amanda was captivated by the name.

"When I did my rotation last year I heard there was an Academy Award-winning actor doing a rotation at the same time," Dorothy confided.

"Who? Did you meet him?" Paul leaned toward Dorothy.

"I can't remember his name," Dorothy admitted, "but it was someone I never heard of."

"I noted five famous actors and actresses on the roster when I had my rotation," Janet put in. "There were also famous authors, scientists, and war heroes."

"And millionaires and CEOs of large corporations, along with bus drivers, coal miners, and waitresses. Everyone was young once—even me!" laughed Phyllis.

"Yeah, we know that intellectually, but it's easy to forget." Bill was feeling guilty about his earlier desire to have a mentor younger than his grandfather. For crying out loud, his grandfather had been a tail gunner in the Second World War—and a mountain climber. That's where his own father got his love of the outdoors and passed it on to him—the grandson.

"I think we all saw the oldest generation in another light today. I know from living with my grandparents that a lot of kids sort of ignore older people or even fear them," Bill said.

"Absolutely!" Paul agreed, "But Gus and Bill changed that for me and my friends for sure!"

"There's far too much emphasis on youth in today's world. Many TV commercials poke fun of old people, making them into ridiculous caricatures," Mr. Hoffer declared.

"Well, the best thing that happened to me today," said Amanda, "is that older people became real. I learned that they are generous and have a lot to give and a lot to admire."

Amanda never knew her grandparents. Her father's parents had emigrated from Jamaica in the 1920s and had died one after the other when she was still a baby. Her mother had been born in Jamaica, the twelfth of fourteen children and had been sent to the United States after her own mother's death to be raised by an older sister, Aunt Gloria.

"I still can't get over Len's presentation," said Mario. "You guys have fantastic opportunities in Mapleton. I would give anything to actually work on a book that is going to be published."

"I'm going to volunteer for a rotation and work on the calendars," exclaimed Paul. "I can scan artwork and photos into the computer and use the new Adobe software that has cool special effects. I noticed some serious equipment when I was exploring."

"How did you and Mario manage to be so nosey?" Amanda asked with good humor.

"We eat fast," Paul answered, good-naturedly tossing a paper wad across the table at Amanda.

"The children's theme parties is what I'd choose," said Megan wistfully.

"Learning accounting, or at least bookkeeping skills would help me through college," Lisa added enviously.

"Don't forget," said Phyllis, "if you donated time, you would be collecting stamps, redeemable for college tuition, books, and so forth, all the time you were learning the skills you wanted. I think the rotations accept people as young as thirteen, so that's a lot of years to collect stamps."

"Thanks, Phyllis. That really makes me feel better," Lisa kidded.

"I hate to be a wet blanket, but there are no trading stamps with rotation jobs. Stamps are trades only for the jobs offered by the individual nonprofits, not the center." Janet said.

"Well, you've worked at the center and I'm sure you're right. I'll have to be more careful." Phyllis smiled. "But there are mentors listed on the Dream Machine to train you, and bookkeeping can be done through nonprofits as a regular Another Way job." She turned, still smiling, to Janet. "Why don't you and Dorothy tell us what you chose for your rotations?"

"I worked in the office with Joyce," Janet answered, "and absolutely loved it and her."

"I received training and worked in the cafeteria my first month," Dorothy volunteered, "And spent the rest of my rotation at one of the center's restaurants near my home. I didn't have my driver's license—and still don't," she smiled, "but I needed to work someplace that didn't require transportation. That's the main reason I chose the restaurant project."

"Did you like it?" Raeann pressed, with a thought for her own rotation in the future.

"I loved it. We made tons of money. Plus, I acquired experience, which is impossible for a fourteen-year-old to get any place else. I'm sure it will make it easier to get a waitress job, if I should ever need one in the future," Dorothy replied.

"You know when the Rotary Club came up in the discussion on the way to the Center," Bill said, "I thought of my grandfather and all his friends who belong to Rotary in Bloomfield and I remembered something that was said in a class discussion in preparation for today. It has been bothering me and I thought I'd mention it. Apparently, there has been a recent decline in membership in fraternal groups such as the Rotary, Elks, Lions, Eagles, and Moose. Self-help and community service are woven into the fabric of these groups, which Bloomfield relies so heavily on for volunteers. What will it be like in places like Bloomfield if service clubs go under?"

"I wouldn't worry about it," said Mr. Hoffer. "I read an article in the *Wall Street Journal* and according to Frank Sarnecki, who heads up the Moose, new women members and the presence of children have given a new character and life to at least sixty of the 21,000 Moose lodges. He favors opening up membership and is changing lodges to family centers across the country. This is a trend which focuses on some of the best aspects of Another Way."

"I was most impressed by the alternative school." Harrison hadn't been heard from for a while. "I read about kids who have used computers to advance at their own pace. This kid, Jamie, was only twelve years old and studying molecular biology, and another kid was learning Akkadian when his class was studying about ancient Egypt and Akkad."

"Computers are great for learning languages," said Raeann, "although, I don't know about Akkadian, which is a dead language based on hieroglyphics, but all the newer computers have audio capabilities and you can get the inflections for languages like Japanese, French, or Russian, and even carry on better conversations with computer pals in other countries. There is even a book out called, Virtual College, by Pam Dixon. She says it may soon be possible to get a Harvard Law degree without going to Massachusetts. Apparently, several professors at Harvard Law School are developing a virtual college course called the Bridge Program, working through Lexis-Nexis. Lectures are videotaped and delivered with electronic casebooks."

"We were all justly impressed with all the exciting entrepreneurial projects, and as a senior, I'm kicking myself for not volunteering earlier for a rotation, but I would like to put a plug in for the presentations of Mr. Simmons and Miss Atkinson," Lincoln said. "I'm convinced that one-to-one mentoring is the only thing that can really change things."

Lincoln touched a nerve with Mr. Hoffer who said, "I, too, think mentoring is the most important thing any volunteer can do, but I'd like to add a word of caution to dampen the euphoria a little. I have two points. First, being a volunteer doesn't have instant rewards, and second, just having an opportunity doesn't guarantee success.

"We make the mistake of letting our children think if you do this, you'll have instant success, like on the movie and TV screens. Making a difference takes patience, perseverance, and hard work. In volunteering, there are disappointments, just as there are in the rest of life. There are not always thank yous and smiles; what you do is not always up to the other guy's expectations—whether that guy is a parent, friend, boss, or the target of your goodwill.

"I set out in Bloomfield to show others that young people can do the job society needs right now. I thought a big part of the problem was that adults were not giving young people the opportunity to show their stuff. I may have forgotten the part about everything being possible, but not necessarily easy.

"The visit to the Mapleton TVC Center today assured me that we are all learning every day and just as on the hard drive of a computer, experiences are being stored as long as we are alive, so, although kids today know a tremendous amount, they simply have not built up as many megs on their hard drive, and what they have stored in their memory isn't always relevant to the job at hand. So we must be patient and train them, take the time to explain, and let them practice what needs to be done, as Joyce and George and May and Len are doing with their volunteers.

"It sounds fairly easy to make calls to set up appointments, but aside from the logistics of the job, you have to be understood. When English is not your native language and you are lacking confidence and low on self-esteem, it is neither natural nor easy to speak clearly, distinctly, and in a confident manner, correctly pronouncing names and even ordinary words. You might think there is no big trick to making phone calls, but any person starting phone work has to consider, what if they ask me some questions I don't know? We all like to be prepared and dislike sounding stupid. Even if information is written down and answers rehearsed with the main one being, 'I'm sorry, that is all I know. I was just asked to…' some youngsters and adults do not read!

"People who have raised bright, successful children can tell you about the temptation to do household chores themselves. Why argue with children over making beds, taking out garbage, cleaning rooms, when it is so easy to shoo them off to play or sit them in front of the TV. But I assure you—the people who raised the bright, successful children did not give into the temptation. They worked with their children, listened, gave suggestions, and made them perform tasks over and over until they got them right. They insisted that the important child in their care spell ten words in a row without mistakes, or shoot ten baskets without a miss, or perform ten perfect scales on the piano before going on to the next passage. They resisted the temptation to overlook a mistake on number eight and hope the last two would be perfect so they could get on with their own schedules. If they had succumbed, instead of learning how to do something right, the child would learn a series of unproductive things: he would learn people don't mean what they say. He would begin to think I'm not that important, the task isn't that important, you can get away with things, it's okay to do less than your best, everyone does it.

"Better an adult not assume the task of working with a young person, than to do it poorly. Everyone wants to be a champion; to be the best he or she can be; but from time to time we all let ourselves, and those in our care, get away with less than it takes because we don't always care enough—care enough to spend all that time and energy. And that, my friends, is what it takes to make a difference in the lives of many of our kids who now spend their days aimlessly shooting pool, smoking pot, watching TV, or committing violence against themselves or the community."

The silence when Mr. Hoffer paused was evidence that he had indeed dampened the euphoria around the table. He concluded, "Computers and the Internet open up unbelievable opportunities, but opportunity without one-to-one contact—without mentoring—is not enough."

"Well, I suppose that's it then," Phyllis said. "If there are no further questions or comments about Another Way or anything that was said this morning, let's..."

Lisa didn't let Phyllis finish her sentence, "I don't understand why the money from the rotation projects are distributed in the 20/80 split."

"Can anyone explain it?" Phyllis asked.

"I'll give it a try," said Janet. "The pro-rata distribution was discussed a lot during my office rotation. It seems those small startup organizations, with new ideas and the energy of an impassioned founder who is constantly on the scene, do wonderful work in the community; work that definitely deserves assistance and applause. Donors who want to get more bang from their buck would love to know about these groups. People who want to really make a difference in the community would like the opportunity to volunteer services and other resources to these organizations. However, these organizations used to have very short life spans because most people, even organizations doing the same type of work, never heard about them until it was too late. They spend little or no time on public relations. Almost all staff and volunteer time is spent in the field pursuing their mission. The pro-rata sharing of rotation funds and the coordination of volunteers and needs, gives these organizations a fighting chance.

"While at the Center, we passed someone in the hallway who I recognized as being from the Home of Hope. Although this organization has recently enjoyed media coverage in Mapleton and has proven that it has staying power (the founder is still impassioned), it was floundering when I was on rotation and was the subject of a lot of discussion."

"I assume the Home of Hope is a small startup," Bill said.

"Well, as I said, I sure heard enough about it while I was at the Center. Let's see—the Home of Hope started with one woman, who innocently volunteered to go to juvenile hall with her church group to give the gang kids support. She found she had more to give than most people and she went back and back and she extended her hours and began talking with these gang members in her car, letting them know she cared and was there to listen to them. Kids of all ages responded and brought their friends and soon, there were too many to fit in the car, so she met with them in a series of donated places and finally ended up renting a building; a run down, former store, located in the midst of gang and drug activity where the kids hung out. She had trouble keeping the phone turned on, not to mention heat and electricity. The kids did odd jobs to bring in money, but the temptation to deal drugs was always present. She held Bible study classes and helped them with their homework and generally acted like the mother most of them didn't have.

"There is a lot more to the story. There are things that need improvement and there is a lot that is praiseworthy, but the point is the attitude of the kids. These kids, some of them still involved with gangs, had low self-esteem, many had little command of the English language, most were illiterate and unskilled, and the Home of Hope was their lifeline. They were eager to cut grass, wash cars, run errands, and it was plain that if they had the skills to match their desire, they could do anything. Len's entrepreneurial training and projects were ready made for them. They didn't know anything about the Another Way; they were inspired by the dedication of the wonderful woman many of them still call mother.

"There was a pioneer spirit there; a willingness to sacrifice for one another and for the future; there was a shared dream of what the Home of Hope could become, not just for those involved at the moment, but for younger brothers and sisters." Janet paused and leaned into her audience: "Have you ever felt a promise? Have you ever encountered the promise of America, maybe in an old movie?" She seemed embarrassed and quickly wrapped it up: "Anyway, I was there once before they joined the Another Way and you could definitely feel a promise at the Home of Hope.

"Look, the Home of Hope would have gladly played by the old rules; writing grant proposals and operating on money contributed by grantmaking foundations or government subsidies, but they didn't have the time, the skills, or the money to compete in that marketplace. Even a discounted course in grant writing takes a week to complete and costs three hundred and fifty dollars, and that's without travel and hotel expenses. Grant writing is a business—that is the old way of thinking about it. Becoming self-sufficient and independent of the starts and stops of grants is Another Way.

"There is a new crop of innovative and awesome ideas every day. To me, Home of Hope is a symbol of all the young organizations that might result from those ideas. Fundraising by the Kangas gives those organizations a chance to survive. I remember the three months that I was in Joyce's office, preparing checks for just under two thousand dollars to several of the smallest organizations, who only contributed the minimum number of volunteers—one adult and two young people, to the Center rotation. A couple of the large church groups who sent more than fifty volunteers to the Center got checks for over fifteen thousand dollars a month. You can follow the pro-rata break down for twenty-five fictional entities in your handout when you get back to Bloomfield."

"Nicely done, Janet," Mr. Hoffer said exuberantly.

"Yes, indeed," Phyllis agreed. "Okay, people," she said, with an eye on the clock, "are there any other comments before we call it quits?" She looked fondly around the room. "That's it then. Thank you for coming. Good luck and let's meet again soon. Today we only scratched the surface of the many implications of Another Way."

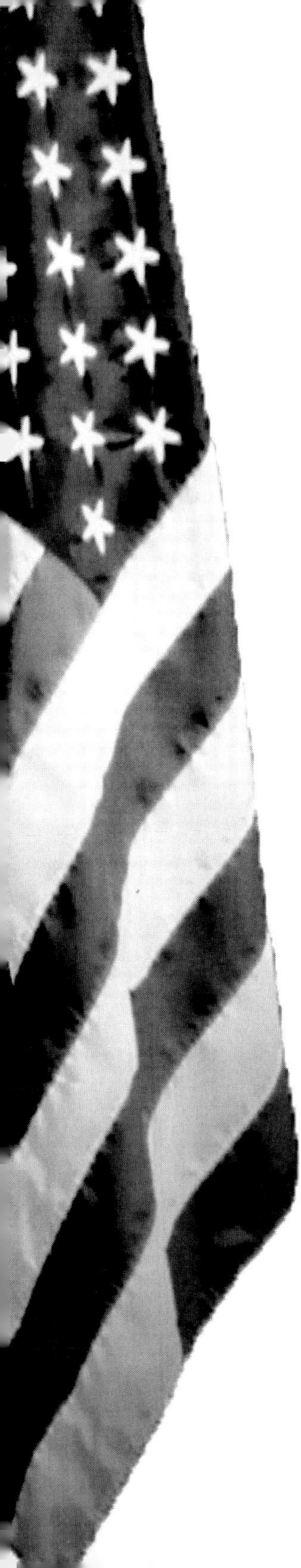

2003
A Tragedy

"Could you come with me, please? Could you come with me, please?"

The words kept repeating themselves over and over in her head. Through her numbness she understood the police woman sitting next to her was trying to comfort her, to ease her pain—but she felt no pain, not yet—she was in a fog, surrounded by a thick, protective numbness. She was in a stupor that was, in its own way, comforting but could not silence the revolving tape in her head.

"Could you come with me, please? Could you come with me please?"

Dorothy had no sense of time. One moment she had been happily singing in the shower and the next, she was at the door watching the red lights revolve over the policeman's head and hearing, "Will you come with me, please?"

In between, she had been asked if she were Mrs. Davenport and told that there had been an accident. Her husband was involved, which was not surprising, since he was the chief intern at the hospital in town. Tonight they were going to celebrate their first anniversary and David had volunteered to pick up her dress at the dry cleaners while she finished her shower. It was the dress she had worn on their honeymoon. She had given into nostalgia and had it altered now that the baby was demanding more room. It was natural that he should rush to help at the scene of an accident.

"Is there a relative we can call?" Then, "Is this Doctor Avila?" That's all she remembered.

2011
Opening of the Bloomfield NE Community Center

The perfect day, Bill thought, as he walked briskly toward the center. Just as he had pictured it! The sky was blue, the sun was bright, the birds were singing—everything was coming together. The years of hard work were paying off and he wondered if it could have been done without Lincoln Williams.

Bill Adams ran over his introduction. As usual, it was brief and to the point, so he continued to let his mind wander while his body absorbed the warmth of the sun.

What if Lincoln had accepted the more tempting basketball scholarship from the University of Kentucky instead of the Bloomfield scholarship? Would the Bloomfield NE Community Center be opening its doors today, without Lincoln's talents?

Everyone who knew the situation admired Lincoln for making the responsible choice. As if the sudden and tragic death of his father and the loss of his mother's lifelong companion were not enough, the insurance didn't cover expenses and his mother couldn't work outside the home because Lincoln's younger sister required special care. Since Mapleton was only a few minutes from Bloomfield University, Lincoln was able to stretch the

99

proceeds from that scholarship to cover the family's living expenses. The scouts found him anyway, and his responsible choice was rewarded.

After graduating, he had played pro-ball with the Portland Trail Blazers for five years and coached at Bloomfield part-time for the last four. Because Lincoln was a celebrity in the sports world, and a passionate and persuasive advocate of the project, Another Way had finally taken root in Bloomfield. Another Way had become Bill Adam's passion fifteen years ago and there was no better promoter of the Another Way concept. Nevertheless, there had been no media coverage, no publicity before Lincoln came onboard.

"Hey Bill—this is the big day! How're you feeling?" It was Mario Lee, one of the original instigators of Another Way in Bloomfield. He and Mr. Hoffer were going to introduce some of the volunteer mentors from Mapleton who had contributed their time to Bloomfield.

"I'm feeling great! Even the weather is cooperating. Long time no sun. Did you pick up the awards for the honorees?"

"Sure did. They look terrific! The engraver did a good job."

The two friends climbed the steps to the new community center. They had arrived early intentionally, as they were jointly in charge of this event. As they closed the large carved doors, salvaged from a church that was demolished last year, they were immobilized for a few seconds while their eyes adjusted from the bright sunlight to the overhead lights that were temporarily dimmed while the lighting was tested for the afternoon's activities. The space they entered was the heart of Bloomfield's third community center and today, its partitions removed, the 10,000 square-foot area would accommodate just under a thousand chairs; slightly more without the temporary stage that was now decked with flowers, banners, and a podium. When divided in half, each of the two 100-by-50 foot spaces usually contained five long tables, with a total of 190 workstations. There were smaller rooms in adjoining buildings used for a variety of activities and larger spaces to accommodate small groups collaborating on projects. The Center was versatile. It had been open on a twenty-four hour basis for the past six weeks. Many adjustments were made during this trial period and Bill was sure many more issues would come to light that would require solutions in the future. The Another Way concept, like its newest building, was flexible. Another Way in Bloomfield was modeled on Another Way in Mapleton, but there were differences, just as each of the other two centers in Bloomfield differed from one another. However, like any franchise, the basic structure remained the same.

The two young men ran around assuring other volunteers that the flower display was perfect, the curtain pull was now installed, and complimenting the arrangement of the eleven chairs that had been placed behind the podium in a gentle curve.

The first seat was reserved for the master of ceremonies, Bill Adams; the second two, for the Mayor and Superintendent of Bloomfield's schools—both speakers; the next pair, for the Bloomfield presenters, Mario and Mr. Hoffer; the next five, for the Mapleton honorees and the last, for the third speaker; Lincoln Williams.

Bill tested the microphone on the podium, borrowed from the Rotary Club, and before he knew it, the auditorium was half-full. Soon, guests were standing in the back and along the sides of the huge room. The honorees, all but Raeann Cotton, were seated, and the speakers and presenters were behind the curtain waiting to be introduced. Mrs. Ortiz had been playing for several minutes on the grand piano her family had donated. Bill figured Raeann would slip in discreetly before the presentations began, so he gave the signal to dim the house lights. He thought he would be nervous, but he was simply enthused and proud. He climbed the movable stairs to the stage as Mrs. Ortiz launched into the classical tune they had earlier agreed would be his cue.

"Welcome! Welcome everyone to the grand opening of the Bloomfield North East Community Center. This is the pay-off for all who worked to make this center a reality and we deserve to celebrate.

"First, I'd like you to meet today's speakers, the honorable Mayor Charles Christopher." Bill paused for applause as the Mayor entered smiling and waving as he crossed the stage and took his seat.

"The Superintendent of Bloomfield's schools, Edward Ellison." There was more enthusiastic applause and when the presenters, John Hoffer and Mario Lee, took the stage, their entrance was accompanied by cheers from current and past students and friends, and cat calls and whistles from the younger members of the audience.

Bill had planned it so Lincoln Williams' entrance was last. He knew, from past experience, what would happen. Pandemonium broke loose in the makeshift auditorium. Lincoln waved and smiled while Bill tried his best to restore order.

The Mayor was just getting into what appeared to be the beginning of a long speech, so Bill settled back in his chair and let his mind wander.

Lincoln was still the thoughtful philosopher whose ideals had expanded the concept of Another Way. Another Way meant as much to Lincoln today as it did that day at Mapleton High School back in 1996, even though he was now a self-described libertarian capitalist. Lincoln's sincerity had attracted Bill that day and he continued to believe that sincerity was one of Lincoln's best qualities. Bill had learned over the ensuing years that Lincoln didn't believe in self-sacrifice; he believed in freedom, not obligation. Lincoln advocated voluntary giving based on compassion and a desire to help as opposed to governments' mandatory redistribution based on force and endless need.

The Candidate

Bill looked around and noted the Mayor was barely in the middle of a speech he had heard before, so he relaxed and went back to his reminiscing.

An attractive, young redhead in the third row caught his eye and made him wonder what had become of Lisa Wainwright, the senior representative from Bloomfield to Mapleton High back in 1996. It had been her first year at Bloomfield High. He remembered because it was something they had in common. At the time he had wondered why two newcomers were chosen. But now that he knew John Hoffer so well, it was obvious. Mr. Hoffer, a sensitive man, had been Lisa's homeroom teacher and probably realized that it was difficult for a young girl to assimilate into a senior class where everyone had known each other for years and were already anticipating the pain and joy of separation at the end of the year. No seniors seemed to mind; their agendas were full and the Mapleton meeting had not stirred the same competitive fervor at Bloomfield that it had at Mapleton.

The mayor had completed his speech and the clapping brought Bill back to the present; but only temporarily. As the superintendent began his own congratulatory address, Bill let his mind drift once again. He was enjoying it.

Bill was amazed that the glimpse of red hair in the audience could bring up such vivid memories. He recalled Lisa's comment that it's harder to gain the trust and cooperation of the people social programs are intended to reach if those people think you're only helping them for the money. He also remembered that Mario had dismissed the newcomer's comment by claiming that if a community was to turn down federal and state subsidies those subsidies would just be distributed to other communities. Bill had pegged Mario as a mercenary back then, but after working with him over the years he was now willing to bet that Mario was the most spiritual person in the room that day. Bill smiled as he considered how he would describe the adult Mario he knew today—a spiritual capitalist.

Bill turned to look at Mario, just as the superintendent finished speaking and the clapping began again. He regained his bearings and introduced Mr. Hoffer as the first presenter to bestow awards.

After Phyllis Clarry was given her award, Mr. Hoffer described some of the programs that Arthur Ragsdale and Mae Atkinson had implemented in Mapleton and intended to introduce into Bloomfield. He went on to explain Arthur and Mae were only on loan from Mapleton until they had trained volunteers in Bloomfield to take their places. Mr. Hoffer spent most of his time relating their accomplishments. Then, he dispensed two more awards and sat down, secure in the knowledge that Mario would pick up where he left off.

Mario Lee was chosen to present awards because of the mammoth number of hours he had contributed to the effort that culminated in the opening of this newest Bloomfield Center. Mario had been devoted to Lincoln since that first day in Mapleton when, as a lowly ninth grader, he felt privileged to be in the room with the charismatic basketball star. Mario put in as many hours as Lincoln did, trying to get Bloomfield residents to give Another Way a chance because Another Way meant so much to Lincoln. Mario's allegiance was to Lincoln, not to Another Way.

Mario, like John Hoffer, enumerated skills and accomplishments, but this time, the awards were for the technical people who had already volunteered many, many hours and pledged to continue to volunteer the technical expertise that the Another Way concept was dependent upon. Mario was good friends with both Paul and Raeann, and he sincerely liked and admired Joyce Ryan and Leonard Deltan, who were the heart of the Mapleton Community Truly Volunteer Center and were mentoring their counterparts in Bloomfield. Mario was surprised that Raeann hadn't shown up. She was so organized that he would have expected her to notify him if she couldn't be there for the presentation. He, like Bill, had noted her chair was empty when the program began and had expected her to slip in at the last moment. He had been prepared to add a bit of humor to her introduction. Instead, he found himself improvising Raeann's disappointment that she couldn't be here today and went on to acknowledge her hard work and praise her skills and past accomplishments. All in all, Mario did a good job.

Lincoln followed with a brief, but enthusiastic, speech. After the cheers and stamping of feet, he was immediately enveloped by a hoard of fans and whisked away to a smaller planned event in honor of two of the Center's largest donors. The crowd had dispersed and Mario was busy directing the clean up contingent when he felt a rough hand on his shoulder. He turned to face a furious Paul Egan.

"What's up, Paul?"

"That's exactly what I want to know," Paul replied angrily as he encroached on Mario's space.

Mario stepped back a pace. "I don't know what you mean."

Paul poked a finger at Mario's chest. "I want to know just why Raeann was excluded from the ceremony at the last moment. Wouldn't she blend in with all your fancy flowers and fanfare?"

Mario was astounded. "She's my friend, but you're closer to her than I am, and if I'd seen you first I would be asking you the same thing. It's not like Raeann not to show up without a word, but it looks like that's exactly what happened."

"Don't give me that!"

Before Mario could answer, they both heard a breathless voice behind them. "I'm really sorry I missed the presentations. I ran out of gas and when I tried to call, I discovered my cell phone was dead. I know that's hard to believe but…"

"See? I don't get you sometimes Paul." Mario turned to Raeann. "Are you all right? You're the last person I'd ever expect to run out of gas, let alone let a cell phone go dead. But, it's good to see you and you look terrific."

Raeann was dressed as a woman who expected to be in the limelight. Nevertheless, Paul was skeptical. "How'd you get the gas?" he asked, staring at her fashionable high-heeled shoes.

"Well, one thing did go right. A highway patrol officer gave me enough gasoline to get me to the Chevron station on Wilder and Tenth. How'd the presentation go?"

"Everything went just fine. But we missed you, and Paul was worried about you."

Raeann crinkled her nose and Mario gave her a knowing wink.

Margie's

"Good job, Mario—congratulations, Paul—we missed you, Raeann," Bill addressed all three of his friends in one breath. Without waiting for a response, and with a sheepish look on his face, he blurted, "Guess who I've got here?"

All three were baffled. "No worries," the young woman interrupted. "It has been thirteen years and I'm not sure that I recognize everyone."

"Oh my gosh. I can't believe it. Janet Norwood!" The two women gave each other a hug.

"How've you been? What have you been doing? Where have you been?"

Mario and Paul immediately put their differences behind them.

Bill took charge. "Let's go down to Margie's and get a cup of coffee and get caught up. They're busy cleaning up here."

⁂

Settled around the table in the back of Margie's, Janet related the highlights of her past fifteen years. She had gone back east to Smith College, her grandmother's alma mater. Her mother had gone there too, but had left her sophomore year. She had warned Janet that anyone who had grown up in the west might find the east coast stifling and the Ivy League's air of self-importance hard to breathe. Janet had stuck it out; at first, to please her grandmother. She, too, noticed the feeling of superiority in many of her classmates, but preferred to call it a legitimate sense of pride in the hard work they were doing and the superior education they were receiving. She had ended up enjoying the four years and made many good friends; one that had connections to a magazine editor that led to her first job as a reporter in New York.

After answering a series of questions about New York and correcting their illusions of the glamorous life led by reporters, Janet told her five newly discovered friends that she had gone back to school at NYU and, after earning master's degrees at Stern School of Business and at the Wagner Graduate School of Public Service, she was accepted at the new John Brademas Center for the Study of Congress. This prompted more questions, since none of her old friends knew there was such an institution. The group was relieved to learn that they were not alone in their ignorance; that even those elected to the United States Congress didn't fully understand its responsibilities, the extent of its power, and the fundamentals of making policy. The Center's goal is not only to help future politicians better grasp the reasoning that goes into policy-making, but also to produce bi-partisan research for the edification of scholars, students, current and past members of Congress, and the general public. Janet described several of the events she had attended and everyone around the table was impressed.

In answer to their constant barrage of questions, she admitted she had fallen in love with NYC and truly enjoyed her stint in the nation's capitol, among the movers and shakers. Although she had kept in touch with her family, (parents and siblings had come to NYC for extended visits from time to time) she was homesick and her parents were getting older, so she searched for a job closer to home and landed one in record time at the city manager's office right here in Bloomfield. She was to start next week.

Janet was a down-to-earth person and was uncomfortable with the situation her litany had caused. It was clear she had awed her friends. The last thing she wanted was to be impressive, so, to deflect the attention, Janet asked for a report on the exploits of those around the table. It just happened that she had run into the five most devoted patrons of Another Way and that meant that none of them had been out of the Mapleton-Bloomfield area for more than a day or two; maybe to San Francisco or somewhere else for brief family vacations.

Each contributed to the conversation, but it was obvious they all felt their last fifteen years were extremely dull after what they had heard from Janet. It was almost a relief when Mario included seeing some movies in his report, and the conversation revived. Soon everyone was involved in a discussion of *Avatar*.

"Does anybody know what Avatar means?" Bill asked.

"I googled it right after I saw the movie and there were five hundred million pages, so I narrowed the search to definitions," Janet volunteered. "The one I liked best was from Princeton wordnet.web: avatar (a new personification of a familiar idea)."

Paul cupped his hand and leaned toward Raeann. "It figures," he said under his breath.

In case Paul was referring to Janet's propensity for research, Raeann quickly asked, "What did you all think of the movie?"

But it was Paul who took the bait. "I thought it was dumb."

"You're kidding—explain please." Mario was genuinely surprised.

"Well," Paul began, "This is the embodiment of nothing new under the sun. There are loads of movies, video games, and comic characters with the same theme and even the same name; some in Japan, and a few other countries. I'm betting on some law suits."

"What? For copyright infringements?" Janet asked.

"Maybe; but that's only a start," Paul replied defiantly. "The producer should be sued by the viewers that innocently sat through the dialogue. A fourth grader could have constructed a better story line."

"I loved the drawings and technical aspects," Raeann interjected in a conciliatory tone.

"Yeah, the imagination that went into the forest and wild life," Mario added.

"Most of that was stolen from previous work done some fifty years ago by others," Paul retorted.

Raeann kept trying to make peace. "Many stories are similar. Compare *Avatar* with one of my favorites, *Dances With Wolves*, and you'll see that both have a hero who is a member of the military and chooses to go take part in an unusual assignment, befriends the indigenous people, learns their language, believes his fellow soldiers are acting unjustly toward the tribe so he joins the indigenous people's fight against the soldier, marries a beautiful member of the indigenous tribe, and turns away from his former life."

"My point. Nothing new under the sun."

Bill jumped into the conversation. "Genius is in adapting bits and pieces from those who have gone before and constructing a new masterpiece. Musicians have been doing it for hundreds of years. My grandparents often play music from the fifties and I notice how many of those tunes can be traced to classical origins."

"I was bothered by the story too—or should I say, lack thereof," Janet said. "I think Paul's got a point. Without all the special effects, Avatar was a B- movie with C acting."

"You mean overacting," Paul grumbled, although he was pleasantly surprised to have Janet as an ally.

Raeann defended the movie again. "I think the actors did the best they could with the script they were given."

"The fictional instigator of all this destruction was the CEO of a private company who wasn't fleshed out enough to be considered a real character. We don't know anything about him," Janet replied.

"Yeah. Instead, they turned all that digital expertise into a Michael Moore propaganda piece of…" Paul paused and looked around sheepishly and added, "You know what I mean."

"What? You don't think big business and the military should be responsible?" This time it was Bill.

"I don't mean they have clean hands," Paul countered. "Historically, the most advanced nations have their period of imperialism, exploiting, even occupying other nations for their resources."

"That was the point of the movie. Exploiting Pandora and disrupting the harmony the Na'vi achieved. A lot of people think the Na'vi were living the ideal life and presented a righteous goal for all humanity. I'm one of those people," Raeann intervened. She thought the dialogue between Paul and Bill was going too far over what amounted to nothing. "Most of our parents were idealists who dropped out during the Vietnam War."

"Great—let's discuss the Flower Children of the sixties and seventies." Paul was disappointed in what he perceived as betrayal by Raeann.

"Raeann's right. The Na'vi were a perfect example of something the so-called Flower Children would admire." Mario pursued his thought. "I believe we are one with nature and it is a matter of appreciating the importance of life at all levels and tapping into each other's energy."

"That may be a comforting belief and one I might subscribe to, but I think Paul has a point. You've got to admit there is an anti-technology feeling that goes along with our current anti-development, anti-growth culture. I think Paul sees it as threatening private property rights, which are a prerequisite to our freedom and jeopardize the raison d'être—the original purpose and uniqueness of the United States. That might explain the success of Avatar."

Raeann was surprised, but not intimidated by Janet's response and offered her own opinion. "The plunder of Pandora had nothing to do with private property rights. In fact, it was quite the opposite."

"Then forget the property rights for a moment. What we have is business and the military depicted as brutal, greedy, and insensitive beasts who, in search of profit, use their nasty technology to rape the environment and destroy primitive, but spiritual cultures."

Paul was pleased to have her support but wished it had been Raeann instead of Janet who had come to his defense. Nevertheless, he backed her up. "Okay—the U.S. isn't perfect, but I've had enough of blaming it for everything evil that happens in the world."

"You think greedy businessmen had nothing to do with the financial crisis the present administration is trying to solve—or the exorbitant expense and expansion of the wars in Iraq and Afghanistan?" Bill persisted. "There was evidence that both Blackwater and Halliburton took advantage of the federal government under the Bush–Cheney administration."

Mario took over. "Halliburton has numerous subsidiaries. It distanced itself from Houston-based KBR, which is the engineering, construction, and military contractor subsidiary you are probably referencing. Blackwater recently began operating under its new name, Academi."

"I thought we were talking about a movie here." Raeann tried once again to suppress the confrontation. "How did we get off on this tangent? *Avatar* was a movie that took in millions of dollars and received five Academy awards for its technical/digital aspects and not its screenplay. Enough already!"

"Yeah, well, I'm sick of this redistribution of wealth and the demonization of America—the most generous nation in the history of the world. I'm wondering if it's the greedy corporations you object to or the military industrial complex?"

Bill was astonished by this turn in the conversation. One moment Mario was admiring the Na'vi and now he appeared to be defending Blackwater. "What's up?" he said, echoing what a calmer Mario had asked Paul earlier. "Did you join the Tea Party or what?"

"What yourself! Do you think they'd have me? I heard they are a bunch of racist neo-cons. But, putting that aside, at least they are voicing a concern about unemployment, terrorism, illegal immigration, education, and most of all the country's mounting debt."

Raeann tried to forestall the developing situation once again. "Of course, they'd have you—and they're not racist. They might do a little name-calling. Both of the major parties are guilty of that."

"Marxists, Socialists, Neo-cons, McCarthyism—otherwise, normal adults are beginning to sound like little kids in a name-calling contest, throwing whatever is handy at one another. This has got to stop! On the other hand, bi-partisanship, trans-partisanship—whatever you choose to call it—is not a reasonable approach when two groups honestly believe what the other is proposing is harmful to the country. To ask for compromise, under these circumstances, is ignorant and ridiculous.

"I think the Tea Party folks have their finger in the dike and think it is their duty to hold back the tide of social policy when they believe, as they do, that it will irreparably damage the country. I don't mind saying I believe they are absolutely right in their belief and that it is their duty to be the Party of No. I've been an Independent for quite some time now and, like a larger and larger number of voters today, I don't want either major party in power. Unfortunately, there is no viable third party to take their place. Democrats clamor for more and more government and Republicans haven't had the guts to do what it takes to reduce the size of government. As a consequence, government spending at all levels is out of control. The programs the present administration is advocating have no chance of reducing the mounting debt. Meanwhile, like the most disgusting gossips, media pundits focus on disruptive rumors and potential voters have resorted to name calling like unruly children in any schoolyard.

"And by the way—the so-called Tea Party advocated an orderly, peaceful people's revolution by the use of principle and persuasion."

Everyone was stunned by Janet's passion and her willingness to state such strong political opinions in a group whose political views had not yet been identified. Most Americans, even at the beginning of the twenty-first century, were still reluctant to talk about salaries and net worth. Political views fell into the same category, unless all were certain they were among people of the same political persuasion.

Most of the population had given up their reticence with regard to intimate sexual matters two generations ago and religion had not been a sensitive topic even for the parents of those who sat around the table in the back of Margie's. Yet, here was Janet eliminating the last taboo—Janet, who likely knew more about the subject and less about the group, than anyone at the table. The friends were surprised to find the diversity of the conversation invigorating. It was obvious that all longed for honesty, and most were willing to seek truth even at the expense of harmony.

Eventually, everyone agreed it comes down to what voters think of people—are people basically good or bad? Would they choose to live with trust, skepticism, or fear? What is government, after all? A set of laws a group agrees to live by. As long as the rules permit them to leave voluntarily, people who are born here, or even brought to this country against their will, by remaining, are required to abide by the rules of the group. There is an implicit agreement.

The group agreed all people should have as much control as possible over their own destinies. They disagreed over the why and how. Some wanted more distribution of federal and state dollars to local communities and others wanted to keep dollars for social programs at home and reduce federal and state taxes. Some wanted tax dollars returned based on population, not need; all wanted these communities to keep all the tax dollars they were able to save.

They debated whether wealthy communities should be treated the same as low-income communities. They discussed the opposition's alternative to the free market and Marx's dictum—*from each according to his ability, to each according to his need.* They argued freedom and property rights vs. redistribution and agreed the best any government could do is provide equality of opportunity and acknowledge the impossibility of giving every human an equal start. Most were not affiliated with any particular political party and those that were, were not happy with it.

As the conversation continued, they asked one another if there were any men and women running for office they could trust. They left with three questions: (1) Could an Independent win a national office in a state like California? (2) Could she/he be persuasive enough to accomplish anything if elected and sent to DC? (3) Where would they find such a person?

Campaign Manager

For the next six weeks, Mario, Paul, and Janet were drawn to each other, compelled by the desire to answer those three questions. Lincoln Williams' name came up more and more in their discussions—subtly at first and, not surprisingly, enthusiastically advocated by his long time devotee, Mario. Janet and Paul had known Lincoln since elementary school. Since Mario had lived in Bloomfield most of his life, he had met Lincoln Williams for the first time at the 1996 Mapleton-Bloomfield meeting. When Lincoln had returned to the area and began promoting Another Way, Mario became his right-hand man. It was obvious to everyone, including Lincoln, that there was nothing Mario wouldn't do for his hero.

When he was young, Mario had been small for his age, but in the middle of his freshman year he had suddenly shot up and was definitely a large man. He had never taken time to socialize with his peers and made no effort to fit in. Many adolescents feel isolated, but it didn't help that his mother was Latino and his father Chinese. It wasn't the stereotypical cultural and gender differences that competed for Mario's identity. His father ran the business and his Latino mother was the oriental chef. She was not overly concerned that Mario should study hard and make something of himself. She *was* worried, however, that Mario might be harmed—maybe killed or indoctrinated into a gang in their rough Chinese neighborhood. It was his father, an intellectual and political dissident who had emigrated in his teens, who encouraged Mario to get a good education. These were the justifications for Mario's long, daily commutes to Bloomfield High.

Mario had always been capable of taking care of himself on the street. His dad had introduced him to Wing Chun—a martial art form—at an early age. The bond between father and son was strengthened daily, via their morning meditations and sparring. That added to the devastation Mario felt when, at the end of his sophomore year at Bloomfield High, his father was shot during a robbery at the restaurant and died before the police and paramedics arrived. His mother was consoled by the fact that Mario wasn't present that night. That was the summer of 1998. The loss of his father drew him closer to Bill Adams. Bill, at that time, was a senior working feverishly to get the Another Way program started in Bloomfield. Today, thirteen years later, was evidence of their success

After his father was killed, his mother had notified Mario's brother in Taiwan, who was nine years older than Mario and had a different mother. Mario was in shock. It was bad enough for a fourteen-year-old to have to deal with the sudden death of the father he worshipped, but now he discovered he had been deceived. For fourteen years Mario thought he was the only son—he felt his father had betrayed him. He knew nothing about other significant relationships in his father's life.; the most important person in Mario's life had been a stranger. His mother must have known—why didn't she tell him? He was the only one that didn't know. Why wasn't he told? He couldn't help feeling like an outcast—an outsider! He had no place anywhere.

The brother, Phillip Lee, was at the funeral and robbed Mario of his rightful role. Mario was the one who should have been consoling his mother and promising her that everything would be all right. Now, a stranger was taking his place, and his mother accepted it. It was as if Mario had died along with his father. Mr. Phillip Lee had taken over; at least that's how Mario saw it at the time.

Phillip had graduated college in 1994 and had been working in the investment division of Bank of America; the Taipei branch on Nanking East Road. He had volunteered to manage the Bloomfield restaurant and the family finances until the life insurance money came through. Mario's father had anticipated robbery, if not murder, because of the area and the nature of the business. Consequently, he had paid additional premiums to cover that risk. That's why the proceeds of the life insurance policy were enough to send Mario through college and take care of his mother for life. On top of that, Phillip sold the restaurant for a good price. Although he was not a beneficiary of the sale or insurance policy, Phillip moved from Bloomfield to San Francisco because he had a better chance of advancement. At that time, San Francisco was the headquarters of his bank and he could liaison with Taiwan and China.

Phillip was married and had a daughter by the time Mario graduated high school in 2000. When Mario went to UC Berkeley—Cal—his mother left Bloomfield to live with Phillip's family, by then in Berkeley too. By 2009, Phillip Lee was working for Merrill Lynch, now part of Bank of America, and had two young daughters who Mario and his mother loved dearly. Mario lived with them part-time between 2000-2004, but his relationship wasn't the warm relationship natural to brothers who had grown up in the same family and shared the same secrets. Mario and Phillip liked and admired one another once they got to know each other, but Mario spent most of his time on campus and hanging out with a couple of close friends in the Great Hall or library at International House at the top of Bancroft and eventually moved in.

Mario and his dad had often talked about education. His dad believed that the talk among students was where the most learning took place in college, and he was right. Mario had some great discussions with the foreign students at I. House. Lisa Wainwright was the only Bloomfield graduate Mario met at Cal. He hadn't known her very well in high school because he had been a freshman her senior year and had only seen her at a distance at Bloomfield High. The only time he had actually talked to her was at that Mapleton meeting in 1996. They went out a few times, but she was only at Cal a semester for some special courses. Once he ran into Dorothy Avila from Mapleton High in the Great Hall and they had lunch sometime later.

Mario graduated from Cal with an English major and ended up getting a masters in political science. He decided he wanted to live in Bloomfield because, by that time, Lincoln Williams was back from the pros and coaching there. He wasn't at all sure what he wanted to do with his life so he hung out with his old friends and got involved in Another Way. Since the insurance proceeds had been invested wisely by Phillip, Mario had all the time in the world to decide on the right career.

The financial means and the degree made it not only possible but plausible that Mario would end up as Lincoln's volunteer campaign manager. As far as Paul and Janet were concerned, Mario was the natural choice. With a little persuasion, Mario consented and agreed to accompany Paul and Janet, if they would approach Lincoln with the idea that he run for public office.

"Look, Lincoln; Mario tells me you have been going around promoting Another Way to cheering crowds. You obviously know how to give a persuasive speech and have a base of fans already. I remember in high school you honestly believed Another Way was the answer to all of America's domestic problems, so you've got a platform with well-researched and well-rehearsed answers to anything today's discontented voters can throw at you."

"Sure, Janet, that sounds great; and even if every bit of it was true, the political pros have their candidates lined up years in advance. I remember Phyllis telling us that back in 1991 her friend Marta was tagged by the group who had recruited Ronald Reagan. They introduced her to the most successful campaign manager in the Republican Party. He agreed that 1992 was the 'Year of the Woman' and, to his credit, five women were elected to the Senate that year."

"To his credit? Most of them were Democrats."

"Hmm. I didn't think of that. Anyway, this not so extra special campaign manager informed Marta and the Big Whig who accompanied her to the meeting, that the appointed incumbent, John Seymour, already had the backing of the doers and shakers in California's Republican Party. That's how it works."

"That's how it *used to* work. The Republicans may have learned their lesson by now. Anyway the national Parties have lost a lot of their former strength. No matter how you look at it, 1992 was an extremely unusual election year in California." Janet had written a research paper on the political Parties in California. "John Seymour was appointed when Pete Wilson vacated his seat in the U.S. Senate after winning his race for Governor. Seymour occupied the seat until a special election could be held to see who would be elected to finish off the final two years of Wilson's six year term. The Party wasn't going to kick the just-appointed guy out just like that. That's how in 1992 John Seymour faced Dianne

Feinstein, the Democrat's candidate, as the official nominee of the Republican Party."

"That's why there were two open seats for the U.S. Senate in California in 1992." Mario had wanted Janet to take over but he now had something to contribute to the conversation. He had only been ten years old at the time but his dad had been fascinated by that election and shared his enthusiasm with his son. "Dianne Feinstein ran against the temporary appointee and Barbara Boxer ran against Bruce Herschensohn for retiring Senator Alan Cranston's long-held seat."

He had been able to get those few words in before Janet interrupted. He decided to let her and Lincoln take over. "The same Herschensohn, who, in the primaries, barely defeated northern California's preference, Stanford Professor Tom Campbell. He lost the nomination by 70,000 votes thanks to the 420,000 ballots which would have gone his way but for the celebrity of another opponent, Sony Bono who lost the nomination anyway. I don't remember anything about another woman running for the nomination."

Lincoln was showing impatience. "I've been trying to get to that. When Marta learned she would just be running to gain exposure and experience, she said she didn't see how she could possibly rally enthusiasm and raise funds under what amounted to false pretensions."

"Sure. She had just been told the fix was in. So what happened?"

"She registered as an Independent, hoping for Ross Perot's support. It made sense because she had written books proposing solutions for the national debt and Perot was running on the national debt that year as an Independent too. She talked to folks in every one of California's, then fifty-one, congressional districts. Marta never hooked up with Perot; he had his hands full. Obviously it didn't work out." Lincoln rested his case but Janet didn't let it go.

"Ross Perot's name has endured but few recall Marta *Whatever* or Senator Seymour. We were kids so it's not really surprising that you don't recognize his name. Even if your parents voted for him, I bet they can't recall the name of the incumbent that Dianne Feinstein defeated in 1992."

"You're right. Herschensohn and Seymour aren't memorable names.

"But I have some trivia if there's ever an opportunity to use it."

"Go ahead—live it up. Use it now."

"You're on." Lincoln grinned. "I bet even *you* don't know what John Seymour's profession was prior to 1991."

Janet knew she should resist, but didn't. Instead, as she told Mario later, she rose to the occasion. But Mario could tell she was secretly ashamed of herself. He knew she despised braggarts and was inwardly modest, but somehow she couldn't hold back when it came to information—at least academic information. He made a mental note to be cautious with private information just in case she succumbed in that area at some point. "Before he was a U.S. Senator, John Seymour was a Marine, a real estate investor, President of the California Association of Realtors, and Mayor of Disneyland—you know..."

"You mean Anaheim," Paul made the correction.

"Anaheim—right."

This last was news to Mario and he was supposed to be the political junky of the three at this meeting—at least on Seymour, Herschensohn and the 1992 election. But, what did he really have to offer? Janet's interest in politics was evidenced by her time in DC and choice to study the workings of Congress at the Brademas Center in New York City. Although Paul didn't really contribute to the conversation he was half of a technical team with serious public relations experience. Mario couldn't help feeling out of his league and wondered if he'd really be doing a service to the cause by volunteering to be Lincoln's campaign manager. He was plagued by the thought that he might not be the best person for the job.

To regain his composure, he confronted Lincoln head on. "Where did you get the idea we'd be getting you on the ballot of one of the major political parties anyway?

It may be the major parties have their candidates lined up well in advance of the elections, like you said."

Janet came to the rescue again. "Never mind; the 2012 election will be occurring in another Year of the Independent. Don't you remember what happened to Scott Brown in Massachusetts at the start of 2010? As an Independent he would have had an easier time than he did running as a Republican running for Senator Kennedy's seat."

"The *main* difference is that you're not running for the United States Senate." In a split second Mario made his commitment. "You'd be running locally for the retiring incumbent's House seat, and you will have plenty of backing.

"I feel like I'm being hijacked. I've got to take some time to think about something like this. Sure, my family set-up is under control now, but I've got plans of my own. I was planning to help Bill get Another Way instituted in communities throughout the state and I've got a network already established."

Mario tried to help. "What we are proposing will help you do just that; in fact, it will accelerate your plans. Just as Janet said, Another Way *is* your platform."

Janet saw that Lincoln was blindsided, so she quickly added, "I understand you have to take some time to think it over. Do what you've got to do, but we need to have this settled one way or another by the end of the week. We don't have much time."

That was Janet, the organizer, still in top form. Mario felt more confident as they went their separate ways. He was sure this could be done! His first task was to look up the members of the famous 1996 Mapleton meeting. He was sure they would all be enthusiastic supporters. Unbeknown to Mario, this was an idea Janet had covertly planted in his head.

Recruiting

Paul claimed that he and Raeann were already excited about setting up a web site if Lincoln became a political candidate. Janet had, at least on paper, already lined up influential contacts at City Hall. He knew Bill would hold rallies and speak on Lincoln's behalf, and the teachers, Phyllis Clarry and John Hoffer, would be behind Lincoln all the way. Including himself as campaign manager, and Lincoln as candidate, there were eight accounted for leaving only five of the thirteen left to locate.

It was too good to be true when Janet called with the news that Lisa Wainwright had been an accountant in the comptroller's office at City Hall for the past five years and Amanda Miller had recently been hired as an assistant to Jack Campbell, the District Attorney, located in the same building. Amanda was scheduled to arrive at the end of the week. Janet volunteered to meet with both, leaving Mario to track down Megan Goodwin, Harrison Davis, and Dorothy Avila. He hadn't spoken to Harrison or Megan since the 1996 Mapleton meeting and only had that one conversation with Dorothy at International House at Cal. He started with the alumnae offices at both Bloomfield and Mapleton High and added Cal Alumnae for Dorothy as well.

On the other side of town, Bill agonized over the decision to tell Mario what he had heard about Dorothy Avila—now Dorothy Davenport. He had been attracted to her in 1996 and knew he hadn't been the only one. Dorothy was one of those legendary, dark-haired beauties, even at fifteen. To no one's surprise she had been the class valedictorian. They had dated for a year. She wasn't full of herself the way so many gorgeous girls were. She was just the opposite. She was always friendly and kind to everyone. None of the women were jealous when she was crowned Miss Mapleton a few years back and her former suitors earnestly wished her well when she later married a medical student she had met at college and moved a hundred and fifty miles to the coast.

A few weeks ago Bill had been privy to what he had convinced himself was a mistaken rumor. When Dorothy was seven months pregnant, she witnessed a car crash that killed her young, career-bound husband. She was crazy with grief and attempted to kill herself. She and the baby survived, but her father, Dr. Avila, urged her to give the baby up for adoption. At that time, she could barely care for herself.

Bill hadn't believed a word of it. He just couldn't believe Dorothy could actually do such a thing. But now she couldn't be located. What if the rumors were true?

Why do horrible things happen to good people like Dorothy? Dorothy, more than anyone he had ever met, deserved to be happy. He still clung to the hope that it was all a rumor and decided to do some research on his own before spreading something that wasn't true.

Bill discovered Dr. Avila had retired in 2004 in order to spend full time with his wife the last year of her life. She had been fighting cancer for several years; even before Dorothy was married. She died in 2005. The young woman, who had taken over Dr. Avila's medical practice, claimed not to know his whereabouts but was perhaps protecting the good doctor's privacy. It was certainly understandable after all the doctor had been through. She claimed the house was now rented to a nice family and referred Bill to the landlord; Dr. Avila's attorney. The only information the attorney could, or would give Bill, was that the doctor's will left the family home to his daughter if living upon his death. Bill couldn't be sure the attorney actually knew the location of either Dorothy or her father, but if he did, it was privileged information which he would not divulge.

Bill searched Face Book using the list of those who graduated with Dorothy and gathered a lot of information that couldn't be confirmed without definite dates and names of people and places. Nevertheless there was enough corroboration to enable Bill to construct a probable story.

Dorothy's child was born in 2003. Some thought it was a boy and others were sure it was a girl. The child was adopted by a family in Berkeley. No one knew the name. Dorothy was institutionalized after the attempted suicide and was under the care of Dr. Bradley, a physician with a fine reputation chosen by her father. Dr. Bradley released Dorothy from the institution in 2005 several months after she learned of her mother's death. She was not ready to reunite with her father so an older doctor, who had become quite fond of her and her father, found a job for Dorothy in New York with some magazine. She still harbored shame and blame for attempting to kill her unborn child and was furloughed on the condition she continue receiving therapy. She didn't attend her mother's funeral and it was unlikely her father knew of her whereabouts. Bill was able to contact Dr. Bradley and was assured that Dr. Avila knew that Dorothy had been released and was not ready to unite with family and friends; not even her father. Dr. Avila had reluctantly agreed to be patient as long as Dr. Bradley continued to monitor Dorothy. Dr. Bradley refused to divulge any privileged information. That was it.

At the end of the week Bill pulled himself together and called Mario and told him the story. He added that he would continue to run down leads and would eventually find Dorothy and her father or at least the truth. The good that came out of that conversation was the confirmation that the original thirteen, or those members who could be found, were going to be the support system they needed. Mario was even more motivated to push on with his search for Megan Goodwin and Harrison Davis. The names were so common that a Google search was useless when it went beyond California, which it did.

He entered Dorothy Avila and Davenport to the list.

Lists

Lincoln, too, was mobilized. He realized plans were being made by his friends and he had to make a decision soon.

As customary, the first thing he did was make lists.

Care Most About

- Freedom
- Spreading the idea that people are basically good
- Personal Responsibility
- Human Potential
- Self-Respect

What I Want To Do

- Get the Another Way concept working in society

Pros of Running for Public Office

- Incorporates everything I care most about
- Provides a wider audience for the Another Way concept
- I have a public following—i.e. fans
- I have debating and public appearance experience
- I have friends who have contacts in the media
- I have a huge desire to change the disincentives of current government

- I believe I can offer positive alternatives for society's current woes

Cons of Running for Public Office

- Have no positive feelings for professional politicians (getting paid rather than speaking out as a responsible citizen)
- Not easy to re-package image from hero-jock to villain-politician
- Have less time to emphasize merits of Another Way
- Don't relish the spotlight—had enough—enjoying some relative privacy
- Don't take criticism well
- My temper may come back
- Don't know how to schmooze or raise money
- I'm too honest and straight forward—I will alienate too many—no lies
- Compromise—the art of politicians—is something I don't want to do (can't?)
- I'm sick of traveling and being in the spotlight
- I'm not in the condition I once was and may not have the energy it takes
- I'm not positive about my chance to win—I don't take failure well
- Don't like to waste time or make enemies
- Could set me back in promoting Another Way later (bad publicity is part of campaigns)
- I'll have even less time to spend with family and friends

Lincoln wasn't particularly surprised to find the cons were double the pros, although he had to admit many of the cons were shallow. He was surprised to find how compelling the first two pros were. He suspected anyone he showed the list to would have the same reaction; the strength of the first two pros easily outweighed the large number of lightweight reasons not to become a candidate.

Another surprise was that there was only one item in his want-to-do list. He decided on the spot not to share the lists with his mother, but only with his more objective mentor, Phyllis. His mother would be concerned by the last item on his con list and the absence of career on his Want-To-Do list and especially, no mention of wanting to get married and have a family of his own.

He had limited himself to only five before starting his care-most-about list and was proud how quickly the top five had come to him and that he had no desire to add or delete when he reviewed it.

It was time to pay visits to his mother and Phyllis—so far, the two main women in his life.

Consultations

Lincoln appeared at his mother's front door with the idea of seeking advice, but ended up acquiring information that led to more insight into his family and, ultimately, himself. He never brought up the issue of his potential candidacy.

It was a strange visit. His normally warm and light-hearted mother had a certain aura about her today. Did she have a feeling he had something special to discuss with her? Perhaps she had some inkling of what he was about to do and was somehow trying to warn him. Even so, why would she tell him personal things about herself for the first time today and for no apparent reason? It didn't make sense. What prompted the revelations?

The first surprise was the discovery that his mother had always been religious. Lincoln didn't remember going to Sunday school so he was surprised to hear he had been baptized. He found out his father had also been a practicing Christian, but didn't allow mention of God after his sister was born with severe disabilities.

His mother had found solace in her religion and had Josie, his sister, baptized secretly. She claimed to have read the Bible to Josie every day of her life. She told Lincoln that his father was a good man and he should always remember that. He had worked hard and taken good care of his family.

Lincoln had already decided not to discuss his lists, so he was content to let the visit take its course. He was glad he had brought up the subject of freedom and confirmed that it was always number one for his mom and dad. His mother suspected it would be number one for most people of color. Lincoln was quick to point out that Caucasians also had been slaves throughout history—using conquered people as slaves was common—but his mother wasn't swayed by this new information.

Lincoln had never been exposed to this side of his mother. It was natural that she was still missing her husband. He had a momentary pang of conscience; she might be lonely. Now that he had his own apartment he wasn't around as much. But, he dismissed the idea quickly recalling his mother's many friends, and that Josie kept her busy; they were always laughing. It was just until now he had only been exposed to her strong can-do happy side.

He and his sister had always received warmth and encouragement from both parents. Today, the rather somber conversation gave Lincoln an eerie feeling. He tried to shake it off. As always, he was able to find a bright spot. He now knew where she got her usually sunny disposition and strength. He was grateful she had been able to cope with her daughter's condition and the death of her husband while conveying a sense of peace and love to the family and others over a good many years.

Lincoln usually looked forward to his discussions with Phyllis, but this time he was apprehensive. He didn't know if Phyllis would approve of what he was about to do, and worse, he didn't know if he really wanted to do it. Sure, at the beginning he had felt like he was being railroaded and had protested. Janet and Mario had backed off and urged him to take his time. He had always respected their opinions, although he was aware they put him on a pedestal and held him in an esteem he didn't yet deserve. He allowed for this distortion and took their evaluation of his abilities as encouragement and inspiration. Their belief in him was empowering.

He hesitated for a moment before ascending the stairs to the condominium Phyllis had moved to last year. Although he had prepared for this meeting, he didn't feel prepared. Phyllis had a way of getting to the core of his soul, asking the tough questions he knew he needed help answering. Ahead of him was one of those moments of truth.

He laughed at himself as he rang the doorbell. Talk about being overdramatic! Relax, buddy—Phyllis is an old friend. No reason to be so uptight.

They gave each other a hug and settled on the same comfortable couch that had been reupholstered twice in the last fifteen years. The first thing he noticed was the notation on his lists, which she had spread out on the coffee table. Lincoln began to relax as the two friends engaged in pleasantries. His favorite cookies were still hot from the oven.

When the small talk ended, Lincoln got down to business. "The two women in my life who have had the most influence on me, see things quite differently," Lincoln began.

"Oh?" Phyllis urged him on.

"Except for freedom. That is very important to both you and my mother."

"And what do you intend to do through your candidacy to preserve freedom?"

"I don't intend to do—I intend to undo—to undo the massive increase in the size of government and reinstitute the free markets essential to capitalism. I want to sunset outdated and repressive legislation and give people the opportunity once again, to decide and do what they think is best for their unique situations."

"That may sound admirable to you, but do you realize that only half the population even believes in capitalism? Twenty percent out-and-out advocate socialism—although they don't call it that—and a full third are actually undecided, according to the findings of a 2009 Rasmussen poll I used in class recently. That tells me there is a job of educating and persuading that needs to be done before a significant number of Americans will choose the opportunity to provide for themselves, over being taken care of by government."

"Of course, I will use the campaign to present and persuade people. I don't expect instant success—it will happen over time."

"Well," Phyllis paused thoughtfully, considering where to start. She wanted to guide and protect Lincoln. Protect him from what? Disappointments? Life is full of disappointments. No—something more specific. She was reminded of Marta's story again. Does Lincoln really understand what it means to compromise, and the necessity for a politician to do so? Does he know how? Will he learn—or want to? Is it a role he can play or must he be a natural? She knew the answer to that one.

"I think you are a natural—that you have what it takes to take on this leadership role and all its responsibilities. You are able to see and consider many points of view in any number of circumstances. This is necessary for any leader—to be able to call the good out of any situation and leave the bad without ill feelings.

"I believe you analyzed yourself and the situation well, but I'd like to go over the con list with you if you don't mind. You'll see I've numbered the items to make discussing them easier." Phyllis handed him a copy of the list he had spotted earlier on the coffee table.

"Of course. That's what I'm here for; to get your input."

"I think it might help if you picture yourself as a symphony director who understands that each instrument has its part to play. A good conductor knows how to emphasize the importance of each to the whole, and when to bring each into the process in order to produce a masterpiece."

"I've never even played an instrument." Lincoln was immediately embarrassed by his stupid comment, but Phyllis understood better than he did that he was nervous and short on confidence. She continued with a more suitable analogy.

"As I said, I believe you have that ability. All coaches need that ability and you have been a fine coach. I believe you know how to speak the truth without offending. I admire your disdain for name-calling and slinging dirt, which is so much of the political game now days. I think it would be worth you running, to show a better side of politics and politicians—you have always been a trendsetter. That way, you won't have to worry about turning into a villain-politician, as you put it.

"I dismissed the next four con items right off because you are involved in all of them right now anyway. But it's true, you may have to put some effort into accepting criticism and controlling your temper, and I'm afraid raising money comes with the game, unless our election process is overhauled in the next few months—something to put on your agenda. I would like to spend our time together discussing numbers eight and nine. I dismissed ten through fifteen as irrelevant, or frivolous, but will be glad to entertain a discussion if any of them are really holding you back and you want to talk about them."

He skimmed the newly numbered list and stopped at eight and nine.

Cons of Running for Public Office

1. Not easy to re-package image from hero-jock to villain-politician
2. Have no positive feelings for professional politicians (getting paid rather than speaking out as a responsible citizen)

3. Have less time to emphasize merits of Another Way
4. Don't relish the spotlight—had enough—enjoying some relative privacy
5. Don't take criticism well
6. My temper may come back
7. Don't know how to schmooze or raise money
8. I'm too honest and straight forward—I will alienate too many—no lies
9. Compromise, the art of politicians, is something I don't want to do (can't?)
10. I'm sick of traveling and the spotlight
11. I'm not in the condition I once was & may not have the energy it takes
12. I am not positive about my chance to win—I don't take failure well
13. Don't like to waste time or make enemies
14. Could set me back in promoting Another Way later (bad publicity is part of campaigns)
15. Less time to spend with family and friends

Lincoln took an audible breath and plunged in, "I don't want to take too much of your time but would certainly like to hear what you have to say about numbers eight and nine—honesty and compromise. Those two things are very important to me, and I know they are important to you also."

"Let's do it! To begin with, I was surprised to see that you think there can be such a thing as too honest. I'd like you to look at some videos of that new governor Chris Christie on the East Coast. He is both loved and despised for being straightforward—telling it like it is. So far, it has worked for him."

"Maybe, but it has worked against him too. He is using what I would call slash and burn tactics. He sees his state's debt as a crisis that needs immediate attention. I have seen him in the media and on YouTube where he admits, in one episode, that having a Sicilian mother and Irish father—who accept conflict as an essential part of life—has formed his personality. Well, I came from a peace-loving family and that has formed my personality. I believe in a more gradual approach to solving problems."

"Nothing wrong with that. So where does the problem of being too honest come in?"

"I believe if you plan to use gradual change you can't afford to alienate anyone before you accomplish your task. That means, gaining trust by consciously avoiding bad press. It's no secret that honest, unfiltered answers often attract bad press."

"In my opinion, that will be an asset rather than a problem. Your home may have been peaceful, but basketball has been a big part of your life and I believe has instilled the go-for-it attitude that will serve you and the governor well, especially in this economy, when hard decisions cannot wait. I don't think anyone can go wrong by telling the truth."

"Even when that truth is something that nobody wants to hear or believe?"

"Even then, as long as it is explained in a forthright, factual manner, followed by an easily understood and carefully laid out solution."

"Ah, there's the rub, but I think you have successfully destroyed number eight on my list. I don't know why I thought I might have to lie. There's really no safe route because the truth is subjective and facts are constantly manipulated in the political arena."

Phyllis smiled as Lincoln confirmed what she thought she knew; Lincoln was nobody's fool. "On to nine—compromise. Compromise is not so much a can't or won't situation, as it is knowing when and what to compromise. *When* occurs if you can't get something done by yourself and the other people involved don't all agree."

Lincoln nodded. "*What* is harder. There are some things I definitely won't compromise."

"That's exactly as it should be."

"So, you don't see that as a problem?"

"As I said before, you have a talent for recognizing common ground and those are the things where compromise is permissible. Common ground is your personal *what*. Some issues can't be decided on the spot and that works into your natural preference for gradual reform; plus it's taking a page out of your opponents' book."

"What opponents? I'm not following you. What page?"

"From what I know about your political perspective, your opponents are those advocating what they're calling today, progressive policies. Doing things gradually at this time in American history is like fighting fire with fire. Those who call themselves progressives have been content to accomplish their goals a little at a time. That goes back to both Roosevelts and Lyndon Johnson. The Obama Administration is following in their footsteps by compromising—getting the camel's nose under the tent when it can be certain that the rest of the body will imperceptibly work itself in overtime."

"I'm assuming the camel signifies the expansion of the federal government. If so, it seems to me that FDR and President Johnson each got far more than the camel's nose under the tent by instituting Social Security and Medicare. There was nothing gradual about it. And, President Obama's health care bill amounts to at least half a camel in my book. The effect will be just as earthshaking as what we have to encounter today with the impossible burden of Social Security and Medicare/Medicaid."

"You're right. All these far-reaching pieces of legislation have always been time bombs, but their effect was gradual and almost imperceptible to the recipients and their families. I believe you understand what is meant by gradual. That's why your use of the word gradual convinced me you have a natural instinct for what you are about to do. Your preference to effect change gradually is an opportunity to beat your opponents at their own game."

"I see what you're saying. Fighting fire with fire refers, in this case, to fighting gradual with gradual. Something huge and daring starts it off and the long-term effect is gradual so the doomsayers are discredited. The damage is at first imperceptible, as you say, and is only revealed over time."

"Something like that. Politics brings strategy and cunning into play. People stampede when they hear revolution, but they gather when there is a call for reform. Words are important. Reforms occur over time, while revolutions are sudden and destructive. The reforms of the past century have led to an expansion in the size, expense, and power of the federal government at the cost of state sovereignty. One by one the states failed to stand up for themselves. This was not an accident; it was thoughtfully planned by those who would inspire confidence in, and reliance on, the federal government."

"Certainly the expansion of Social Security and the more recent entitlements fit the bill."

"Not to mention the numerous federal departments and administrative agencies that have changed the landscape of DC gradually over the last hundred years and employed thousands and thousands of public sector workers at the taxpayers' expense, but without their input. We're now facing a crisis as public employees begin to retire en masse, with generous pensions and other benefits that the public cannot afford.

"The nation's debt is being fueled by these generous pensions and numerous other expenditures, of course." Lincoln was gaining respect for the benefits of gradual change.

"Just remember President Obama sees the 2010 healthcare bill as only the first step in overhauling the entire healthcare system."

"A critical first step." Lincoln understood. "Gradually, one step at a time, is at the heart of the strategy. I can see now how piecemeal reform works—it's like raising the temperature under that much-maligned frog in the pot of tepid water, until the water is boiling and it's too late. One of the numerous benefits is that it doesn't alienate ideologues on either side of an issue."

"You can see then, how foolish and futile any attempt to repeal that health care bill would be."

"That would be tantamount to revolution rather than reform. Got it!"

"Look, why don't you and Mario give your candidacy a trial run before firming up your platform? I can arrange to have you appear with one or two of the Democrat and Republican hopefuls who are already on the stump trying to win the nomination in their respective primaries. You can get the feel of it and give Mario some practice before you both actually commit. You'll get a better idea of what the voters care most about and can work their concerns into your platform and stump speeches from the beginning. What do you say?"

"You really think I've got what it takes, huh? I've got to admit I'm on the fence and it would probably help me make the decision. You know me—I don't like to fail. You know how I hate to waste time and energy that can be put to productive use—not just my time and energy—I'm thinking about my supporters. If I run, I will run on heartfelt principles. I won't take the easy way out and pander for votes. It's up to the voters of this district to decide if they want to be represented by my principles. They must decide if their principles are in line with mine and not the other way around." Lincoln glanced at his watch and added, "You have a way of making time fly, Phyllis."

"*We* do," she corrected him.

"Well, I think that about covers it," he said, slipping the numbered list into his pocket. "Don't you?"

"I'd say we covered a lot in a comparatively short time. So go then, with my blessing, and tell Mario I'll be in touch with him when I have a time and place for an Independent candidate to try out his wings." Phyllis gave Lincoln a big hug and stuffed a bag of cookies in his coat pocket as he prepared to leave.

"Thanks for the advice—and the cookies," he called as he descended the stairs two at a time.

As Lincoln hurried down the street, he mentally went over the two visits.

Phyllis, like his parents, put freedom at the top of her list, but he assumed she didn't believe in original sin, i.e. people are basically bad, as Lincoln now supposed both his parents did. He suspected his father saw Josie's condition as a form of punishment for who knows what. Lincoln had a flash of satisfaction and pride as he entertained the possibility that his father had taken his son's prowess in academics and sports as the reward for his own responsible, hard work in providing for his family. He may have viewed it as some sort of balance in his universe.

Lincoln reflected long enough to convince himself that he received his sense of personal responsibility, belief in human potential, and a craving for self-respect, equally, from his own family and Phyllis.

Arthur and Kirk

"I'm sure I speak for everyone here when I say we're sick of hearing about the problems somebody else caused. We're used to politicians kicking the can down the road so it lands in someone else's yard. We want to know what you guys are going to do about it."

That statement was followed by loud clapping and feet stamping. Lincoln winced at yet another use of that over-used phrase, *kick the can down the road*. At least this time, it was used by a member of the audience and not another politician.

Kirk Jamison recognized an easy retort and picked up on it. "Well, there are no incumbents on the stage this time, and each of us is asking you for a chance to open that can and see what we can make of it."

Lincoln felt his eyes roll and hoped no one had noticed. The older man continued. "Okay then, what do you make of the fact that the ratio of federal spending to our gross national product is now twenty-four percent when, for over thirty years, the ratio has averaged close to eighteen percent?"

"Well...what do they call you?"

"My name's Hal."

"Well, Hal," Kirk went on, "the President has called for a spending freeze on one-sixth of the federal budget."

"What about the other five-sixths? He keeps raising the debt limit. Everyone knows he's spending like a kid in a toy store and the credit card is in our name. He's exempted Social Security and Medicare—the two largest items in the budget."

"The spending is to stimulate jobs and encourage lenders to supply capital so entrepreneurs can increase their hiring. This will lead to an increase in the gross domestic product, although not overnight, I agree, but I assure you it will get the economy back on track."

Hal was no believer. "In the meantime, those that shoulder the largest part of the tax burden now will find their taxes increased. Did it ever occur to any of you Democrats that to penalize those who have the capital and the ability to provide private sector jobs is comparable to shooting yourself in the foot?"

Hal wasn't satisfied so Lincoln thought he'd have a go at it. "You're absolutely right Hal, to be concerned about the ratio of spending to GDP and to understand that taxes will have to be raised to sustain government spending until we get our GDP in line. Until then, we can't depend on the rest of the world to keep supporting our spend-borrow habit. If I understood, you are concerned with the studies that show that during periods with high tax-to-GDP ratios, economies grow much slower than they do during periods with lower tax-to-GDPs. Is that right?"

"I can't say I know about any studies, but it is just common sense to recognize that high taxes are going to stifle economic growth.

That, and uncertainty about what the government is going to do next." Hal sat down after relinquishing the microphone that was being passed among those seated in the folding chairs that filled the large modern high school gymnasium.

An older lady had the microphone in her hand now. "I'd like to know how you define high ratio and low ratio tax years. As far as I'm concerned, all taxes are too high. That's just for the record."

There was some stifled laughter in the audience as Arthur Harris decided it was his turn. Polite as usual, he deferred to Lincoln. "It's my understanding that high tax-to-GDP ratio years are those where the ratio is above eighteen percent and low tax years are those when the ratio is below. Is that your understanding, Lincoln?"

Lincoln nodded pleasantly. He and Arthur had become good friends on the campaign circuit, and although Kirk had very different stances on issues, there was a sense of comradeship among the three office seekers. On second thought, it probably took second place to the tension. Kirk was scared that the prevailing wisdom that the president's party always loses seats in off years—years without a presidential election—was true. Arthur feared that the Tea Party and Independent voters, he couldn't tell the difference, might go with Lincoln—or worse—split their vote and give the election to Kirk, the Democrat.

Arthur continued, "I'm familiar with a study by Professor Lazear at Stanford, which shows that if the ratio were maintained below that eighteen percent level over twenty-five years, the country would achieve a fifty percent larger GDP per capita." Arthur leaned toward the audience and indicated a young man in the front row. "What's your name, sir?" and when he had the answer, he went on. "I see you have a couple fine boys with you. Are they your sons?" The man nodded assent. "I imagine you have big dreams for those boys and it bothers you when you hear talk about the huge debt we're putting on our kids and grandkids." The man nodded again. "But that's only one part of the problem.

Worse than that, if we just maintain our debt—don't even attempt to reduce it—we will be spending an immense amount in interest on that debt every year. Some of you in the audience know exactly what I'm talking about—the pain of paying and getting nothing in return. If you're a religious person you might equate it to penance for past sins—in this instance, the sin of spending beyond your means. Paying only the interest doesn't amortize—doesn't reduce the debt and additional spending obviously makes the situation even worse. That's why any new program that is supposedly financed on a pay-as-you-go basis, is not sustainable."

Someone who Lincoln suspected was a student at the high school had a loud enough voice to ask his question from the back of the gym without the aid of the microphone. "How much is the interest on the national debt, sir?"

Kirk rushed to answer for reasons that became obvious from his first sentence. "It may surprise you to know that in fiscal year 2009 the total interest on the $11.9 trillion debt was down to $383 billion from the record $451 billion interest paid in fiscal year 2008, before President Obama was even elected."

But Arthur wasn't going to let Kirk get by with telling half the story. "That's because the interest on that debt dropped to two tenths of one percent—an interest rate we will never see again."

"That was the year average interest on three-month T-bills," Kirk reminded him.

"May I point out that half our debt now matures in less than one year?" Arthur was ready for Kirk today. He pulled out a sheet of paper, told the audience they could find more information on the web site of the National Debt Clock, and then began reading:

> *This means that if rates on three-month T-bills went to just one percent, interest on just this short-term financed half of our debt would increase by a factor of at least five times by the end of the year. Interest on half of 11.9 trillion (6 trillion) at .2 percent was about 12 billion. Five times that is 60 billion. If rates went to just 2 percent, the*

interest owed on this short-term financed half of our debt, would be 120 billion by the end of a single year. All other maturities would increase by greater amounts depending on the time length of the instruments. Since Moody's recently announced they are considering downgrading their rating on U.S. debt, rates could skyrocket to banana republic levels.

Arthur put the paper back in his pack and added, "Near the beginning of 2010, the United States was the 22nd highest out of two hundred and two countries when it came to our public debt as a percentage of GDP. That percentage was 63.6."

Lincoln hated it when Arthur pulled something like this. He knew that many members of the audience were rightly confused now. Those that understood the ratio of federal spending-to-GDP earlier now were given the national debt as a percentage of GDP. The GDP to spending ratio was twenty-four percent and the GDP to debt ratio was 63.6 percent. He only knew this because, initially, he was confused by the antics that Kirk and Arthur engaged in and had gotten some input from Lisa Wainright back in Bloomfield. Lincoln thought both Kirk and Arthur were trying to impress the audience and that they didn't know themselves what they were talking about. He wished they'd stop using the GDP to confuse people and start talking about something they could understand—the GNH—Gross National Happiness. Maybe he should run on bringing a little happiness back—happiness that didn't depend on material goods.

A young woman picked up the microphone. "In view of the fact that President Barrack Obama signed another increase in our national debt ceiling; this time to $14.3 trillion, is it possible to pay the debt off while leaving room to spend more? I love the President and his family and I voted for him, but I just need help understanding how the new programs can pay for themselves. If they can, then, wouldn't we have done that before? Maybe one of you can explain that new PayGo bill the Senate passed earlier this year."

Lincoln had explained PayGo numerous times before. As he began to speak, he had a premonition—a warning of some kind—and determined to follow up on it at the next opportunity.

"PayGo means Congress can only spend a dollar if it saves a dollar elsewhere. And, just to remind you, in DC lingo, a dollar tax cut is a dollar spent as far as the government is concerned. All dollars belong to the government and when they give you some of your earned dollars back, they *spend* it. Draw your own conclusions.

"Some of you may remember Ronald Reagan had a *you cut-spending, I'll-cut-taxes* deal with Congress. Everyone knew it took both actions together to make his program work. The Congress reneged on its part and he got the blame for the budget deficits. There's a lesson here: equal decreases in spending and equal decreases in taxes increase economic growth. PayGo does the opposite. Equal increases in spending and equal increases in taxes reduce, not increase, economic growth—period. So, any time a politician claims increased government spending will stimulate the economy, run the other way. And recite this to yourself until it is burned into your memory: More spending equals more taxes equals less growth."

꧁꧂

What was suppose to be a short trial-run had gone on for two weeks, with the three potential candidates for the district's House seat appearing before two or three audiences a day. Kirk and Arthur were up against other primary candidates, but the decision to run or not run in the general election was up to Lincoln. As far as he knew, he was the only Independent running so far. There were a few candidates from the minor parties fighting it out to see who would represent the Libertarian, Green, Peace and Freedom parties; those who usually got a candidate on the general election ballot.

Alone on his drive back to Bloomfield, Lincoln puzzled over the earlier premonition.

He, Kirk, and Arthur had gotten into a routine of handling the questions they could each answer the best. Each had his specialty. He acknowledged they hadn't discussed it; it was something that just happened—an unspoken understanding—a gentleman's agreement that not one of them should have engaged in. Now that he saw it clearly, he felt ridiculous. By taking the easy route, they had been unfair to their supporters. They were competitors. Lincoln vowed to have a better answer for every question and not wait until a particular question came his way. He would stop playing this gentleman's game—stop being differential—stop being lazy! Just think how that would be on the basketball court. "Excuse me. Is it time for me to take a shot at the basket yet?" He burst out laughing right there, alone in the car. But it wasn't funny. He realized if he continued in this vein, he'd be letting Mario, Raeann, Janet, and all his supporters down. If he decided to get into this, it would be to win, and that's what he had been trained to do on the court. People believed in him. He could do it—he would do it—win. He smiled as he felt the competitive blood surge through his veins again. He relished the familiar feeling.

The Third Floor Meetings

Amanda and Janet began meeting in the small restaurant on the third floor of City Hall to compare campaign notes and exchange information. Both had new, demanding jobs and were donating all their time outside the office to the fledgling campaign. They reminded each other that Lincoln had only agreed to a trial and was not really committed. They acknowledged Lincoln had only been on the circuit three weeks and all their effort might be for nothing; but they didn't really believe it. It wasn't long before the

143

brief campaign meetings led into longer, friendly lunches. The third floor became their retreat. They had a view of the park from their own table which Jenny, the waitress, reserved for them. The campaign and other business were relegated to occasional coffee breaks and confidential lunches became the norm.

Janet would be thirty-two this year and Amanda was four years younger. They both wanted families someday but were still too young to feel pressed. At the moment, the campaign was their mutual time pressure. Although neither had time to date, they didn't exclude males as a topic of conversation. Amanda talked about Magna1628. They had been virtual friends since college. She had read something he wrote in the mailbag of the Annenberg website, www.factcheck.org, and tracked him down and commented on it. She thought he was wrong, and they had been debating issues online ever since. They seldom agreed, but they admired each other's intellect and frankness. They mutually thought of getting together and also mutually decided against it. That's when they made a rule not to ask each other personal questions. For all Amanda knew, Magna1628 could be an old man or an adolescent boy. Neither knew where in the world the other lived.

Not much of a romance in Janet's book, but she didn't have a lot going on either. In fact, Amanda had to explain to Janet the effect she had on several guys in the building and even among the 'ol 1996 group. Whereas Amanda had plenty of dating experience in college and in San Francisco prior to coming to Bloomfield, Janet had none. She had been too busy and she didn't count meetings in coffee shops or restaurant meals as dates—the conversations were either intellectual or about business matters. Maybe that's why they both coaxed Lisa Wainwright to the table when she entered the restaurant one day. Each had secretly hoped Lisa had a love life that could add some spice to their conversations. They got more than they bargained for.

At first Lisa was reluctant to reveal anything about herself, but Amanda and Janet were persistent. Lisa was a mysterious challenge to the two young women. It seemed that none of their acquaintances knew anything about Lisa either. Little by little, her story came out. Each new bit of information was accompanied by a sworn promise by Amanda and Janet that none of what Lisa revealed was to be passed on to anyone else.

Both parents and several other members of Lisa's family were in and out of prison and drug rehab. Most of her older siblings had made messes of their lives. Lisa had taken a bus at the end of her junior year of high school and gotten off in Bloomfield because that was as far as the money she had saved for transportation would take her. She had been saving to escape her environment for years by taking on odd jobs like gardening, babysitting, and even waitressing at fifteen by lying about her age. She had planned to leave town right after high school graduation, but felt her future, and perhaps her survival, depended on getting away a year earlier than planned. She had stayed at a cheap motel for the first couple nights after arriving in Bloomfield, but soon found a large room in a lovely Victorian, owned by an older lady who was looking for a companion and occasional helper. After her senior year—her one and only year at Bloomfield High—she had accepted a math scholarship offered by Harvey Mudd College—one of the smaller Claremont schools in California with less than a thousand students and nine majors, all in math or science. She had come back to Bloomfield to take her current job five years ago.

Everything about Lisa was a surprise to Amanda and Janet, who had both come from warm, loving homes. Lisa's experiences were foreign to them; like watching a movie. They discovered later, when comparing notes on a day when Lisa was absent, that they agreed the biggest shock had been Lisa's certainty that no one in her family would miss her. Both women had gone through the same emotions on hearing Lisa's story—disbelief, sadness,

145

sympathy, admiration, and tenderness. But the real surprise to both was the fact that Lisa had been engaged to be married! Her fiancé had unexpectedly left her and the job he had accepted, only a few weeks earlier. Amanda had been offered that same job and was now the replacement for Lisa's fiancé. Who would have thought? Lisa's was a tale worth retelling. Too bad they were sworn to secrecy.

Campaign Disaster

Mario hadn't accompanied Lincoln on the campaign trail for an entire week. Lincoln didn't mind, but everyone else was incensed. Wasn't that what a campaign manager was supposed to do—monitor the performance of his candidate?

Mario isolated himself from the mutterings of the well-meaning supporters because he knew that something drastic had to be done. He needed time off to reorient the campaign—they were not getting through—the campaign was not focusing on Lincoln's ideas. Lincoln had declared his candidacy only a month ago and so far, the campaign had been reactive—answering the media's questions, pontificating on their agenda and in gatherings arranged by the campaign staff.

The initial goal was to be accepted as a legitimate Independent candidate and that required equal billing with, and acknowledgement by, the media and the two major political parties. Lincoln's celebrity enabled the quick accomplishment of that goal, but Mario could see now that the acceptance was solely due to the public's love of sport and Lincoln's star status. Lincoln was holding his own and surprising his audience with a brain to match his brawn, but he was fielding questions that had nothing to do with his platform. Mario didn't agree with Phyllis that this was the best use of Lincoln's time, but had learned from his father that there was no such thing as a waste of time. On the plus side, Lincoln was getting comfortable with a different type of audience

The Candidate

and their concerns, and that was something. On the negative, Lincoln was being recognized before they had strategized the message—a rare position for a novice politician to be in, and one they had counted on, but it had happened too quickly.

It wasn't that Mario hadn't been doing his homework. The incumbent congressman was retiring, so the seat was up for grabs to all comers. For the past two months Mario had gone over tapes featuring the performances of the Republican, Democrat, and Libertarian contenders for their parties' nomination. Mario knew their issues and their parties' platforms and they were not the issues and solutions of Lincoln and his supporters. Mario knew this because he knew Lincoln so well. Unfortunately, because Janet and Amanda were just breaking into full-time responsible positions at City Hall their team hadn't finished preparing outlines for issues to bring up at town hall meetings. That didn't slow down Lincoln and Mario had mixed reactions to that. He had noted how easily Lincoln got pulled off track. As an independent candidate he had no party platform to embrace so was free to make limited government his focus. He was eager to show how adapting the principles of the Another Way project would make limited government not only possible, but plausible. Bill's coaching would be invaluable in this area.

It happened during the Q & A period. Looking back, it was a blessing that it happened so early in the campaign.

"I want to know what you think about a court declaring that a nursing home can't allow its patients to discriminate against employees." The questioner was a young man, possibly a graduate student, or worse still, a law student at the nearby college.

"I'm not a lawyer, as you all know." Lincoln grinned as fans in the audience clapped and hooted. "But off the top of my head, I'd say I'm against discrimination in all places and I bet you all wouldn't be here if you didn't feel the same way." More clapping.

Lincoln asked the young man his name. "I'll make a deal with you, Jim. If you give me more information about that nursing home case, I'll give you my honest layman's opinion."

Jim nodded agreement and explained that an elderly woman was found on the floor in the middle of the night by one of the most competent staff members, who just happened to be black. He wasn't sure if she had gotten the patient into bed and the patient sued, or if it came to court for some other reason, but the patient had specifically asked that she not be cared for by an African American and a note to that effect was in the nursing home's files. It could be that the black staff member sued because she was discriminated against—Jim wasn't sure—but, he knew some judge ruled that a nursing home cannot allow patients to discriminate against employees.

Mario recalled holding his breath as Lincoln began his response.

"I'd say that localities should be able to make their own rules when it comes to getting along in a neighborhood. Rules for: zoning, curfews and roping off streets for special activities and such, and there should be a set limit—maybe no more than a dozen of these community conduct rules. That way unpopular regulations would be discarded and updated frequently. but I don't think anyone, not even a judge, can force or prevent a person from feeling or thinking a certain way. They used to call something like that legislating morality. A court ruling is law—right? I believe the courts should address specific harm and not hurt feelings. The staff member didn't lose her job, did she?" Jim shook his head and Lincoln continued. "In my opinion, job loss would be something concrete that the courts could rectify. Nursing homes exist to serve patients and have a duty not to physically harm their employees. However, when it comes to feelings, it seems to me that the patients come first and a nurse would be trained not to take the eccentric preferences of an old woman personally. Private personal preferences are part of freedom."

Lincoln made a sign to silence the applause as Jim countered. "What about keeping blacks or redheads off teams like basketball…" He was interrupted by laughter from the audience. Jim continued, "baseball and other sports?"

"It would depend on whether a team is professional or attached to a school and whether the school is public or private. Was the rest home run by a private or government agency?"

"What's the difference?" an older man in the front row wanted to know.

"In the treasured documents that define us as a nation there is mention of liberty and justice for all—we've expanded that over the ages to include opportunity."

"Of course, it took the Fourteenth Amendment to see to that." The audience snickered at the unidentified speaker's comment and Lincoln went right on.

"Nowhere is there a suggestion that people are equal in their aptitudes or acquired skills, just as they are not equal in health or appearance. It would be absurd to suggest that everyone has the same upbringing, home life, and amount of love or wealth; property. We recognize private property rights in this country. I interpret 'created equal' to mean everyone should have access to everything subsidized by taxpayer money. Sports in public schools have regulations and standards and one of those regulations is that every applicant has an opportunity to meet those standards via practice and hard work. A private school that takes no tax dollars can have regulations that specify that only people with blond hair can try out for a team. Since blond hair can't match speed and accuracy on the field, they wouldn't win games with those regulations. The same free market that operates in the business world would see to that. The same is true of a privately owned professional sports team."

"Aren't you forgetting the Civil Rights Act?" This came from a middle-aged black woman to Lincoln's right.

Unfortunately, Lincoln saw this is an opportunity to educate. "William Bradford Reynolds, the Assistant Attorney General during the Reagan administration, tried to get rid of group entitlement and equal results and move toward equal opportunity. He felt strongly that the use of forced racial preference to make amends for past racism did more harm than good."

The same older man took up the conversation again: "Didn't Reynolds try and use the victim specificity doctrine to invalidate affirmative action? I recall he used to infuriate his opponents when he quoted Martin Luther King Jr., who maintained that the Constitution should be racially neutral. There are a lot of people out there that believe color-blind policies might cool racial passions."

But the woman on Lincoln's right was not through. "Well, don't count former NAACP executive director Benjamin Hooks as one of them. Bless his soul; he declared to the world that "the U. S. Constitution was never color-blind."

Lincoln and the rest of the audience seemed content to ignore her comment (probably because everyone already knew it was true) and let the man in the front row continue to enlighten them. "It seemed like big business was afraid of negative publicity and sabotaged the Reagan administration's efforts right from the beginning. I remember the Civil Rights Division asked fifty-six government employers that had court-ordered or privately negotiated affirmative action programs, to fight them in court. Only three agreed to do so. Many large corporations, and even some local governments, were already comfortable with court-supervised programs that guaranteed a portion of their available jobs to minorities. In fact, the National Association of Manufacturers praised affirmative action mandates. They thought the goals and timetables were an effective means of bringing minorities into the workforce and they let the Reagan Administration know that they had no desire to attack these affirmative action programs. Their spokesman even went so far as to insist that voluntary compliance wouldn't work."

"I think the best thing that minorities can do is get government out of their lives; ask for less of it because it makes a mess of things," someone in the second row volunteered.

A young man near the back of the room added a bit of humor. "Just think, the Boston Celtics would only be allowed four blacks and would have to include women and other minorities if it were forced to attain racial balance. People wouldn't buy tickets."

The older man, who by this time Mario suspected was an attorney, responded with a smile. "You're right—statistical parity is not good economics. Lawyers make a lot of money in legal fees via civil rights legislation. When there was segregation you had rich, middle, and poor blacks all living together. Good role models were available. Sadly, desegregation was forced and blacks unwittingly stopped patronizing black businesses in their hurry to patronize white businesses, which had previously been off-limits. That led to the disintegration of a lot of neighborhoods. Then, there was that lawsuit brought by a Michigan schoolteacher who claimed layoffs were based on race instead of seniority."

Lincoln got back into the conversation. He had heard about the teacher lawsuit from his father. "That was the 1986 case where the teachers' constitutional right to be treated as individuals was argued against a race-conscious policy. The School Board claimed that the faculties had to be desegregated before schools could be considered desegregated. Justice Powell said discrimination in hiring can be tolerated because racial exclusion in applying for a job is not nearly as bad as loss of an existing job."

"You're absolutely right. The 1986 rulings by the Supreme Court made it legal for white males to be subject to racial and sexual discrimination, in favor of people who had never personally suffered from it in the past. This ruling ended up giving blacks and Hispanics priority for promotions as city firefighters. Naturally, this increased resentment. It looked as if the affirmative action forces were definitely gaining ground. U.S. vs. Paradise continued the trend, in favor of reverse discrimination. The issue before the Supreme Court in 1987 was whether equal protection of the law was now being denied to whites. Were racial quotas permissible under the U.S. Constitution?"

Lincoln interrupted, "Back up there for a minute. Wasn't that based on a 1984 ruling somewhere in the South?"

"You're right again. An Alabama judge ordered that at least fifty percent of the promotions to corporal in the state troopers be awarded to blacks, if qualified black candidates were available. In February of 1984, the state complied and then appealed to the Supreme Court. The 1987 decision was 5-4, in favor of quotas."

Lincoln expressed surprise that these rulings had occurred, despite the judicial appointments by the Reagan administration. The older man elaborated on his comment.

"Sometimes wheels turn slowly. The effect of the Reagan appointees became apparent later. In 1989, the cases began to proliferate." Lincoln mentally noted that progressives were not alone in their use of gradualism. The supposed attorney continued, "In Martin vs. Wilks, the Court swerved and ruled five to four in favor of workers filing new lawsuits, claiming reverse discrimination under court-approved affirmative-action plans. The five-to-four decision in the Patterson case said that the 1866 civil rights law, giving the right to contract equally to all citizens, doesn't permit lawsuits involving harassment on the job or other conditions of employment."

"Wait a minute." This time it was Jim who interrupted. "Wouldn't you say that case in Virginia, which ruled against set-asides of government contracts for minorities, was pretty much a reversal of the Slaughter-House cases that justified governments' playing favorites?"

Mario had noticed the audience was getting restless and was hoping Lincoln would call for an end to all the legalese.

"You must mean the City of Richmond vs. Croson, which severely limited the power of government to favor women and minorities in public contracts. In that case, Justice O'Connor said race-conscious remedies must be subjected to strict scrutiny. In Richmond, Virginia, minority participation in city employment contracts fell from thirty-two percent before the Croson decision, to eleven percent in the fall of 1990. The Croson ruling was too narrowly defined, leaving us with the possibility of good and bad discrimination. Federal set-asides for black contractors are good, but municipal set-asides for black contractors are bad."

Lincoln made a note to include the Croson case in his request to Amanda. Nevertheless, Lincoln bravely reentered the conversation. "Discrimination by government is wrong and I know of no one who believes two wrongs make a right. If, as politicians are so fond of claiming, Americans (the American people is the term they most often use) really want to see minority firms get a helping hand and stand on their own, they will extend that hand. If they don't, and I'm aware that some don't (only politicians seem to know what all the American people want), they will insist that minorities compete in the market place without special favors. I personally, believe a majority, maybe a small majority, do want to help, but pretending by politicians will not make it so."

Lincoln gave way to a woman who stood and introduced herself as Gale. "How does anyone imagine that discriminating against white-male-run businesses can make up for past discrimination against minorities?"

That left an opening for the supposed lawyer: "Obviously a lot of people don't because after Croson, nine more programs were declared unconstitutional and twenty cities and states voluntarily ended their set aside programs. That limited the use of set-asides somewhat, but limited does not mean dead. If the right analysis is done, it may still be possible to justify set-aside programs."

Jim was just getting started: "It's still possible all right, if the plaintiff has the time and money to compile a statistical paper trail showing a minority-owned firm has been frozen out of local construction contracts in the past. I heard of one law firm in Seattle that was paid four hundred thousand dollars to do just that. The Supreme Court tried to make a distinction between individual rights and rights. In 1987, the Supreme Court allowed benefits to individuals who were not, themselves, victims of discrimination. The minority of justices agreed that was trampling upon the rights of innocent whites, but the majority felt the decision did not impose an unacceptable burden on innocent third parties because the hiring mandate was to be severely limited, both in scope and duration."

"But, when it comes to race-conscious hiring and promotion practices, timetables and goals are allowed. I would have thought the Reagan appointees to the Supreme Court would have made more of a difference." Gale seemed a bit dejected as she took her seat.

Neither Mario nor Lincoln had ever heard of the Slaughter House cases. Lincoln resolved to quiz Amanda the next day, but now he ceded to Mario's more than subtle signals and determined to gracefully end the discussions among lawyers, real, imagined, or wannabes.

"Sometimes patience is required." Lincoln was reminded of his earlier conversation with Phyllis and attempted to console Gale. "The Reagan administration may not have won many affirmative action battles, but it promoted its reverse discrimination theory and I find it hard to argue with their logic. You don't cure discrimination by discriminating against an innocent individual. Two wrongs don't make a right."

Lincoln caught sight of someone on the right-hand side of the room trying to get his attention. The same three or four people had been engaged in conversation for so long he had stopped looking for hands. He acknowledged a well-dressed older woman who claimed to be a refugee from Indianapolis where she had lived until twenty years ago. "While the Reaganites had logic on their side, proponents of affirmative action had emotion." She remembered Richard Hudnut, then, mayor of Indianapolis, saying on TV that affirmative action programs were a general American commitment to the fulfillment of the American dream, which is one where everybody has equal opportunity. He suggested that without hiring mandates the nation would be taking a step backward into a world where only white males had jobs. She said, "You should be ashamed of yourself. Columnist Carl Rowan did his part by telling readers across the country that good Americans, exemplified by Mayor Hudnut, care about justice and know when something mean and destructive is being foisted upon them."

In reply, Lincoln said something next that Mario wished he could erase from his memory: "I only wish this was the case because affirmative action has been just that—mean and destructive and harming those most that it purports to help. In a truly color-blind society, people readily admit to superior, normal, and inferior members of every racial group. The superior and normal members of the black community suffer because of the innuendos that blacks could not succeed without the extra help provided by affirmative action laws. People aren't the same just because they are members of the same group. All blacks aren't underdogs; some are very successful members of society. To imply that a group cannot have successful leaders because its members are all underdogs hits at the self-esteem of both the group and individuals within that group.

"Although Ronald Reagan was ridiculed when he touted the merits of a color-blind society, I'm absolutely convinced that should be our goal. It seems to me that we were a lot closer to reaching that goal before the affirmative action legislation interrupted the progress that had been achieved. A color-blind society is fairer and, in the long run, more beneficial for everybody."

Already, some members of the audience were making audible comments among themselves. One of the younger men spoke up, "What makes you think this color-blind thing could work?"

Lincoln didn't hesitate. "At one time, the Detroit Symphony had all white musicians. They used to test behind a screen, only listening to the music with those who auditioned being given a number so there was no chance of knowing the player's sex or race. The screen is gone now so that race and sex can be considered. Which is fairer, and which makes a better symphony?

"I try and put myself in the other guy's shoes. I realize it's hard, but somehow we have to communicate. Let's, for a moment, forget the differences and concentrate on the sameness. All of us, when we work hard, want recognition and feel cheated when others denigrate our work and suggest our success was due to something other than our own effort. As things stand now, some people assume, even if they don't articulate it, that a successful minority is the beneficiary of a special program. These attitudes often lead to more than hurt feelings; they can lead to loss of jobs and opportunities. That's why well-meaning people advocate for laws to protect against discrimination rather than telling people to ignore what is happening and just go about their business. But, laws are force and force will not work in this situation. Besides, if you think the majority of white employers in this country would be influenced by the openly expressed racial hostility of a few people, then you would be showing a bias against the white race, attributing an ugly propensity for bigotry to a very large group. You would, in fact, be expressing a belief that white employers would go out of their way to treat a minority badly. It seems to me that people who hold those assumptions are as guilty of accelerating racial tensions as those who assume members of a minority race are less capable than whites and, therefore, must be given a crutch via mandated preferences."

Lincoln was oblivious to the signs to desist that Mario was now frantically sending. The younger man was noticeably angry now and it was infectious. "So, what would you suggest?"

"I'd appeal to the best instincts in the population. Change the goal from achieving equality through force to achieving a color-blind, creed-blind, race-blind, sex-blind society through faith and trust in the basic goodness of mankind."

"You've got to be kidding!"

"You think it's naive, but I'm not alone. Martin Luther King, Jr. and Ronald Reagan were both correct in their denunciation of forced preferences and in their support for a color-blind society.

"Let's go back to Carl Rowan again. He declared that the call for a color-blind society was a call for maintaining the special privileges of Whites. What do you say to that Black boy?"

To Mario's dismay, Lincoln couldn't be stopped.

"Referring to people as Whites, Blacks, Hispanics, Asians, women, and disabled is in itself separatist and confrontational. Every Bobby, Ted, and Mary Ann within a specific group is as different as the Bobby, Ted, and Mary Ann outside that group. We're all human beings so let's support one another. I say being human is our common thread, but I celebrate and respect the diversity. It may be trite to say it, but diversity is America's advantage, although foreign observers often assume it's her curse. Diversity needs to be emphasized, but not the diversity of groups, the diversity of individuals. America has always been a nation of individuals; that is the uniqueness of our political heritage and our culture. Let's not lose that. Let's remember all Blacks are not alike; all Whites are not alike; all Hispanics are not alike; all Asians and other ethnic minorities are not alike; all challenged people are not alike; all older people are not alike and all teenagers are not alike; all men are not alike; all women are not alike. This is something policy makers have forgotten. I believe individual rights, not group rights, should be protected under our laws—period."

Gale earned Mario's gratitude by breaking in, "Highlighting rights and privileges makes people touchy. When anyone goes around with a chip on their shoulder daring others to knock it off, tensions rise. Employers understandably become more reluctant to hire workers who seem to be waiting to catch them in some infraction of a law. For years and years it was commonly, and I believe wisely acknowledged that morality cannot be legislated. I believe the races would have achieved a greater harmony, naturally, if certain aspects of the civil rights laws had not been enacted. The process would have been slower, but the foundation would have been stronger and today, race relations would be the better for it."

The young man didn't try to suppress his disdain in his response, "Don't you think two hundred years was long enough for black people to wait for white people to accept them and treat them as equals? Appealing to this crap about society's best instincts got many good people lynched!"

Mario was on his way to the stage when Lincoln replied. "If you're going to appeal to emotions, I give up. I'm looking for alternatives to help the situation we have today. I can understand the desire to speed things up—who can't? People of goodwill, naturally, want to see justice achieved today, not tomorrow. And although I believe many people forced racial relations in the past because they cared about their children and future generations, it is exactly these future generations that are now suffering because of their haste."

"Again, I ask you what you personally would have done differently or will do differently if you get elected to a position of power."

"I would have attempted to focus the legislation on the public sector only. Maintaining the distinction between public and private property is essential to the political and social structure of this country and I believe policy makers lost sight of the rights of private citizens to control their own property."

"I don't believe that's true. We don't let a person take his car just because it's his own private property and run over someone, or use a paint brush he owns to deface someone's property."

"Now we're getting down to the nitty-gritty. The question, supposedly answered by our Constitution, is under what, if any conditions can a group of individuals impose its will on another individual or group of individuals?"

"So, what's the difference between telling a person he cannot discriminate in his hiring practices and that he has to hire minorities in the proportion that they are represented in the local community?"

"The most obvious difference is practicality. One can easily see by the numbers that the proper number of minorities are being hired, but one cannot see if the reason someone was not hired, or advanced on the job, or whatever, was due to his religion, skin color, sex, or age. In other words, without some pretty sophisticated thought-police, we cannot tell if the employer discriminated when hiring."

"That's precisely why policy makers have suggested that numbers be used as a presumption of discrimination. What's wrong with that?" The young man thought he had gained the upper hand, but Lincoln wasn't through.

"By asking what's wrong, you are introducing morality and ethics into the discussion, and, in my judgment, morality is at the core of the civil rights issue and it cannot be discussed or solved without examining where we stand as a nation and, perhaps, suggesting where we as individual citizens believe we should stand. Because, as we all too often forget, there is no king at the head of our government with divine rights—these decisions fall upon the shoulders of individual citizens."

"Once again, I don't agree. Individual citizens don't have the time to analyze and ponder over issues like civil rights. We delegate these discussions to our legislators and then if we don't like what they come up with we give the courts a go at it. And/or we don't re-elect them," he added.

"And that is why we are experiencing tensions and witnessing a polarization of groups in America today. If individual citizens don't make the time to think seriously about such issues, they better be prepared to waste a good deal of time trying to lead a fulfilling life in a discordant society."

"Okay, at least you and I can spend some time wrestling with these ideas, but I seriously doubt that you'll get more than a comment or two off the top of most people's head. They just won't think these things through. The most you'll get is undigested opinions, not even the speaker's own opinion, but more likely a parroting of the sound bite heard on the six o'clock news."

"Again, we exhibit a difference in our attitude toward people. You think I'm naive and I think you underestimate people," Lincoln replied pleasantly.

"Okay, okay. I asked what is wrong with using numbers as an indication of discrimination." Anger was giving way to impatience.

Lincoln remained calm and, to Mario's dismay, focused. "You can tell how I would answer just about any question if you remember my premise; people are always going to act in their own interest. So, if a penalty were imposed for discriminating, a person would want to avoid the penalty, and therefore, if numbers are used to determine discrimination, he would make sure the numbers were in his favor and would adjust his hiring and advancement policies accordingly. In other words, it would lead to quotas."

"Let's cut to the chase. Would you at least stipulate that discrimination exists and that it is wrong?"

"I know you want a short answer, but I can't oblige. First of all, since I believe people are self-controlling, the ability to discriminate should be theirs. We're talking about preferring one thing over another and I believe a person is entitled to his preferences no matter the reason."

"Get real! You know good and well by discrimination I'm referring to restricting someone's rights because of race, age, sex, and so forth."

"It's impossible to have such a discussion in a hurry. You use words imprecisely and their definition is extremely important to the outcome. To continue, I would have to define what you mean by rights because I would not stipulate that anyone has a right to work for a private party unless that party wishes to hire him, nor do I believe any individual has a right to live in a private property that the landlord does not wish to rent to him."

"I had you figured from the start."

"Hold on; because I don't stipulate to it, does not necessarily mean I don't think it's legitimate. It's just not as obviously true as you seem to think. As for wrong, there is a distinction to be made here between (A) against the law, which I believe is the manifestation of a collective moral code, and (B) against the moral code of a given individual. In the first are laws against people committing physical bodily harm against one another and the taking or destruction of one another's property. The second category is reserved for things like integrity, character, truthfulness, courage, and goodness. There are no public laws in this area—no state prosecutes a person for not being good."

"Get over yourself. Lying under oath is prosecuted as perjury."

"That's different. I would put discrimination in the second category instead of the first. Ethics require self-examination—in other words, thought."

"Meaning, we shouldn't have civil or criminal laws to regulate it?"

"I believe the fact that we have such laws is part of the wrong turn I mentioned earlier."

"This is getting ridiculous." Mario too was confused and was ashamed he had to agree with the young man.

Lincoln continued, "I'm not trying to discuss what is—that can be seen by going to the Internet or a law library in any county in the country and looking up civil rights—I'm trying to discuss what should and could be. It would be a fruitless exercise except that in the United States we the people have the power to determine these things."

There was more muttering in the audience. Several people had already vacated the room and more were standing as Mario rushed to the stage and thanked the audience for their participation and invited them for refreshments in the reception room. For the first time, he didn't add that the candidate would be available for more questions and discussion. Instead, he smiled, waved, and efficiently ushered a surprised Lincoln off the stage and down the inside stairs in back of the kitchen. He opened the door of his Ford and ordered Lincoln to get down in back, which was not easy for the seven foot Lincoln to do quickly.

Before Lincoln knew it, they were in the fast lane headed toward Bloomfield. Mario looked as pale as a man of Chinese-Mexican descent can look.

"What's up?"

Mario slowed the car a bit. "We're still not ready for prime time," he replied. "We've got a lot of work ahead of us."

Emergency Meeting

Mario called an emergency meeting with Janet, Amanda, Lisa, Paul, Raeann, Phyllis, and John Hoffer. Bill was away on a speaking engagement promoting Another Way, and Lincoln had gone along to pick up some tricks and make a brief campaign speech of his own. Mario explained that last night, Lincoln had been distracted from his main issues and sucked into a heated discussion of civil rights; a topic even a novice should recognize is right next to entitlements in terms of delicacy. He was playing catch with a time bomb, positioned to go off with a single, careless miscalculation. Worse of all; he was oblivious. Mario went on describing the mood of the audience and negative atmosphere that led to walk outs near the end of the Q & A.

"We need to devise some way to keep Lincoln on message, and it wouldn't hurt to be briefed by Amanda on law; current decisions likely to arise—find out what case the boy was referring to in the seventh circuit and prepare Lincoln for other popular cases that might be brought up—or better still, let him bring up a few. That will give him credibility."

Amanda suggested, instead, that the campaign gain more control of the Q & A periods. There was disbelief all around. Phyllis warned that Lincoln was not likely to go along with more control, and Paul assured everyone that Lincoln wouldn't go back on his beliefs—he'd drop out first. John Hoffer told the rest of the group that Lincoln trusts Phyllis—he then turned to Phyllis and addressed her directly. "He respects you. You've been his mentor for almost twenty years."

Mario said, "I'll tell Lincoln you want to see him. When can you be ready?"

Phyllis nodded. "Of course, but I want to know what Amanda has in mind and get input from the others first."

"That's why we're here," Raeann assured her.

"What have you got? Let's hear it." Janet had her iPad out and Mario could see her fifteen years ago, taking notes on her laptop in Mapleton High's conference room.

Amanda launched into it: "I thought maybe we could collect written questions before the speech and pick and choose which ones to feed to Lincoln during the Q & A."

Janet chimed in: "They do that at the Press Club in DC The president, or person in charge, reads the specially pre-screened questions to the speaker after his presentation."

Mr. Hoffer reminded everyone that they'd need time to sift through the questions and remove any potential time bombs. Paul suggested the questions be turned in at a break, which Mario nixed. "We usually go straight through with refreshments and mingle with the crowd right after the question period. Remember, the presentations are usually scheduled on a workday and most of the audience has to get home and to bed. The most benefit generally comes from pressing the flesh."

Raeann came to the rescue. "We can include pads of serrated paper for questions, along with the campaign material that is laid out on the chairs before the audience arrives. Someone could collect questions just before Lincoln begins his presentations."

Paul, always ready to praise Raeann, was sure this time the praise was justified. Mario, or another member of the team, could preview the questions while Lincoln was speaking. The others weren't sold so quickly, claiming questions were logically prompted by the speaker's presentation. Mario insisted that the campaign remain on message. "Lincoln is flexible and has opinions on just about every issue."

"I personally agree with most of Lincoln's ideas, but I've got to say some are way beyond what an average audience would consider acceptable." Janet shrugged. "It's going to be hard to keep him on course in order to avoid what happened last night. On the other hand, Raeann's idea allows for some prearranged questions in case enough suitable ones aren't collected at some events."

Now Phyllis balked. "Some of you know how Lincoln feels about calculating politicians. He doesn't like rehearsed discussions. He's told me how much he despises prefabricated evasive answers. It's not that *I'm* against the idea; in fact, I've explained, to no avail, that the media loves to put words into the mouths of politicians by getting them to agree to the interviewer's words and then use those words out of context."

Raeann attempted to convince Phyllis that Lincoln would see the difference in an evasive answer and an opportunity to get more of his convictions across to the audience.

Mario saw the time slipping by and took charge. "Let's take a vote. How many think it's better to have some prearranged questions to give Lincoln more time to get his message across, but only to be used when enough appropriate questions are not collected from the audience?"

Apparently Raeann succeeded in convincing Phyllis because all hands were raised.

"It's settled then. You'll meet with Lincoln as soon as possible?" Phyllis nodded and Mario proceeded. "Next on my list is compassion. Lincoln doesn't show enough of it. Wasn't he supposed to be running on the Another Way platform—didn't one of you say that was Lincoln's answer to everything? Janet? Do you think you can get Bill and Lincoln together more often? Maybe have Lincoln join more of Bill's presentations."

"Good idea! Bill sees the innate goodness in people and their willingness to volunteer as the heart of Another Way. His talks have become almost messianic lately. They need each other. I'll get them together and you come too John—you've been great rehearsing with Lincoln, but it might help if you could come to Bill's Another Way presentations. Then we can go over what we think should be integrated into Lincoln's campaign, plus Lincoln might add some realism to balance the preachy feeling that has crept into Bill's appearances lately."

Mr. Hoffer looked surprised—yet pleased. Everyone was surprised to hear Janet address him as John—she and Phyllis were the only ones that had ever called him John. They all assumed Janet wasn't aware of the customary address because she had been back East so long and had only met John Hoffer that one day in 1996 at Mapleton.

Mario was oblivious. Turning to Lisa he asked, "Is there any chance you could join the contingent too, Lisa? You are not as familiar with the Another Way concept so could pin point areas that need clarification better than anyone else. We really need that. Think it over and let me know at the end of the meeting." Lisa nodded and Mario continued. "The last item is the Constitution—freedoms, liberty, capitalism, free markets. Lincoln has most of that down, thanks to Phyllis' classes and hours of discussion. But somehow, Lincoln got tripped up on his zeal for freedom. If you can stay after for a little while Mr. Hoffer, I'll explain the problem I witnessed in more detail. And I'd like to meet with you again too Amanda, as soon as you can arrange it." Mario had to remember Amanda was still learning the ropes of her new position and, therefore, her schedule was less flexible than most of the others.

When the others left, Mario and Mr. Hoffer got down to business. Lisa had committed to the Townhall metings as her schedule allowed. That was something. The format was the problem—Mario wanted to make sure Lincoln was getting his main points across at each gathering. He wanted to know the numbers in each audience. He wanted to schedule radio and TV spots to emphasize the points that were getting less than optimal coverage. Mario complimented Mr. Hoffer on his rehearsals with Lincoln and that he tried to fit as many campaign events as possible into his teaching schedule.

As overbooked as he was, at the end of their discussion, John Hoffer had agreed to take over some of the strategic planning that had fallen through the cracks. Mr. Hoffer promised that before the next meeting he'd have a time line and agenda mounted on the wall, showing all the campaign events between today and the election in November of 2012. Each would be marked *confirmed* or *planned*. These charts would be discussed and modified at each meeting. It was clear to both former student and teacher that need trumped lack of time. As they parted, Mario made a mental note not to abuse this valuable lesson by planning ahead to minimize the desperation implied by need.

Mr. Hoffer left the meeting realizing he had committed to put more activity into the same twenty-four hours. Just by luck, he had recently come across the critical thinking lesson plans offered on the Annenberg classroom web site. A circumstance like this made him believe in old bromides like, luck is what happens when preparation meets opportunity—the platitude appropriate to his present situation. Normally he wouldn't consider adopting another teacher's lessons plans for his classes. Why not? John

Hoffer was not one to consciously fool himself; the reason was pride—he had never seen a lesson plan that could match his own.

He saw his mission as a teacher analogous to that of a blacksmith firing up the forge, as opposed to so many of his colleagues who saw themselves as gas station attendants ready to fill the students up with information and predigested knowledge. Mr. Hoffer's job was to open their minds by insisting his students research and present the pros and cons of a minimum of two sides of any issue. They had to find a variety of sources offering different viewpoints and both use and describe these sources. In their written papers they were required to defend their own reasoning and show how it logically led to their personal, rationally explained, conclusion. His goal was to give his students enough experience thinking critically in class, so it would become ingrained. Classroom discussions didn't fill them up; they ignited their fire.

After looking over the eleven-page lesson titled *Amnesty*, on the Annenberg Institute for Civics, he had been so impressed that he felt comfortable assigning it to his classes—just this time. He'd still get to read the papers and lead the discussions.

Mr. Hoffer hated to give up any part of his teaching, but he felt good about this. The author of the plan had previously been a researcher for one of his favorite publications—*Congressional Quarterly*. There were almost thirty plans posted on a variety of subjects. He would definitely recommend the Annenberg Institute for Civics to his colleagues as a worthwhile resource.

Now his students would benefit, and so would the campaign. A win-win!

―――

Lisa was working at her desk when her cell phone rang. She knew it must be a friend as she didn't give her cell number to business acquaintances. She was concentrating on a project and almost let the call go to voice mail but answered at the last moment. "Hey

Lisa. We've missed you. Where are you eating lunch these days?" It was Janet.

"At my desk. I took on one more project for some unknown reason. How are you guys doing?"

"We're overloaded, just like you, but we aren't about to give up our lunch dates. Those forty-five minutes keep us sane. You've got to have some relaxation, and aimless chatter helps."

"I'm helping John with the timeline he promised Mario. He's such a conscientious teacher he couldn't conceive of shortchanging his students plus he's trying to mentor Lincoln as well as helping Mario out. He's amazing."

"Yeah. He's a good guy. What's this about a timeline?"

"It's a huge custom calendar to be mounted on the wall, showing the time, place and agenda of all Thirteen meetings and all the campaign events scheduled between this month and the election in November of 2012."

"I guess you'll be filling it out over the next year."

"You've got it. I bet Raeann or Paul could have designed and printed something with all their latest software much faster and better. John just doesn't know how to say no to any request, even if it is something he doesn't know how to do well. I'm not so good at it either, but better than he is. We split the project. He does the research and I input the information as he relays it. Believe it or not, he's a lot of fun to work with. Even clowns around. It's hard to think of him as the serious teacher sometimes."

"All right! Well I don't want to keep you from your regular work if you've got all that going on the side."

"Before you hang up, how's Amanda doing?"

"Amanda? You know her. At the moment she's having one of her most frustrating online debates with Magna1628. This time it's about the Federal Reserve. It's hilarious. I don't know why she keeps corresponding with him; he makes her so mad. When I tell her to forget that stuff because she's already got too much on her plate, she says how understanding and encouraging he is and she'd really miss his *consultations*. She's hard to figure."

"Tell her hey from me. I'll see you at the Townhall meeting this week and we can catch up afterwards. I think another Thirteen meeting is coming up soon too, so maybe the three of us can go somewhere to talk afterwards."

"Does that mean you're not coming to the third floor anymore?"

"Of course not. This is temporary. Hey; thanks for calling."

"Yeah. Take care."

The Condensed Platform

Lincoln had found that the time was right for implementing the ingredients necessary to establish Another Way. He was trying his best to introduce it into his trial Townhall meetings. He could see no other candidates were offering concrete solutions to unemployment, excessive debt, education, health care, crime, mental illness, and loneliness, that didn't involve more big government. His absence gave Mr. Hoffer the chance to have the team do some more work on platform issues. He hoped to give a couple new proposals to Lincoln when he returned at the end of the week.

Mr. Hoffer sat at the head of the table and made a list while some of those who were now identified as the Thirteen, talked among themselves. Most thought the mood was right for changing the tax code, and perhaps the demand for the versatile Another Way program would provide the momentum. The necessity to trim the budgets of federal and state government might be the incentive needed to get the ball back in local hands. The tax code needed to be revised to allow local communities to keep the dollars saved by substituting local volunteer labor, donations, and efficient innovations when and wherever it could be done. The chump factor had thus far been the biggest obstacle to the Another Way project—why should A save, when B would just squander the savings. People may be basically good, but they weren't stupid.

First, they needed to convince enough voters of the benefits that could be derived by sending to Capitol Hill only the taxes needed to accomplish the responsibilities enumerated in the Constitution. They thought the State should tax residents only for the services jointly shared by the fifty-eight counties in California, leaving the collection of local taxes to be determined by individual communities.

They argued about the inequalities of such a plan—whether a free market could take care of the disparities between the rich and the poor. To alleviate concern, someone cited a survey that showed that enough parents preferred to raise children in diverse neighborhoods to almost guarantee the predicted ghettos would not materialize.

Most agreed, not sending the dollars to Washington, DC, in the first place, made the most sense, as it allowed residents in local communities more control over how their contributions were spent. Others were not so sure. Some thought it was fine to send all taxes to Washington and let the federal government distribute federal and state dollars to local communities based on population, not need. That would end the Robin Hood policy of taking from the rich and giving to the poor. Others considered it noble to redistribute from those that had more than they needed to those who had less. Even more found it neither worthy nor legitimate, claiming need will always outweigh supply. All stipulated the importance of definitions. One person's wants are another person's needs.

Raising taxes on business will lead to less revenue for the government; raise taxes on everyone making above $250,000, including the trillionaires, and it would not begin to cover the need. That led to some hot words, like slavery, socialism, and ended up with a word everyone agreed with: *voluntary*.

Every one of the Thirteen wanted less federal control of local government and more freedom for the individual. All were pledged to work for it. Someone claimed that freedom was becoming a code word for selfishness. Of course, the libertarians among them didn't see that as a problem. To them, selfish meant everyone acting in their self-interest, with the good consequences documented over two hundred years ago by followers of Adam Smith. In the end, Mario and Janet were able to convince them that perception was important and to most people selfish meant lack of compassion. They got sidetracked for a while on the nature of man; whether the instinct to help is innate or learned and so forth.

Lincoln had explained his reasons for running for a seat in the House of Representatives at the initial meeting of the Thirteen. Phyllis saw his candidacy as a chance to find others who believed the nation's ideals had been misinterpreted and manipulated over the years and needed to be reconciled to basic principles. She admitted it would take time. Mapleton and Bloomfield had taken that first step and proven that local control provided more opportunities for a warmer fellowship among residents as they worked together to apply local solutions to local problems.

They all agreed the main job was to show why and how the Another Way program was the solution.

As for education, some claimed the state had a responsibility to ensure equality. Others were convinced local education would work just fine in a free market. Most parents want the best for their children. There is ample evidence that many home-schooled children are accepted in the toughest, most competitive universities. In Chicago, in a low-income housing project, children were taught in a single unit and excelled when given the same objective tests taken by children taught in a traditional school environment. That many Bloomfield schools were now on a level with Mapleton schools was considered a testament to the efficacy of the Another Way Community Centers open twenty-four hours a day and monitored by volunteer mentors. Residents of all ages gained access to online courses, provided by the best teachers in the world. These teachers were nominated by former students and subject to the rigors of the selection process used by the acclaimed Teaching Company. Residents were beneficiaries of more resources than any one school or library could hold.

The Another Way virtual school had come under attack from skeptics. It offered classes suitable for preschoolers, as well as those with postgraduate degrees. Students had the opportunity to be evaluated online by taking a nationally standardized test in any number of subjects. Scores led to a gradation of awards in the subjects tested. It made no difference where or how the knowledge was obtained as long as the scoring was objective. Too many certifications and degrees had been given for too long based on subjective merit taking into consideration the age, effort, race of the student and the reputation of the school. Employers had been fooled too many times by the range of competence among those who could present 4+ grade point averages. The virtual classrooms were not dumbed down to preserve the self-esteem of the slowest in Another Way classes. Everyone progressed at their own pace and there were no stigmas attached to age or performance.

Raeann was not one to back away from a good, opinionated discussion, but was not tolerant when it came to loud attacks where no consensus is sought. She steered the group toward Lincoln's main precept—that people are basically good. The discussion went on for some length. A number of supporters thought the basically good talk made Lincoln look naïve and, at the very least, it was controversial.

Others believed the real issue was people who love power or people who love freedom. Would they choose to live with trust or fear? Someone has to have some power unless you believe in anarchy. What is government, after all? A code that a group of people agree to live by. People who are born here, or brought to this country against their will, by remaining, have tacitly agreed to abide by the rules of the group as long as the rules permit them to leave voluntarily.

Mario recognized that his peers, and those younger, had grown up with the attitude: anything goes—live and let live. California had been settled by those seeking gold, to be sure, but tolerance, also. He had sat patiently through what he considered nonsense, with one purpose in mind. He had to energize this small group before sending them off into battle. He analogized it to the drum ceremonies primitive tribes engaged in to whip their members into frenzy—ready to strike—in this case, the war was a political one.

When he thought the time was right, he picked up the paper Janet had prepared and read it aloud.

The Plan

- Smaller government
- Why?
- More freedom
- How?
- Redefine government's function per the U.S. Constitution as only national defense, interstate commerce, law, and international relations
- What about social welfare?
- Local Another Way programs are capable of picking up the slack while the current federal/state system is gradually reduced over fifty years.
- How?
- The local opportunity databases and community centers with tax relief from government and with local and national private philanthropic organizations.

"I want you to analyze your own copy of Janet's condensation of a proposal for Lincoln's platform and be prepared with your comments on Friday when Lincoln will be back. He'll be ready and is willing to work over his proposals with us.'

Friendship

"Hey Early Bird. Why so gloomy?"

Lisa looked up as Janet and Amanda joined her at the view table in the corner of the third floor restaurant. It was true; this was the first time she had arrived before her friends. Somehow she just couldn't wait to get out of the office today. The boss was at a meeting and the clerks on the floor were using his absence to go over the details for a surprise party for one of the receptionists who had announced her wedding date earlier in the week. Lisa couldn't help overhearing the lively banter between the young women and a few of the male clerks. They were sitting on each other's desks and having a great time. It wasn't that she hadn't been included that bothered her. Lisa had her own office and wasn't part of the clerical staff. She was aloof and always had been and it hadn't bothered her before. Today it depressed her.

She had seen a rerun of *My Big Fat Greek Wedding* over the weekend; maybe that was the trigger. She loved movies like that—*Delancey Street, Moonstruck, While You Were Sleeping,* —all those ethnic movies with all the warmth, teasing, love and support that families from a variety of backgrounds expressed so freely were foreign to her. Even *Mask* revealed caring and comfort from the motorcycle gangs that were there for the character played by Cher; the maids were a family of sorts in *Help*, a more recent release. Whether it was true or not, Lisa believed these movies depicted real people. It intensified her feeling that she didn't fit in—didn't belong in a family, school or workplace. She was grappling with possibilities and emotions when Janet and Amanda entered.

"I think she's dejected about the possible inability of a tax plan to ensure equality if taxes are not redistributed by the federal government, Amanda teased. Am I right?"

"Hardly. It's more than likely the very mention of such a plan will sink the entire Another Way concept."

"Well if that's not getting you down, what is?" Amanda only knew how to be straightforward.

Janet made an attempt to lighten things up. "I think Lisa's wondering how the fate of the Federal Reserve will be affected by the results of the online debate by Magna1628 and our own genius, Amanda Miller."

After a brief, but awkward pause, Jenny appeared to take their order and Lisa quickly offered to go first. Even Amanda could not miss what Janet perceived immediately. Lisa was delivering a mixed message. She didn't want anyone prying into her private life yet she did or she wouldn't have showed up for lunch. Janet was used to making decisions and seized the moment when Jenny left the table.

"Look; you probably think you don't like to talk about yourself because it's your nature, but that's just not true; it's your *nurture*. You're a warm sharing person but you were either ignored or slapped down every time you tried to communicate. We're your friends; we honor your privacy but we want to nurture you like friends do for one another. Friends are the next best thing to family in that area. Trust us."

Lisa had already admitted to herself what Janet was saying. The banter this morning had only intensified her longing for friendship but she didn't know how to go about elevating her relationship with Janet and Amanda and the rest of Lincoln's supporters. Lisa was smarter than most and adept at survival. She didn't want to be hurt and was ready to admit that she had nothing to fear from Amanda or Janet. She had become exceptionally good at analysis over the years but she was hungry for collaboration or input to many of her ideas. She was ready to acknowledge her loneliness and ready to give it up. It was with relief that she started to share.

"It's been a long time coming but I do trust you. I'm sorry it took so long but I think you both understand. I admit I was embarrassed after our first meeting. I still have no idea what prompted me to tell you my life story. I still can't believe you didn't despise, ridicule or look down on me afterwards. And you kept your word. At least I don't believe anyone else knows my story." Amanda's brow furrowed and Lisa quickly added, "I *know* you didn't tell anyone else about my past and I doubt anyone else would be interested."

"Someday you will realize your story is extremely interesting. You have been an inspiration to us and would/will be to countless others. I'm sure Amanda feels as I do; we cherish your friendship and are grateful to you for broadening our outlook."

Amanda reached over and hugged Lisa as she seconded Janet's statement and added, "I really admire you. We both know we can learn more from you than you will ever learn from us."

Lisa wanted to share more but because they all had to get back to work she was only able to relay how much Mr. Hoffer's kindness and attention had helped her back in 1996. She had never met anyone like him. He had taken her under his wing and made her feel more at home in a strange new environment than anyone had done in all her previous sixteen years.

Lisa went back to work satisfied that she had shared her gratitude toward Mr. Hoffer with two other human beings and Amanda and Janet left with a greater respect for him and teachers in general.

Janet had overheard a conversation in the office back in 1996 between Mr. Hoffer and Phyllis during the planning stages of the Mapleton-Bloomfield meeting. John Hoffer had told Phyllis that he had chosen two new students to represent Bloomfield. He thought it would get them established quickly and accepted into their new surroundings in a leadership capacity. One was a senior. That was Lisa. He figured the other Bloomfield seniors understandably would have little interest in a program that they would never participate in as they would be off to college before it was fully instituted. Their extracurricular energies would be directed to planning their senior trip and prom.

Janet had to admit she was eavesdropping by then. She had learned about the ski resort and the death of Bill Adam's parents but had never told anyone. She supposed she had felt guilty. She couldn't swear to it but she did recall the sympathy she had felt for the good looking boy who only she and the two teachers realized had gone through such a recent tragedy. She wondered if any of the others knew about Bill's background now.

As for Raeann—Phyllis had volunteered background on Mapleton's one new student who had also suffered a recent tragedy. She was maimed in a car crash in which her father had been killed. Phyllis admitted she hadn't met the student but she had been told by the 11th grade home room teacher that the students had chosen the new girl to represent them.

Raeann was already known to everyone except Mrs. Clarry as the girl from Texas who was a whiz with hard and software. She had already taken over the school's web page and was rumored to be both patient and willing to help the numerous students who lined up to get technical help. As far as she knew no other student knew about the automobile accident. Everyone was focused on Raeann's skills and never thought to question her looks.

Janet recalled her mental note to be more discreet in the future when confiding in Mrs. Clarry. She never expected teachers to discuss students' personal information. The whole episode was strange and probably why it lay dormant in Janet's subconscious memory until now. Janet wished she had thought to connect with Raeann sooner but everyone was already so busy—especially Raeann back then *and* now. It would probably be difficult for Raeann to find the time to join them. She didn't work in the building that made it so convenient for the others to meet for lunch. Janet discarded that thought and made a mental note to discuss the possibilities with Amanda. Amanda would find a way if she put her mind to it.

Lincoln's Platform

As the group went over copies of Janet's draft together, it occurred to Mario that this could be the finished product. The Thirteen had previously agreed the shorter and more specific the platform, the better. They were tired of the political hype that had become the standard in campaigns and were betting that enough voters felt the same way. What Mario held in his hand could fit on a postcard and was, he speculated, the result of hours of condensing by Janet. He was reminded of Samuel Clemens' *If I had more time I would have written less*, and concluded that Janet had spent quite a bit of time on this platform.

Janet graciously accepted the praise that came from all corners of the room for her compact platform, but secretly wondered if Lincoln would know what to do with it. Lincoln wondered too. He had appreciated all the goodwill and offers to help, but wasn't accustomed to being spoon-fed. He had already been working out what he wanted to say in order to persuade voters. Janet was sensitive to Lincoln's hesitancy to embrace her work and responded by urging him to take over and fill in the blanks.

Lincoln apologized, in advance, for the time he knew his explanations were going to take. He thought the team should know the what and why of his proposals because he was soliciting their opinions and suggestions.

He intended to run on a platform which he claimed contained the steps toward the freedom and smaller government Janet had presented. Copies were, at that moment, being passed around the circle of friends.

If Elected:
1. I will never vote to raise the debt limit but will work to require balanced federal budgets with a time table goal and clause that will stop all borrowing until the current debt is paid off. It will require an overhaul the tax code so

taxes are gradually reduced to no more than ten percent of the nation's gross domestic product (GDP).
2. I will work to ensure the federal government irrevocably affirms its commitment to all citizens who have become dependent upon its social programs prior to 2015. Those eligible for Social Security between 2015 and 2020, will have the option to participate or choose from other practical alternatives. Thereafter Social Security will be phased out via attrition.
3. I will present a list of reforms that would maintain the extent and quality of care, but reduce the amount currently budgeted for Medicare and Medicaid by giving more market-based choices to all health care consumers.
4. I will present a plan to gradually replace Medicare and Medicaid based on the same principle and timelines as that proposed for Social Security.
5. I will work to gradually decrease the number of military bases around the globe.
6. I will work to ensure the citizens of California attain a fairer representation in the United States Senate by dividing the state into three: Southern California, Central California and Northern California and ensure the governors of each have a line item veto to control their budgets.
7. I will work on legislation that would prevent any government agency from awarding a contract to any foreign entity that would be paid with American tax revenues.
8. I will work on legislation that would require that a hundred laws be sunset for every new law passed and that no new law should be longer than the Constitution, i.e. fourteen pages, 12 pt Times New Roman type and standard spacing.
9. I will present a plan to phase out the Internal Revenue Code, substituting instead, a flat tax or a new version of the transaction tax as government's primary source of revenue.

10. I will work on legislation that would require the federal government to balance a budget that includes a rainy day fund so it can cease borrowing until the current debt is paid off and the budget amounts to no more than ten percent of GDP in the year of the borrowing.
11. I will work on legislation that forces the federal government to appeal directly to the people for emergency funding, beyond the capacity of the rainy day fund—i.e. in case of war or catastrophes.
12. I will work with others to close federal departments and all federal facilities that do not perform functions specifically enumerated in the U.S. Constitution, and especially those that compete with similar programs in the private sector for profit or nonprofit. (Illustrative list available)
13. I will encourage colleagues to honor their constitutional obligation to reclaim the responsibility to declare war.
14. I will lobby to replace GDP (Gross Domestic Product) with GNH (Gross National Happiness) as the leading indicator of the health of the nation.

Lincoln said he had been studying the field and believed he was the only candidate that would be giving specific solutions. That was strategic. He understood that specifics were sure to offend one group or another but figured that's why politicians infuriated voters, by refusing to discuss the serious, most controversial issues, let alone take stands on them. He had given it a lot of thought and believed people were ready for a decisive leader that had a program and a timeline. He thought the public was looking for representatives that would take the bull by the horns, even though the plan might include the so often referred to *pain and sacrifice* making the prescribed medicine go down hard. What they wanted was solutions.

There were no eyebrows raised, or gasps of despair, as Lincoln had anticipated. He knew his way was not the way these things were done and had prepared to defend his position. He waited for a reaction from his supporters—even derisive laughter would have been preferable to the silence he faced. He had to admit they were stunned—every one of them.

Phyllis broke the embarrassing silence by pointing out that Janet's and Lincoln's platforms complimented one another. Amanda, perhaps a little too quickly, suggested they were two different views of the same platform. She analogized the two platforms as paintings of the same scene by two artists, as different as Picasso and Monet. That comment was so bizarre it relaxed everyone and sparked a step-by-step analysis.

They started with Janet's condensed version—smaller government and more freedom could be handled by Another Way. Someone reminded the others the solution to social welfare was also Another Way.

The group agreed that Lincoln could explain how adapting the Another Way concept to local communities would lead to smaller government, superior education, more employment, more competitive business, and more freedom, and that it would do more than just replace social welfare; it would improve the existing system. But there was a catch. The success of Another Way as a national program was heavily dependent on #12 in Lincoln's platform.

"Restricting the federal government's role to national defense, interstate commerce, law, and international relations is mandated by the Constitution, so what's the problem?"

The spontaneous laughter made it hard to pinpoint who had asked the question. However, it was obvious to Phyllis that at least one of the group was living in a dream world. Not that there wasn't some truth in the declaration by the unidentified questioner. The intention to limit government *was* surely at the core of the Constitution.

Phyllis thought it was important to make everyone in the room realize what they were up against.

"Today the idea of limited government is not necessarily valued or considered to be at the core of the Constitution by many—perhaps by most voters. Do you think enough Americans would be willing to eliminate all the functions *not* enumerated in the Constitution that the federal government has assumed over the years? I think not. Definitely not without a better alternative that they can believe in. Although those who have been introduced to the Another Way concept agreed it was a better way, only in two communities—Mapleton and Bloomfield—has it taken root over a twenty year period. All who heard about it were willing to try it in their communities as long as others would get it up and running. *They* were personally too busy.

"But even if they *were* convinced that Another Way could do the job, too many Americans have an enormous stake in the current, large, entrenched government. Besides livelihood for many, the expansive government also offers power and prestige.

"The only way it can be reduced is by reversing the numerous rulings by the Supreme Court that permitted the expansion in the first place. Time is not on our side, but at least we've isolated the crux of the problem. Revisiting the constitutionality of the interpretation of several clauses in the U.S. Constitution and assuring voters that, if declared unconstitutional, the good that had been done could be retained via Another Way. It might be difficult—but it *could* be done."

Raeann had some ideas but wanted examples for herself and some of the others who looked perplexed. "What's the good you see that would be threatened by reversing Supreme Court decisions?

"*Good*, as you all know, is subjective. Although the Supreme Court is supposed to be objective, the members are human and swayed by the predominant mood in the country over successive generations. This guarantees that, in finding certain decisions unconstitutional, everyone's favorite ox will be gored—excuse the outdated cliché. They will find that rights that were fought for and attained will no longer be protected by law."

"For example?"

"For example minimum wage and labor laws, nanny laws that protect, the numerous restrictions on employers, teachers, landlords employers, farmers—all commerce and trade."

Mario hated to put an end to a conversation that he found fascinating but he had to get the meeting back on track. There was too much to cover and they had barely started.

It was clear Lincoln's list, as it was, wouldn't play well in front of a live audience. They figured most everything on Lincoln's list would come under the heading of more freedom, but the part about phasing out and replacing entitlement programs and instituting market reforms would be a hard sell.

Lincoln was advised not to discuss anything on his list on TV or radio. Even if he could explain his rationale for each item, his words would be twisted. There was no time to train for that kind of combat. The consensus was that Lincoln should stick to explaining his stand on controversial and complex issues in writing. After agreeing there was not enough time to write a book, even with a ghostwriter, they compromised on a series of videos for YouTube. They were all willing to help and, to that end, they critiqued each pledge one at a time.

As for the first plank in Lincoln's platform, the team agreed that Lincoln should mention the amount of the federal debt. Trillions and trillions of dollars was incomprehensible. If the federal government could be honest about the number of trillions, voters would agree that the debt ceiling shouldn't be raised. But, how could you personalize what you can't imagine? Someone had an analogy for $14 trillion so they settled on $14 trillion. That led to a free-flow of analogies—some made up on the spot and others that the speaker had heard.

"Fourteen trillion is fourteen piles of thousand dollar bills, each sixty-seven miles high. Lay the bills on their side and it would take an hour to drive the length.

"If you earned one dollar for every second, you would have:
$1 million after 2 months
$1 billion after 32 years
$1 trillion after 32 thousand years.
32 thousand years! Multiply that by 14."

Lisa reminded everyone the income tax rate had been as high as ninety-two percent in 1952 and some current voters wanted that rate reinstated. Paul sarcastically commented that back then people actually believed in paying for wars.

To get everyone back on track, Raeann offered to find some really good analogies to help Lincoln's audience visualize a trillion.

The second plank seemed most likely to alienate voters. Mario italicized the most dangerous words as the discussion progressed.

I will make every effort to ensure that the federal government irrevocably affirms its commitment to all citizens who have become dependent upon its social programs prior to 2010 and to provide new programs as viable options to those eligible for Social Security between 2010 and 2020 and only alternatives to Social Security thereafter.

No one wanted to understand the government could go back on its word, even though the law had been changed many times over the years. No participants in Social Security would want to identify with the word dependent, and eligible would raise a terrifying question as to who would qualify. Only those who started receiving Social Security benefits before 2013? What about those who planned to receive benefits in 2014? Maybe make the cut off 2020? What about the payroll taxes they had paid? He had to clarify, not only who was to be given the choice of options or alternatives, but what those options and alternatives were. Lincoln was advised to remember that recipients were convinced they would be getting back the reward of lucrative government investment of their own money. Alluding to reality would devastate the campaign.

Lisa volunteered to prepare a chart showing what the historic investment returns would have been if the contributions had been invested prudently in the private sector vs. the returns from the low-yielding treasury bonds the Social Security administration was compelled to invest in. She also offered to document the amount that was not paid, but was retained by the government on the death of each contributor/recipient, instead of passing to heirs. Some might be interested in that information, but all agreed it would not gain many votes. After much discussion, they begged him to leave this issue out of his platform.

The group was initially unanimous in their enthusiasm for any list of reforms that would reduce the cost of health care services. They agreed that whatever was proposed would incur the wrath of too large a number of voters. Lincoln was dismayed. He explained how he despised the cowardly politicians that evaded these issues; issues that were most central to bringing the federal budget under control. No one, not even Phyllis came to his aid. Although Lincoln felt defeated he tried to look agreeable. His friends later described his look as stoic.

They all supported number five, the base closures. Several thought this would be the first pledge that would be backed by the majority of voters. Even so, there would be a good number that would consider many of the bases strategic for defense and diplomatic reasons.

Number six, dividing California, was enthusiastically endorsed, but not considered doable.

As for number seven, most members of the group were incensed that foreign firms could/would be hired and paid with American tax dollars to supply services, equipment, and parts to taxpayer funded projects. It didn't seem possible; especially when creating American jobs was a priority. The materials supplied by China to construct the new portions of the San Francisco Bay

Bridge were the main target of the group's fury. Amanda timidly reminded them that there were international trade agreements to be upheld, and Janet declared that other countries would counter by banning American goods and services. Amanda's unusual timidity and Janet's comments prompted more discussion. Eventually a majority agreed that the world didn't need a series of trade wars right now and that Lincoln's seventh plank would have to wait.

After much quibbling, Mr. Hoffer had enough and told Lincoln, flat out, that fourteen-page bills and retiring one hundred other pieces of legislation for each new bill passed was not only pie in the sky, but would make him a laughing stock. The others agreed, but in a more gentle way, that Lincoln would be ridiculed if number eight remained on his list. Lincoln protested but in the end number eight was also scrapped.

Number nine, overhaul of the tax code—involving the many different versions of the transaction tax—Lisa thought this was taken care of in number one and advised that the word *transaction* be omitted entirely during the campaign. The flat tax could be constructed to yield the same result and was much simpler for voters to understand. Lincoln, with some pent up belligerence showing, explained he had already drafted a two-page paper giving specifics for his own version of the transaction tax.

Number ten generated a long dialogue. The majority found that putting an end to borrowing by the United States government would be both unpopular and dangerous. However, they favored the rainy day fund. Janet suggested that borrowing was covered in the first plank. That made it easy to remove ten from the list by tacking its rainy day obligation onto number one.

After Lincoln explained what he meant by appealing directly to the people by using war bonds, victory gardens and other examples from World War II to illustrate—most of the group were happy with number eleven. Number twelve was also given a pass, based on what departments would be targeted and the way

Lincoln would handle the disruption that would occur in DC's economy when public workers were put to pasture via closure.

They were unanimous in declaring number thirteen a winner. Reclaiming the power to declare war led to a short, but loud discussion that cast blame on every usurping president starting with Harry Truman in 1950 and his undeclared war against North Korea.

Everyone wanted to know where Lincoln got number fourteen —the idea of substituting GNH for GDP—that is almost everyone—because it seems Lincoln heard about it from Amanda, who took an exaggerated bow and told them about her Bhutanese friend. He was living at International House in Berkeley and had come to a ten-day conference at Stanford one summer. Rather than looking for happiness in material things, the way too many residents in the industrialized countries do, Bhutan's Prime Minister was encouraging his countrymen to look for happiness in fellowship and spirituality. Just like Another Way, Bhutan was trying to promote family values, fellowship, and pride in its communities. Rather than collect taxes to support a government welfare system, the Bhutanese safety net was delegated to the resources and personal responsibility of the individual, the family, and local community—another of Another Way's goals. All agreed that the many parties and other community-wide gatherings such as, the rushes and award ceremonies sponsored by Another Way, served to reinforce social ties and offer opportunities to allow each individual to develop the pride and self-respect that comes with generosity and responsibility. The happiness quotient, as Amanda called Gross National Happiness, received a thumbs-up from everyone.

The group had cut Lincoln's platform in half. If he were to accept the consensus of the group—revising number one, and eliminating numbers two, three, four, seven, eight, nine and ten— the new platform would now consist of seven items having to do with budgets, reducing military bases, splitting California, local emergencies, eliminating departments, reclaiming the exclusive power to declare war, and promoting GNH as an American mission. Each plank dealt with either smaller government or fiscal and personal responsibility, and those that were eliminated could be replaced by the implementation of Another Way. They were proud of their work, but truthfully, the majority secretly believed the plank was still too long and too diverse. When Mario, Janet, and Amanda confided in each other later, they were surprised that each had felt strongly that the platform was especially ill-suited for California voters.

The meeting was so long and demanding that everybody was too tired to go anywhere but bed at the end.

Talksalot and Magna1628

A few days later a sleep-deprived Amanda called Lisa to ask her to tell the others she wouldn't be relaxing with them at Margie's tonight as planned. When she hung up she realized she was too hyper to go to bed either. She had a lot on her mind. She opened her email to see if Magna1628 was online. He was. She messaged him:

Talksalot:	"Glad you're there. Do you have time for a discussion of Obama's stimulus package?"
Magna1628:	"You just caught me. Sure I'll stay around. You start."
Talksalot:	"Okay. For starters do you think the stimulus was necessary to stabilize the economy?"
Magna1628:	"That's Keynesian thinking. You know I'm not a Keynesian. I don't think it's the government's job to create demand and it's not necessary. There are demands staring them in the face."
Talksalot:	"I remember that infrastructure was the first stimulus the Administration considered. Actually,

that made sense. But I would have been happier if the government had stayed completely out of it and let the bankruptcy laws and the marketplace do their jobs."

Magna1628: "Do you think it makes sense for the government to send out taxpayer dollars to the unemployed and then tax the unemployment tax dollars?"

Talksalot: "What do you take me for—a fool? Taxing unemployment income is the stupidest thing I ever heard of. I had a client when I was working part time at the volunteer center, who went years and years without collecting a dime from the thousands of dollars taken out of his paycheck. The first time he was laid off he optimistically thought he was going to get back a portion of the money he had deposited to tide him over in a tough situation. I couldn't argue with him about the idiocy of a government taxing a tax. What he received was barely enough to get by as it was"

Magna1628: "Just the idea of pots of money being handed out via the stimulus was enough to make a more prominent place for the term "crony capitalism" in our everyday vocabulary."

Talksalot: "That brings up the government take over of the auto industry. Do you think that helped to stabilize the economy?"

Magna1628: "Well it certainly bought back some jobs. But at what cost?"

Talksalot: "Cost to taxpayers and private sector investors. Just believing that government can moderate or eliminate recessions can encourage folks to take risks and that's destabilizing."

Magna1628:	"It's counter productive, I agree. Anyway I think that stimulating the economy was not the Administration's only objective."
Talksalot:	"What do you mean by that?"
Magna1628:	"It's clear that the Administration wants to redistribute resources and prop up the unions. It's also interested in increasing the scope of government."
Talksalot:	"You've got to admit the tax cuts and transfer increases were aimed at low to moderate income households."
Magna1628:	"True if you consider the stimulus included a payroll tax credit in 2009 and 2010, an increase in the alternative minimum tax floor, increased spending on Medicaid, extended unemployment benefits, and provided more money for food stamps."
Talksalot:	"Be fair. Some cuts were aimed at businesses."
Magna1628:	"Things like the deductions of current losses against profits made in earlier years may have sounded good but since these were not reductions in tax rates, they didn't really improve incentives. The best I could say is they might have been neutral."
Talksalot:	"Like those payroll tax credits and the checks sent to Social Security recipients."
Magna1628:	"Say, where are you getting all this information? Are you going into tax practice?"
Talksalot:	"Don't patronize me. I admit I have a friend who is an accountant—for the government."
Magna1628:	"I don't envy you your choice in friends."
Talksalot:	"Forget it. Seriously, don't you think the proposal to eliminate the corporate income tax made a lot of sense?"

Magna1628: "No kidding. Of course it makes sense to eliminate it."
Talksalot: "Don't be sarcastic"
Magna1628: "Well duh—it's double taxation! It decreases the incentive to save and invest which lowers productivity and growth. The complexity of the tax code means many businesses and some individuals have to pay professionals to keep up with the changes. And that's just for compliance with the tax code."
Talksalot: "It really gets to me. Even those that write it can't understand it."
Magna1628: "So why do we tolerate it? I think a lot of people really want to redistribute income. They realize high earners already own a disproportionate share of the wealth."
Talksalot: "But forget they pay a disproportionate share of the taxes. I'm so sick of hearing about fair share and Warren Buffet's secretary. He doesn't make a salary like she does. His is investment income and of course it's taxed differently to encourage the risk that new ventures entail. Take the risk of drilling an oil well—most of the holes are dry. That's the risk."
Magna1628: "I'm waiting for some candidate to compare the *dollar amounts* paid in taxes by the average wage earner and by the successful super rich entrepreneur."
Talksalot: "They'll see who pays what when even more successful businesses and their owners move their activity off shore."

Amanda heard someone in the background. It sounded like *Get off the computer. C'mon it's ready.* But she couldn't be sure. She wondered again if Magna1628 was married. She could tell he must live in the West, because if the *it* meant *dinner* it was late even for the Pacific time zone.

The Third Floor Conflict

Amanda and Lisa were at their usual table having lunch on the third floor. Janet hadn't shown up yet. "So how's LW doing with the Townhall meetings?"

"Okay, I guess. Did you know Bill only let him handle the introductions for the first one and sort of a rallying cry at the end of the next couple of meetings?"

Amanda wrinkled her nose in disgust. "Rallying cry? You mean Bill's using LW as a cheer leader?"

"Well, kinda. I guess I should have said a pep talk. You know—whatever you call it when the coach gets the team ready to give it all they've got before going out on the field."

"You mean court. LW's game is basketball—no field; just a court."

Janet overheard the conversation as she slipped into the seat next to Lisa. The women exchanged greetings and Janet made a face and said, "I can't imagine Bill ever *using* anybody. He's a wonderful speaker and I think he is doing a number one job coaching Lincoln. Everyone thinks so."

Lisa explained that having Lincoln *inspire* the crowd was John's idea. Janet noted and appreciated the verb change. "Inspired them to do what?"

"You've heard of the ten-ten plan, right?"

"Sure. Ten people recruit ten people and each of those recruit ten more and you've got a thousand and so on. But Bill says it never works." Janet added.

"Why makes you say that? Just because Bill says so? I'm sure John knows what he's doing."

Amanda didn't give Janet a chance to reply. "People never follow through. Sure they think it's a great idea at the time and are all enthused. Then they get busy and it just doesn't happen."

"John took that into account," Lisa snapped. "He discounts ninety percent of the audience. He says if only ten percent of those that agree to participate actually follow through the numbers grow exponentially and we will have fund raisers that will get us media coverage before we know it."

"Amanda stole my thunder. But let's suppose the ten-ten plan worked. Ten thousand recruits and lots of media coverage would be a disaster right now."

"Disaster? How's that?"

"You have to be ready for publicity. You have to be able to handle tough questions. People are always skeptical of new ideas. You have to have the ammunition at hand to convert skeptics or you'll lose the more trusting supporters you already recruited. You'll go backwards if the timing is off."

"What makes you think LW isn't ready for publicity? He's been able to handle it all his life."

"That was different. He knew how to discuss plays—what went right or wrong during a game. We're talking about the heart of his platform; Another Way."

Amanda kept still for once; she actually wanted to listen and let Lisa get to the bottom of this. She was more puzzled than Lisa. Amanda still thought of LW as the main proponent of Another Way. She hadn't been around when Bill took over that role. She had been on the coast and LW had been stationed in Oregon but traveling all over the country and Janet had been on the east coast.

"Lincoln doesn't even mention Another Way in his platform," Lisa argued. "He laid out fourteen items he was going to work on if elected. Those were the means to achieve the freedom and smaller government; the so called heart of the platform."

"Don't you suppose people are going to object to a cut back on all the programs that will have to occur if his proposals are enacted? He will have to show *how* he is going to cut back on the national debt, assure health care is available at a reasonable cost, lower unemployment, provide an environment for a robust economy, decrease crime, improve education and allow people to keep more of their money and have more control over their lives."

"You've said it yourself and we all know how he's going to explain it can be done; Another Way. You're the one who said Another Way is at the heart of his platform. That's Lincoln's answer to everything. It's working in Mapleton and Bloomfield and Bill is trying to expand it. John Hoffer wouldn't let them waste their time and waste his and our time if he thought we weren't going to pick up supporters. That's what these meetings are about. Lincoln is getting loads of applause and potential voters for the primary just by being there."

"I'm sorry Lisa, but you're being naïve. Lincoln's favorable response is a tribute to his skill at basketball. People love celebrities. They are applauding the sports star, not Another Way."

"But the meetings are *about* Another Way; not about basketball or Lincoln. You know Lincoln has only a small part right now. Bill describes the Another Way program and the audience does ask questions—and they like the answers. You're there and taking notes."

Amanda jumped in. "C'mon Lisa. First you insist Lincoln sticks to his fourteen platform pledges and doesn't even mention Another Way and now you claim the meetings are about Another Way. You can't have it both ways."

Janet ignored Amanda's comments. "Yes. And no one has asked what happens to displaced workers, public and private, if volunteers take over their jobs? Has anyone really understood barter and community dollars? Has anyone questioned how small towns without a lot or rich residents or numbers of grantmaking nonprofits can come up with the rewards for those willing to work for the things the community or some of its individuals can't afford? And what about the biggest one of all? Who thinks the federal government will give up first call on *any* of the taxes now paid by the 307 million people who reside in the United States of America and let them—the taxpayers in each individual school district—not the federal government—decide the entities and how much each will get of just some of those tax dollars?"

Lisa was angry. She hadn't been involved in Another Way as long or as deeply as the others in the group but she knew it was working.

Amanda was stunned by this outburst from Janet. She wasn't sure yet what to make of it. Thank goodness they all had to get back to work.

Second Thoughts

There had been two meetings since the initial platform meeting. It had taken a while, but Lincoln had come around and readily acknowledged that he was having trouble concentrating on so many items. He knew his hardest job was to focus. Everyone had agreed that focus was vital. Each member of the team was working furiously on Lincoln's behalf, some working around their full-time jobs—researching, writing pamphlets, drafting speeches, and rewriting to his specifications, creating web sites, and feeding numerous social sites, working with the media, soliciting potential donors, planning videos, and securing gigs.

Lincoln, on the other hand, was having second thoughts about his decision to enter politics. He seemed to be uniquely ill-suited for the job he had pledged to do. He was a professional athlete, a philosopher, and a perfectionist. The perfectionist had been an asset to the athlete—he recalled making himself start over when he was very young, if he failed to meet his goal of ten baskets in a row. When he was older and the goal was one hundred, he still made himself start from the beginning if he missed on ninety-two. He never missed a free shot when he was a pro.

But the perfectionist in him was proving disastrous when it came to his campaign. Everything was moving too fast. He was being asked his opinion on issues he knew little about and there just wasn't time to research all that he didn't know. A week earlier, he had second guessed what he thought he *did* know—his long held opinion that the Supreme Court now occupied a role in the government that put the judicial above, instead of equal to the legislative and executive branches, was just one example. The research he engaged in, hoping to confirm his earlier stand regarding the Supreme Court, led him to the conclusion that the founders initial restrictions on who could vote made sense. Certainly not the archaic restrictions on gender and race, but he could see the wisdom of having only people who took the time to educate themselves on the issues, to vote on them; and also, only those that would be actually paying the taxes, to vote on issues regarding taxes.

He would keep these ideas to himself until he had thought about them longer and discussed them with people wiser than himself, whose intellectual integrity he admired. If he followed through, he would be proposing tests to qualify voters, and eliminating others who were exempt from paying any tax that was being considered, from having a say on that tax. That was not where he wanted to go, but he knew from history that in a democracy, the financially strapped would vote in a minute to redistribute what the financially stable had acquired. There were many reasons the United States was a republic rather than a democracy. If it made sense, why did he feel ashamed of just recognizing the merits of restricting voters?

Lincoln remembered a college course that emphasized the role Sir Edward Coke's interpretation of the Magna Carta had played in shaping the beliefs of the colonists in the years prior to the writing of the American Constitution. In 1628, Lord Coke declared in Parliament that Magna Carta was subject to no king or any ruler. Professor George had claimed that this was the same period that the charters for the American colonists were written, guaranteeing them the rights and immunities of free, natural subjects—laid down in the Magna Carta. Almost a hundred years later, our founding fathers incorporated both Lord Coke's interpretation of the Magna Carta and the 1689 English Bill of Rights into the United States Constitution.

Lincoln still thought it ironic that the colonists used Lord Coke's interpretation of the Magna Carta to justify their War of Independence from Great Britain. He had recalled that most of the class was surprised when a portion of a letter John Adams wrote to Thomas Jefferson was read. He remembered it said that many colonists were thinking about a revolutionary war at least fifteen years before the first battle took place. Other disclosures found in the writings between the founding fathers, in the decade preceding the war, showed, clearly, their goal was to create a place that took the best of the English system, but adapted it to the peculiarities of the colonies. That revelation led to more discussions. Lincoln's thoughts were more focused now, ten years later, and today's insights were heightened by his immediate need to know the truth.

He knew the colonists envisioned a place where individuals of common birth could rise by merit and could have their ideas discussed and voices heard on a par with anyone. Theirs was to be a government of the people—the average citizen would have the final say—but not by a majority consensus, but by elected representation. Just the fact that this new land would be a republic, not a democracy, would be news to many citizens of the United States today.

Lincoln was a regular guy and he liked it. He liked the fans in the stands and hamming it up with his teammates. Most of these guys didn't know the difference between a democracy and a republic or that voting was not extended to all citizens originally and why. But he did know he wanted them to vote and felt guilty that his research had led him to consider that maybe the right to vote should be denied them and countless others unless they could prove they understood the issues. He knew the majority of voters now were not that knowledgeable about the issues they were asked to decide. Was this the reason so many laws that he believed were unconstitutional got passed—the reason the federal government was able to so easily usurp the power that rightfully belonged to the individual states and the people?

He got up and walked around. That's why Problems Solvers at Mapleton schools discussed proposed legislation on the radio. By sharing their knowledge they were making a very important impact in their community.

Lincoln had faith in people. He knew they could be flexible and willing to sacrifice if it were important enough. He remembered discussing Pearl Harbor in class and how the people pulled together in World War II in a way they had not be asked to do during the many undeclared wars that had occurred since, and were still going on in his lifetime. He was glad he had brought that up in defense of number eleven in his platform, which was the legislation that forces the federal government to appeal directly to the people for emergency funding beyond the capacity of the rainy day fund—i.e. in case of war or catastrophes.

As for the United States Constitution itself; he believed it had been manipulated beyond the flexibility purposely written into it. He was certain the vision of freedom embodied in that innovative document had been distorted by the many interpretations of the commerce clause and the necessary and proper clause over the years. He definitely understood the genius of allowing the Constitution to change with the times, but the Supreme Court had reversed itself so often, what was ruled unconstitutional over and over, suddenly became constitutional, and then precedent. *This* Lincoln knew was wrong.

There was much to be undone, but experience had shown no one wants to go backward. Opponents had begun calling themselves progressives, to throw off the tarnished liberal label and had succeeded in linking conservative with the image of an old fogey resistant to change—the party of no, reinforced the image. Lincoln needed to change that image that was meant for the Republicans and Tea Party members, in order to get his libertarian-Independent views accepted. Many of his views were shared by the Tea Party and it was being labeled as radical and irresponsible. There was no doubt about it; revolution was in the air and occurring all over the globe. He stopped pacing and thought about it. The Constitution was set up for peaceful revolutions—could there be peace between those who favored more government and those that favored less? He concluded the war of ideas had first to be fought and won, and he was game.

Lincoln kept the glaring weakness he saw in his proposals to himself. He needed more time to test his intentions before he proceeded. Everything he intended had to be done gradually. The faces and mood of the House were subject to change every two years, the president and his administration—every four, and the Senate—every six years. That meant legislation, if passed, would not remain unchallenged long enough to effect the desired changes.

That remained to be seen. The goals had to be mandated and the only way he could see that happening was via a Constitutional Convention. That meant more persuasion directed to more people than initially anticipated. He had to remove his own doubts; he had to truly believe this could be done in order to summon the enthusiasm needed to persuade others. He had been wearing rose-colored glasses; today he was looking through the clear lenses of reality and realized that, even if he won a seat in the House, he would be one freshman voice among the four hundred thirty-five that could vote and be heard on the House floor. The thought of the character Jimmy Stewart played in the old movie, *Mr. Smith Goes to Washington,* gave him hope, until he recalled Mr. Smith was one of a hundred Senators that could filibuster—besides, it was fiction. In truth, he knew it would be difficult to hold on, without believing in the possibility of a Constitutional Convention.

He didn't have time. Other candidates had a head start on him and he couldn't wait to perfect his platform. He had to do what he had to do—soon.

Voting and Civil Rights

Amanda was going through her email one last time before going to bed. She had Flo Rida in the background singing *Good Feeling.* Amanda was happy with the campaign and her paying job. Life was good.

It had been a busy day at work. She was adjusting to her new boss, Jack Campbell. He was a down to earth guy; handsome with a good sense of humor. He was very intelligent and she had many interesting discussions with him—some outright arguments which was something generally not tolerated between a boss and an assistant.

She had intended only to delete and spam targeted email tonight and open the others tomorrow. She wanted to get to work early and could answer email when she got there. Then she saw she had a new email from Magna1628 and couldn't resist.

Magna1628: "Hey there Talksalot! We've talked about the ignorance of callers to talk shows and those that post online in the past. I've been thinking about the merits of requiring a test to show people have some knowledge of the Constitution, Declaration of Independence and the issues they are being asked to vote on. I'm only too aware of the drawbacks. The opposition is obvious. They

	banned literacy tests in the civil rights legislation thinking the idea was racist."
Talksalot:	"The Civil Rights Acts were just supposed to enforce the rights of all citizens to vote. You can't start prohibiting people who aren't informed. How could you tell?"
Magna1628:	"That's why testing should be required."
Talksalot:	"That's absolutely not acceptable. It wouldn't be fair. It's settled! Government can't make people learn about something if they don't want to do it on their own. This is a free country—remember?"
Magna1628:	"That's fine but at the same time Title II of the Civil Rights Act gave jurisdiction to the district courts and empowered them to tell private individuals and entities how to deal with their own property. That had nothing to do with voting or with freedom."
Talksalot:	"C'mon; it was to prevent discrimination which you know full well means treating every person in the same manner."
Magna1628:	"Not *it*—I mean *they*—all the Civil Rights Acts. The Civil Rights Act of 1875 guaranteed that everyone, regardless of race, color, or previous condition of servitude, was entitled to the same treatment in all facilities open to the public. That meant even private businesses that provided transportation, lodging, entertainment etc. Well the 1964 did the same thing even though the 1875 Act was declared unconstitutional via the14th Amendment."
Talksalot:	"Of course I remember that. I went to law school and I suspect you did too. Violation of that 1875 Act resulted in fines and/or up to a year in prison.

Magna1628: I thought we weren't going to give any personal information. Your rule. Remember?"

Talksalot: Opps—sorry. You could just as well be a history major as a law student. The point is the 1964 Act was legislated based on the 14th Amendment. Just because the 14th doesn't allow discrimination by the states the Supremes pointed out that didn't mean it was okay for the states to stop discrimination by private individuals."

Magna1628: "A lot of the same provisions were included in the 1964 and 65 Civil Rights Acts justified this time, not by the 14th Amendment, but by the interstate commerce clause. Barry Goldwater voted against these acts even though he supported earlier civil rights efforts. For instance the 24th Amendment and legislation that failed in 1957 and 1960."

Talksalot: "If he cared about private property and freedom as he proclaimed, then why didn't he oppose the segregation laws that forced business owners to operate on a segregated basis?"

Magna1628: "I don't know about that but I do know he believed Title II violated both individual liberty and HYPERLINK "http://en.wikipedia.org/wiki/States%27_rights" \o "States' rights" states rights. I also know I agree with him when he said 'You can't legislate morality.' because both acts did just that."

Talksalot: "You missed something. The intent was to keep the newly emancipated Blacks from voting. Definitely racial discrimination. That's what all the civil rights legislation is about. Get it?"

Magna1628: "Touchy aren't you? Truce?

Talksalot: "Don't be silly."

Magna1628: "You know I agree that intent is important and that's why I favor concise laws and fewer of them.

	In this case one law prohibiting discrimination on race and gender and a separate law requiring someone to know something about the legislation they are voting on. In the 1964 Act the written literacy tests used as a qualification for voting in federal elections were only required of citizens that couldn't prove they had six years of education."
Talksalot:	"Remember the kind of education kids were given in the 19th century surpassed what most eighteen year olds get today. I'm not sure about the sixties."
Magna1628:	"Well that's just one more reason to admit the 1964 educational requirement was legitimate. It's just that it should have applied to every voter and should have been separate from the law based on racial and gender discrimination."
Talksalot:	"Well the 1965 Act got rid of all future literacy tests via Article One section eight which did provide equal protection. Individuals discriminate thousands of times a day. Humans are equipped to make choices and that's how it's done."
Magna1628:	"The truth is I do know something about the history of the various civil rights acts because I got to thinking how ignorant so many Americans are about our Constitution and how the government is supposed to work. I'm positive the Founders knew it would take informed citizens to safeguard the freedoms that are the foundation of their American dream and so I did some research."
Talksalot:	"It also takes some honest officials who will refuse to tolerate the bigoted corrupt ones. Back in the sixties Hattiesburg, Mississippi had a corrupt and racist Registrar of Voters. He never allowed a Black to register."

Magna1628: "How'd he get away with that?"
Talksalot: "Easy. Besides making them take the official literacy test he would make up impossible fanciful additional questions. I remember this because of one such question. "How many bubbles in a bar of soap?' On top of that, he didn't require any literacy testing for the over eighteen hundred Whites he signed up."
Magna1628: "I was hoping you'd agree with me about the need for educated voters. At least you confirmed what I guess I knew already. It may be impossible to require voters to be educated on the issues.
Talksalot: "Of course it would be wonderful if we had educated voters but you've got to be realistic. Too many Americans have become so focused on themselves and their individual problems that they can't think of the broader picture."
Magna1628: "I think it's worth an attempt to make our experiment in freedom work."
Talksalot: "You mean self government? I suspct you're one of those that believe the United States' destiny is to be a beacon to the world—to show the rest of humanity that it is possible to live as free human beings somewhere on this planet. I may poke fun occasionally but I respect that. Just realize we are not there yet or anywhere close."
Magna1628: "Thanks for that. I hope I didn't keep you up. We may have different time zones. I too respect your opinions and knowledge and always enjoy our discussions. (Are we nerds?)

Signing off.
Magna1628"

The Meeting in Mario's Office

Janet and Amanda met in Mario's office. Janet had a couple things she wanted to discuss. Amanda was a little irritated with the wait, but Janet was actually relieved that Mario was late. He had left a message with Jamie, a volunteer. It said Mario was consulting with Raeann and Paul in their sanctum at the newest Bloomfield Community Center and got held up. He wanted them to wait for him.

"Good," Janet grinned. "This gives me a chance to discuss a personal matter with you."

"What's the problem? Do I have bad breath?"

"Don't be cute. Remember how belligerent Lisa got at our last meeting? I didn't know she had it in her?"

"Yeah; you're right. Do you think she has a crush on Lincoln? She sure was defending him."

"Not Lincoln, silly. John Hoffer."

"Mr. Hoffer? You've got to be kidding."

"Remember how she stood up for the ten-ten plan?"

"But that was part of the rallying *Lincoln* did at the end of the meetings. I remember Lisa was incensed at the idea that it might make him look stupid. She insisted it would work."

"It would work because *John* knew what he was doing. John, not Lincoln. Those were her exact words. She worships John."

"I think you're wrong. If it's not Lincoln then it's Bill. She said he was the one who described the Another Way program and that the audience liked the way he answers questions. After all, Mr. Hoffer was her teacher. He's way too old for her."

"That's ridiculous. He's not even forty yet. He was a new teacher when we met at Mapleton and I remember he claimed Phyllis was his mentor."

"Wow. If you're right I've got to take some time to get my head around this. Maybe we should do something about it."

"What do you mean?"

"You know. Kinda push them together."

"I've already done that, *unintentionally*, by asking Lisa to attend the Townhall meetings. I certainly didn't do it to get Lisa hooked up with John."

"Well how about providing more opportunities. Like offering her a ride and then asking Mr. Hoffer—I mean John—to substitute for you since you have to go earlier or later than you planned. Or give Lisa a ride and load up the car with some boxes or something so she needs a ride after the meeting. Don't you guys go to the Mucky Duck or some place like that to have a bite and relax after the meetings?"

"You're right. That's a good idea. John's been driving me lately but …"

"I forgot. You really don't like to drive."

"No, no—that's okay. I just got out of the habit during all those years in New York and DC—the traffic and parking is a nightmare. I can start picking up Lisa and if the plan works he'll take over and I can just as easily get a ride with Bill or Mario."

The door opened and Mario entered. "Sorry to keep you waiting." He sank into the big office chair and got right to the point. "What's on your minds?"

"I heard something on C-Span's *Washington Journal* that I think might be valuable."

"Are you kidding? Isn't that on C-Span early in the morning?

"At four a.m. here so I record it every morning and review it when I first get up. They start out with a call-in segment and the other morning they asked callers to share the qualities they most desired in a President. I made a list of some of the qualities the viewers were looking for. I thought they would be assets to a candidate for Congress just as well." Janet reached into her brief case and pulled out three print outs. Amanda and Mario took a minute to skim the list.

"Very interesting. Let's discuss the ones you thought would apply to Lincoln. Isn't that what you had in mind?" Mario smiled at Janet.

"Something like that," she replied. "Actually I'd like your thoughts on how we might use this information."

"I see some are starred."

"That's right. Those are the qualities I'm not so sure Lincoln exhibits at this point. I'd like to know if you agree or disagree and what other ones you might star."

"Sound good. Amanda, why don't you read the list aloud and comment as you go."

"A non-politician, no hypocrisy, reasonable, realistic, brave enough to buck the tide, *Knows the Constitution and ideals of our county." She paused and looked up. "I think that Lincoln may need to get better acquainted with the U.S. Constitution. I'll give him a pocket size version when I next see him." She continued with the list. "Decisive—I guess so—but I'd remove the star from the next one; *Honest and sincere. I definitely believe Lincoln is already honest and sincere."

"I agree." Mario sat upright in his chair. "If Lincoln had only one quality to brag about it would be that one."

"Sorry, I think that was a typo," Janet blushed and Amanda continued reading.

"Determined, *wise. I agree with this star. Lincoln is a little young to be labeled wise, but I do think we can say he does what he thinks is right."

Janet interrupted Amanda. "There was a discussion of checks and balance after 'does what he thinks is right'. Some callers thought the current President exhibited too much of this quality. In fact there were several that turned this quality into a negative calling it autocratic and accusing the President of acting like a dictator. That's where the checks and balances conversation came in."

"That's far fetched, don't you think?" Mario continued without waiting for Janet's answer. "I wouldn't vote for a president that wouldn't do what he thought was right." Amanda and Janet agreed and Amanda continued.

"*Praises and promotes the virtues of the USA. Why is that starred? I think Lincoln is a pro at doing that."

"Maybe so. I know he can, and certainly did it often enough throughout high school. Anyway, I think he could be encouraged to do it more during his campaign. The time is ripe for that kind of thing. So many callers criticized the President for putting America down."

"Good grief. Lincoln's not running for President." Amanda still remembered how inspired and inspiring Lincoln was during the Mapleton meeting. Of course she was only a seventh grader from Bloomfield and everyone and everything was pretty awesome that day. She really didn't know the adult Lincoln very well.

Mario couldn't help adding "Not yet." to Amanda's exclamation. He winked at Janet.

Amanda read on. "Optimistic and against negativity, not a flip-flopper, knows his job and doesn't exceed it..."

"Another blast at the current President," Janet interjected.

"Gotta have heart.

"That's Lincoln alright." Mario beamed.

"Works with both sides—can compromise. I don't know. Compromise? Do you think this deserves a star? From what I've heard and seen and know of Lincoln's professional career I doubt if he's so good at compromise. What do you guys think?"

Janet and Mario both nodded. "You're right. But I don't know that it would be good to encourage this quality." Mario was conflicted.

Janet stated the pros and cons. "Compromise would attract votes from Independents and the Democrats but repel votes from the Republicans. I'd leave it alone. Go on to the next one."

"Passion and love for liberty. No problem. *Appreciates our market economy. Why a star?"

Janet shrugged, "That's why I want your opinions."

"No star," Mario and Amanda agreed.

"Common sense. Definitely. Ahead of his time, also definitely if he's going to propose the Another Way programs. Religious—at least a belief in God. Do you guys know or care about this one?" Both Mario and Janet shook their heads.

"Leave it out," Mario said. "Religion is too controversial; too personal."

Amanda continued. "Is a strong committed family man."

"Leave that out too." Mario added, "Not that Lincoln isn't; but he isn't married with kids and I think that's what the callers were getting at. Did you have something else in mind by including it Janet?"

"Not really. I don't know much about Lincoln's family but of course I knew he wasn't married. It's fine with me to forget about emphasizing family in the campaign."

"Modesty, meaning not politically correct—believes it's okay to hurt some to improve the lot of others—thick skinned meaning can take criticism." Amanda was getting tired and linked the three together and waited for a response. She didn't think any of them were very important and had no idea how they applied to Lincoln.

Since Mario knew Lincoln the longest, he believed he was best qualified to comment and he did. "I think Lincoln is appropriately modest, especially for someone who is a celebrity, so there's nothing to encourage there. He's a softie so I don't think hurting some to help others would sit well with him any more than it does with me. I don't know why anyone should suggest that as a quality."

Janet broke in. "Any leader needs to be able to make hard decisions. I think that's what was meant, although it wasn't stated very well. Anyway to win games with a five man team requires that quality. I guess Lincoln obviously has it. I don't know why I added it to the list as there's no way to use it as something to brag about in a campaign without offending someone." Mario nodded and Amanda continued.

"Doesn't pander," she read and broke out laughing. Mario and Janet joined her. They all agreed the last one described Lincoln to a *t*.

The Fourth Townhall Meeting

Mr. Hoffer, Janet and Lisa were in the audience. This was the fourth meeting and Lincoln had just finished his introduction. Mario was with Lincoln in the wings where they couldn't be seen. Bill had introduced Lincoln at the first presentation and had him speak about his candidacy for about ten minutes at the beginning and finish with a brief wrap up of how Another Way would make lower taxes and smaller government possible. They handled the second presentation the same way. Then they began dividing the time evenly between Bill and Lincoln. By the fourth meeting, they had worked it so both men joined in the Q & A

Bill usually used the same opening, but tonight was different. "I'd like to read a few lines from a paper a student in Seffner, Florida, submitted to the Harry Singer Foundation. I was told it, and similar comments from teens over the years, were catalysts for the Another Way project.

Many people in the community are more than willing to help people that need it, but simply don't know how. I believe that the only way that we will be able to take care of the poor is to let the comfortable people know how they can help. If the opportunities to serve are made readily available to the general public, I believe that the response would be overwhelming. If we work together with obtainable goals in mind, nothing can stop us.

"Another Way is more than another program; it is an infrastructure and mindset.

"What do I mean by infrastructure? Well, what do highways, subway rails, and the Internet have in common?" He paused.

"I'll tell you. They are all delivery systems. Another Way's delivery system is what the Florida student was looking for in 1994—'opportunities to serve, made readily available.' The Another Way concept was conceived two years later when search engines were in their infancy. Lycos, Go.com, and Web Crawler were around in 1994, but, in 1995, Yahoo was a directory. It evolved quickly, but Google, currently the other most popular search engine, didn't make an appearance until 1998. There is no Another Way without the ability to conduct complex searches via the Internet; this is integral.

Another Way's delivery system is a search engine unique to every community and constructed and maintained via high school students, as part of the school curricula. It's not a new program. It will not duplicate or replace the existing programs in any community; it exists to draw attention, to enhance and connect the already existing and often unrecognized resources in every community. It is there to publicize and help every nonprofit—public and private—do what it intends to do even better.

"Now, let me explain the mindset. Another Way doesn't depend on money to reach goals. Too many well-meaning people spend too much time and energy searching for funding, conducting studies, talking about problems and seeking subsidies, or lobbying for new government programs. Another Way acts as a matchmaker and arranges trades rather than grants. When dealing with organizations that are obliged by their charters to make grants, Another Way uses the pass it on concept. This is in keeping with nonprofit law and two additional concepts—trade and leverage.

As usual, Mr. Hoffer, Janet and Lisa documented those items they thought needed more, and sometimes less, clarification.

Bill generally explained that Phyllis Clarry had adopted the idea from a representative of the Harry Singer Foundation (HSF), Marta somebody, who claimed most adults underestimate the capabilities of young people and their eagerness to be productive community members. Marta had edited a HSF book, *Kids R Us*, that used direct quotes from students to that effect. Phyllis had passed the book on to him, but Lincoln admitted he hadn't read it yet, but had read another HSF book titled, *Alternatives: Proposals for Local Governments Struggling with Limited Resources*. Ninety-nine percent of the content was written by teens who had polled ordinary adults, members of the media, and public officials in their community to discover the most pressing issues. He usually explained that each participating school chose one issue from its list and wrote up its own proposed solution.

Lincoln had been impressed with the intelligence, enthusiasm, and willingness of high school students across the nation to help their communities—their work product was judged by several members of the House and Senate, as well as a couple governors and big city mayors. That was his focus tonight. The audience picked up on it and that was a large part of the Q and A session which engendered the most enthusiastic response to date.

Bill couldn't understand why it bothered him, but he had to acknowledge the agitation he felt. He hoped he could hide it when Mr. Hoffer drove Janet home again tonight. It was the third time, and he was afraid it was becoming a habit. Afraid? That was ridiculous! Janet had car trouble the first time and had asked John for a ride; but the next two meetings... Mr. Hoffer must be twice Janet's age; okay—maybe ten or fifteen years older. She should know better—what was she thinking? Worse still—what was *he* thinking? A man old enough to be her father—and a teacher! Oh well, it was none of Bill's business. But it was! Why? He managed to convince himself that he was only looking after the welfare of two friends who were making fools of themselves.

They all went to the Mucky Duck after the presentation. They always met somewhere afterwards to review the presentations and see what went right and what could be improved. The Mucky

Duck was in the center of the Fresno gigs, so it had begun to feel like home base.

Everyone was glad, that instead of conducting the campaign in the direction of an ever-widening circle, they had decided to start the campaign by setting up meetings in a square twenty miles in each direction. They hadn't gone north yet—on purpose. In order to shorten the drive for the Bloomfield-Mapleton area recruits, they would start in the north when the seminar began. Bill had never canvassed that area for Another Way—he had stuck pretty much to the valley north and south of Fresno. He had, unintentionally, stayed away from the coast, with the exception of San Diego and Orange County—oh yeah—and San Carlos. He spent several months in San Carlos…and Spokane, and had sent loads of materials to Dallas and Washington, DC, in response to enthusiastic requests that went nowhere. He even corresponded with young Bosnians who wanted to get Another Way going in their country. He was given these opportunities seven or eight years ago.

Bill wondered what Phyllis and Lincoln had that he didn't. He didn't think of himself as the jealous type, but he was envious of the Pied Piper types who so easily attracted followers. On the other hand, he had been voted Most Popular in high school and had overheard others commenting on his charisma several times since he had moved to Bloomfield. Maybe he was insecure because of what happened to his parents. When he was younger, he had discussed his feelings with Mr. Hoffer, who had slowly become a mentor. Maybe that's why he felt so strongly about Mr. Hoffer and Janet. Mr. Hoffer was one of his favorite people, but he definitely wasn't charismatic, so his evaluation that Bill *was*, hadn't given Bill the confidence and assurance he was after.

Mario was perceptive, and perhaps his best friend. They admired each other, so maybe that's why he hadn't discussed his insecurity with Mario; maybe he would after the election, along with a philosophical analysis of the difference between jealousy and envy. Mario would go for that. Lisa was insightful too, but she was always so busy and he really didn't know her that well. Besides she usually left early and seldom went to relax with the group after the meetings. All accountants seemed to overwork. Bill also respected Raeann immensely. She was kind and perceptive, but he didn't think he'd get the truth from her; she whitewashed unpleasant situations and tended to flatter people. Janet, on the other hand, was maybe too blunt, but she spoke the truth. He put that bit of information in the back of his mind to pull up and consider at a more opportune time.

Matchmaking?

Amanda was sitting alone at their usual table on the third floor. She looked up as Lisa approached. "Janet had to go to San Francisco. Something to do with her job."

"Just the two of us then today?"

"That's about it." Jenny came over with Amanda's salad and a coffee pot.

"How ya doin, Jenny? I'll have a burger and some coleslaw. No coffee," Lisa said, capping her hand over the cup. "I'll have a coke though. Thanks."

Amanda looked impatient as Jenny and Lisa chatted. At last Jenny left with Lisa's order.

"You're late today. I was waiting for you but finally had to order. We're having a staff meeting at one and I've got to get back."

"They kept me longer than usual today."

"I thought you kept your own hours. You have your own office; right?"

"Sure, but this was a consultation."

"That's what you get for being so good at your job. The others pick your brains."

Lisa laughed; then suddenly became serious. "Do you remember that time Janet got upset when I said Bill didn't like the ten by ten plan and Janet went on and on about what a great speaker he was and doing such a great job with Lincoln?

"Well, that's not exactly the way I remember it but I think I know the time you're talking about. I remember you stuck up for Mr. Hoffer and Janet denied that Bill was using Lincoln like a cheer leader at the end of their programs—or something like that. It wasn't very long ago."

"Okay. You're right, but I think Janet really likes Bill."

"Of course she does. I do too. Don't you? Everybody likes Bill."

"C'mon Amanda, you know what I'm talking about. She pretends to ignore him at the Townhall meetings but I see her gazing at him until he looks her way and she immediately averts her eyes and acts funny. No big deal at first but it's getting more and more noticeable. John even noticed it. She does things as if she's trying to make Bill jealous."

"No way. That's not Janet at all. I've been trying for months to get her to notice guys—she's just not into dating or romance."

"I don't think she's aware of it. I think she has no idea how to flirt—nothing like that. Maybe watch her awhile. You see her more than anybody else. See what you think."

"Well, I can tell you right now I think it's crazy—nonsense. I think it's your imagination."

"Promise me you'll think about it."

"I'll keep my eyes open," Amanda said as she buttoned her jacket and flung her purse over her shoulder. "Call me tonight."

Amanda could hardly keep from laughing out loud on her way back to the office. It was beyond amusing. First Janet confides that Lisa likes Mr. Hoffer then Lisa confides that Janet likes Bill. She wasn't so sure about Janet and Bill. Hmmm. Then she began wondering who Lisa and Janet might have put her together with in their minds. Probably Lincoln. Hmmm. That wouldn't be so bad. She felt like she was back in junior high again with all the gossip and speculations.

Training Ends

Mario and Mr. Hoffer were in agreement that all Lincoln's campaign speeches should follow the same format. Of course the Q&As would vary despite their best efforts at control. Once again, Phyllis had warned that Lincoln spoke sarcastically of politicians who gave the same speech over and over. Luckily, no human persuasion was required; Lincoln was persuaded by the schedule that demanded five or more speeches a day. He sometimes felt he was addressing audiences in his sleep. His admiration grew for the candidates he had ridiculed in an earlier life.

This was the last of the on-stage training. At the end, Bill would take over and invite the audience to a one-day-a-week, six-week seminar where they would learn about a different aspect of Another Way in detail. After tonight Lincoln would have to take some time to search his soul and either commit to his candidacy or release his supporters. Janet didn't want to think about the later. She chose to envision the former. By this time next week he should be giving shorter speeches ending with the list of things that needed to be changed, and then describe how Another Way could be the vehicle to achieve that change. Janet was looking forward to it. She, Lisa and Mr. Hoffer continued to sit in the back with their notebooks. Unfortunately, Lincoln tended to go on too long and complicate rather than clarify. Even he agreed he needed to be more concise.

Today, he began as usual: "Everyone thinks government, at all levels, is spending too much money. Many people think government has extended its reach beyond what is desirable in a free society."

Generally, he would describe his platform in a simplified form—what he wanted to do and how—and that would lead into a description of Another Way, which varied with the time allowed and the makeup of the audience.

He almost always started the platform portion off with the following introduction: "Most people think, in view of our current social problems, there is no other way, but they're wrong—there is another way and now, when the federal and state governments are in debt and cutting programs, this is the perfect time to test it out."

He would then explain to his listeners that, with enough communities involved in Another Way, they would have the leverage needed to convince Sacramento that locals could stretch their dollars further than the State could, for many of the same services. A successfully negotiated trade would relieve the state government of certain responsibilities to the locality, and the community would retain a good portion of its tax dollars and use them to regain some of the warmth that their great-grandparents experienced long ago, when neighbors came together to help one another.

Lincoln tackled the options for education available in Mapleton and Bloomfield and gave a long description of the innovative At Your Own Pace program that was an option available at all community centers. All centers now provided access twenty-four-seven and were staffed with volunteer mentors, allowing everyone to access information or take advantage of the numerous online courses and obtain degrees at their own pace in subjects of their choice.

The community centers even provided a warm, safe place for those whose family members occasionally drank too much or got high on drugs and became abusive. The abuser and the abused had a better chance of getting help earlier than before. It was amazing that once the issues of liability, screening, and insurance was settled, volunteers, even in the highly paid professions, came out of the woodwork, as Lincoln put it, and were willing to provide time and services on a regular basis.

During the Q&A Mr. Hoffer was reminded that people didn't accept new ideas easily. A student asked if she specified something for herself as a reward and there was no 501 c 3 organization or public non-profit with an adequate mission for the trade to go through, could she earn community dollars to redeem a reward for her personal use. What she wanted was a new, or even used, computer. She still wasn't clear how the rewards without a nonprofit involved worked and if it was possible to earn something for her own use.

Mr. Hoffer crossed off an entry he had made earlier on his list, after Lincoln gave an explanation that Mr. Hoffer acknowledged he would never have been able to give. In fact, Mr. Hoffer had never considered the situation and its ramifications before and was stumped when it was presented. Lincoln explained that if the speaker didn't qualify under the mission of any of her community's public or private nonprofit's because she chose to trade her time and energy for something for her personal use, as a last resort, the trade would be consider a barter, which might or might not be subject to tax. However, Lincoln reassured the questioner that he was certain the grateful social workers in any community would be able to figure out how to cover these instances with a qualifying auxiliary. Someone else in the audience suggested the Police Explorers was an example of such an auxiliary. In the end the student and entire audience understood it was possible to qualify through a public institution.

A young man, perhaps a college or high school student, asked the next question. He wanted to know if the community centers were really open all night and if they were, he thought the homeless, drunks, and druggies would pile in and the center would be trashed. There was some laughter and knowing smiles from some older members in the audience. Most probably hadn't given it a thought since Middleton was a small country town with little crime. Lincoln asked the speaker where he came from and it was from the largest city in the valley, which made sense. Lincoln explained there was night security at all Community Centers—and daytime security—but in addition to the electronic security built in via access cards, there were an amazing number of screened mentors and mentees at all hours—from the police, who frequently took their breaks there and used the computers or just talked, and the elderly that couldn't sleep and could always get help with their electronic equipment and lots of advice. Lincoln pointed out that during the questioner's entire life his family had enjoyed twenty-four-hour access to groceries. With the onslaught of the Internet, coupled with twenty-four hour TV programming he said he was afraid we had all become part of the modern twenty-four hour society. This was nothing new.

Lincoln ended the Q&A period by inviting the audience to attend the six one-day a week presentations where they would learn everything there is to know about the Another Way project that was so much a part of his campaign.

The series of courses were originally refreshers for Lincoln, though the volunteer stump speakers could benefit from the lessons too. Bill had been giving Another Way presentations for years, in various parts of the state—mostly by invitation. Unfortunately, only Mapleton and Bloomfield were in the district of the retiring congressman—okay, Fresno was too. Bill had tried to get Another Way going there when he was a senior in college, but somehow it didn't catch on. He just wasn't able to find the top-notch organizer—that firebrand, trend-setter that knows the other doers and shakers in a community. Unfortunately, Phyllis was booked at the time and Lincoln was playing pro ball.

Those outside the Thirteen that knew about the training sessions couldn't come to grips with the idea. Everyone in a fifty-mile radius had been exposed to Lincoln's rallies on behalf of Another Way and agreed that no one could arouse a crowd like Lincoln. They couldn't get their minds around the thought that Lincoln Williams would need advice on how to deliver a speech. He was the master. Bill Adams knew more than anyone about

Another Way and was great at explaining it, but he didn't attract the crowds and cheers that Lincoln did. They just couldn't get it.

Lincoln got it and was grateful that Bill was willing to educate him. The truth was that the Another Way program had evolved while he was away. It didn't satisfy Lincoln that his celebrity pleased a crowd whether they received accurate information or not. In fact, a lot of them didn't come to find out about Another Way—they came to see Lincoln Williams.

It's amazing how many people are too busy to get to know one another. Phyllis had tried to explain to everyone involved that Lincoln's ego would not suffer if the sessions were referred to as training sessions. Phyllis wondered how long it took a celebrity to lose that status. By running for a public office, she realized Lincoln was just extending the time, so she gave up the thought as an irrelevant exercise in Lincoln's case.

Lincoln, like Janet, was a humble person, often embarrassed by his own celebrity. He tried to deflect some of the appreciation showered on him onto Bill, who he admired immensely for all the time Bill spent just trying to improve the community—he really cared—an object for his caring was all he really got from his dedication. The guy was something else. Lincoln was anxious to learn from Bill and would do anything he could to help Bill—anytime, anyway—no doubt about that.

Lincoln Confronts Phyllis

Lincoln felt like he was complaining under the pretext of seeking advice. He was ostensibly meeting with Phyllis to figure out why he wasn't getting his ideas across. He felt like a puppet with his strings pulled by both his opponents and the audiences. He needed to regain control of the presentations. In truth, he knew he was letting it happen—perhaps even abetting it. He never left a presentation feeling like he had delivered the message he wanted his audience to hear. He used to be good at this—

the pride of the debate team; sports teams stood in line for his pep talks. What happened? He didn't feel good about himself as he knocked on Phyllis' door. Once he was settled in and had explained the situation, Phyllis took over.

"Your platform tells potential voters what you want to do. Your creed is what you believe.

"I have a question for you: Do people elect their beliefs or yours?" Without waiting for a reply she continued. "Most people today are skeptics. All platforms sound good—promises easily made are just as easily broken."

"It seems to me that most people today elect a person, not on creed, if you mean by that an ideology, but on personality. That's why celebrities are so often recruited to run for office. You saw my celebrity as a plus for this candidacy. I agreed that voters are likely to elect a candidate they feel they already know. That's the advantage celebrities have and one of the reasons political parties encourage them to run. I get it."

"Maybe you get it and maybe you don't. We'll see. I know I never vote for anyone on the basis of personality. In the 1980s I loved Mario Cuomo and Jesse Jackson's way with words, but I would not have voted for either of them because their ideology was almost the opposite of mine. I think your premise is outdated. I believe people in the second decade of the twenty-first century are coming around to my way of choosing representatives. But, of course, to do this, they have to know what they believe in themselves in order to know which candidates are compatible with their beliefs. Unfortunately, few voters have come to grips with their beliefs.

"What I want today is for you to do just that—examine your belief system. In your platform you told us, and yourself, what you want to do. Your friends told you what won't work, at least at this time in history, and most of what was left, you will not be able to do. Now, you tell me you're having problems getting your points across. I'm not surprised."

Lincoln felt like they were talking over, not to each other today. They weren't communicating.

"I realized it wouldn't be easy, but I was sure I could do it. You may remember I made adjustments to my platform I didn't want to make, but I did it. I knew I could do what I set out to do—but, to placate my supporters, I made the adjustments. I did it to reassure them I had my feet firmly on the ground at that meeting of the Thirteen. Didn't I say, 'will attempt' or 'intend' or something like that, several times, in the original draft of my platform?"

"You may know what your supporters need, but your problem is with the public. The public doesn't want good intentions any more than they want false promises. They have been bamboozled—and out and out lied to, too many times in the past. This year, more than any year I can remember, they are seeking truth—they want to know what's really happening; what can be done about it and what can't; who or what was in control of what happened in the past and who, if anyone, is in control of what is happening now—they know what they are told is not what is happening. Worse—they don't know if anybody knows the truth and if it is knowable."

"You're right. I'm in that boat myself. Unconfirmed rumors run rampant and as they rage, they cause confusion, uncertainty, and leave in their wake a feeling of helplessness in all of us. Are dark suns or giant meteors on their way to devastate the earth? Is there an underground site, well supplied to enable certain, selected elites to survive while the rest of the world perishes? Are we on the brink of devaluing our currency? Is worldwide famine around the corner? Should I speculate in land based on the news that the Dakotas and Montana are oil rich? Will civilization, as we know it, cease to exist when the earth wobbles on its axis and the magnetic poles adjust? No one can answer these questions about the future, and uncertainty breeds fear. What can I tell the people that is the truth when I don't know the truth about any of these things and thousands more myself?"

"The truth? Yes, you can tell the truth, as you know it. As I said before, you sought my advice, gave me your platform, and your friends helped you refine it, but they are skeptical, and were then, but won't tell you—they are not sure that you will actually hold fast and do what you outlined."

"The question should not be will I do, but will I try. I'm certain they know I will try my hardest to do what I believe needs to be done. I'm not sure they are skeptical."

"We went through this a few minutes ago. We agree many people will vote for you, but not because you try—they want and deserve more than that. Those who vote for you will do so because they know and like you. But, there are those that have no interest in basketball and have never heard of you, and that you will try is not a good enough reason to vote for you. Your supporters understand that—perhaps not Mario, Raeann, and Paul, but the hard-headed ones like Janet and Amanda understand—and maybe not consciously just yet, they are all too busy, working feverishly on your behalf. But they will see it soon, unless you do something about it."

"Why are you telling me this? It wasn't my idea in the first place—they came to me; it was their idea—and you encouraged me when I expressed my doubts. Why are you telling me this now? What do you want me to do?"

"I think you came to me because you realize you are deliberately distracting yourself from the litany of fears you just went through. Incidentally, they have nothing to do with your candidacy. No one is expecting answers from you regarding any of the ridiculous questions you raised. Your audiences want to know what you believe. They want to know if you have a creed—something that rules your life that they know you depend on before they decide to depend on you.

"I want you to give your potential voters your creed—creed, not your platform. That's what I want you to do."

"My creed? Are you sure anyone even uses that word anymore? What I *believe* in? I don't think they care. Nobody thinks about what anybody believes anymore. It's nobody's business."

"Most of your audience will know about a creed. If not, you can always explain it the first time you use it. I know you're aware that the congregation in many churches recites the Nicene Creed during the service. We discussed it in class. The congregation recites together, but as individuals— 'I believe in...,' not, we believe in. That's what comes through in a creed—individuals taking a personal stand from within and as part of the community. Forget about the word, if you must—but understand it."

"You mean, you think people want to know, or would care, what I believe in? I'm not a preacher. Are you suggesting people want—a preacher?"

"Lincoln, you are trying awfully hard to be difficult today. Most of us don't preach our beliefs—we live them. Most—unconsciously, and those that try to live them, consciously, do not do so perfectly. As I said earlier, the majority of your potential voters aren't conscious of what they believe, and the least that will happen is they will be prompted to acknowledge and own their own beliefs."

"Sorry I'm so disagreeable. I mean it. But I guess I just don't agree with you—as simple as that. I'm confused and came seeking help, but even if I agreed, how would I go about speaking about or living my creed? How do I know what it is? Have you done it—have you discovered your creed?"

"Yes, several times in my life."

"How about an example? If you want me to share my beliefs with thousands of people, maybe you wouldn't mind sharing yours with me right now. Are you game?"

Phyllis didn't hesitate. She admitted she hadn't reviewed her beliefs for quite sometime, but she felt certain the core beliefs remained as steadfast as ever—but had been surprised in the past to find certain, earlier beliefs had changed. She said it took some work and asked Lincoln about his time. Lincoln was surprised at the turn the day had taken. He removed the daily timer from his briefcase and saw Mario had penciled in forty-five minutes with

Phyllis. He called Mario and asked him to cancel the remainder of today's appointments. Mario said he would comply, when he was told the entire campaign depended on it. Lincoln confided that Phyllis had dropped a bomb on him; at least, it felt like it, and he was being truthful. Lincoln realized he had just ruined Mario's day, but Phyllis had ruined his.

Lincoln was troubled, hurt, puzzled, and infuriated—in that order. What was she asking him to do? Why now? They were past the halfway mark in the campaign and she was saying what had gone before was fruitless. The anger gained control—she was getting old; what did she know anyway; she was not a politician, had never run a campaign; why didn't he hire a professional; he should have a party affiliation; he never should have run as an Independent with amateur volunteer help…

Phyllis had returned with three writing pads. She laid them on the table and wrote on the top of each, in turn: What I Believe, What I Think Today, and What I Don't Know. Under the beliefs, she read aloud as she wrote:

I believe:

1. People are basically good
2. No one's idea of God is identical nor accurate, but God *is*
3. Good and evil are real
4. Humans have free will
5. We are faced with many choices every day
6. Everyone and everything has potential; no human exhausts his
7. Forgiving self and others enables us to attain our potential
8. Trust and privacy are our most valuable possessions
9. There is no such thing as an unselfish act
10. It's not wrong to be selfish—to fulfill your potential
11. Everyone's job is to fulfill his/her potential
12. It is wrong to knowingly harm another person or thing

13. It is regrettable, not wrong, to kill if there is no way to avoid it
14. Nature is both beautiful and destructive
15. It is good to express gratitude

I believe in the healing and awe-inspiring power of music; sunrises and sunsets; dark nights with full moons—any size moons and millions of stars; calm waters and crashing waves; majestic mountains—snow covered or bathed in the purple light of sunset or the bright golden promise of a sunrise; the green, rolling hills, dotted with cattle; or the magnificent forests and waterfalls and oak trees—oh, the beautiful sculpture of oak trees.

Lincoln had been genuinely interested and honored by the shared intimacy, as Phyllis made good on her promise. But now he was embarrassed; as if he was witnessing a teacher out of control and he hadn't thought of Phyllis as a teacher, which she was of course, for years. She must have sensed Lincoln's uneasiness. Lincoln noted that the last written words were dark nights; she saw it too and realized, for the first time, she had been carried away. Phyllis had started out writing slowly, obviously thinking thoughtfully as she wrote, and then began writing faster and faster. She was blushing, but that was the only indication she gave that she, too, believed what Lincoln witnessed was inappropriate.

Phyllis didn't apologize, but in a more composed voice continued to read as she wrote on the second writing pad:

What I think today:

1. I got carried away and made a fool of myself.

They both burst out laughing. It relieved the tension, and Phyllis thought it was a good time for a break. She came back with refreshments from the kitchen, saying this was hard work and he would see for himself soon enough.

After the break, Phyllis resumed reading aloud as she wrote; more slowly now, and pausing between lines once more.

2. Everyone is wiser than they think they are
3. Each of us has a role in solving the meaning of life's puzzle
4. No one knows the whole truth
5. No one is given more than they can bear
6. The most evolved souls may not be healthy, rich, or famous
7. Those bearing more difficulties might be more highly evolved
8. Life without purpose is difficult
9. Life with purpose motivates and is superior in every way
10. Cooperation is good, but individuality is part of God's plan

When she came to number eleven she laughed and told Lincoln she was not going to get carried away this time, but did have a legitimately long statement to make about her thoughts—not belief—regarding reincarnation. She proceeded to inform Lincoln that she thought it plausible to believe in reincarnation because it didn't make sense that all the knowledge and goodness we strive to do in the world simply disappear when our bodies cease to function. Yes, she assured him, she was talking about death—and life after death. She didn't think the soul died with the body.

As far as Lincoln could understand, Phyllis thought people continue in some form—that bodies are simply shells and the person does not change as quickly as the body changes. She said she now understood what her aunt meant at eighty when she claimed to still identify with the little girl of her childhood. The main change was appearance; then history and knowledge.

Lincoln meant to pursue reincarnation with Phyllis at a later date and also several items on her list of beliefs; especially the items in number six and number seven and number ten—they seemed so unlike Phyllis. Perhaps she got confused—he would like a more thorough explanation at one of their one-on-one friendly visits after the campaign was over.

Phyllis continued. Once again, she read aloud and wrote:

What I don't know:

1. God's plan
2. How to define the term creation as it relates to God
3. If humans are highest on the evolutionary tree

Then, instead of writing number four, Phyllis asked Lincoln if he thought it possible that a rock, tree, bird, or any form of animal life could turn out to be on a higher evolutionary plane than mankind. It seemed like the writing was through for the day and the conversation began. Phyllis admitted that she often toyed with the idea that the sea lion might be at the highest end of God's hierarchy. When Lincoln wondered what gave her such an idea, she drew him into her own speculation that humans, many who work half their lives to set aside time and money to go lie on a rock or warm sand in the sun, are the laughing stock of those seals, sea lions, elephant seals, and various other mammals, and even reptiles that do that very same thing every day.

Lincoln laughed with her. He hadn't taken her seriously, but he wondered about it afterwards. She had declared there were so many things she didn't know, it was senseless to go on listing them. She only wanted him to understand the difference between speculation, belief, and knowledge. People, she said, were looking for strong leaders and no one without unshakeable, carefully considered beliefs can be a strong leader. She thought most of the Congresses in her lifetime that had been occupied by the wishy-washy pandering, power hungry people that populate the campaign trails; the sad results of ballots cast when few, if any, men with strong beliefs were offered. Still, voters had to make choices from among those that were given, even though most had few, if any, ideas that would lead to solutions.

Sometimes, she said, it's better to vote for candidates with character—character being a trait that requires strong beliefs—even if they pledge to follow policies you don't favor, than it is to vote for candidates without character. At least you know where the former stands and what he or she will attempt and do. If you think your candidates have a chance of being successful, you will know how to plan your affairs if they are elected. Uncertainty stops lenders from lending, businessmen from borrowing and investing, consumers from purchasing, manufacturers from producing, and farmers from planting. In uncertain times the, *what ifs* take over. Intelligent people strive to see the future—current actions are based on past experience and future expectations. Fear paralyzes and uncertainty breeds fear.

Lincoln had assured Phyllis he understood. He agreed that expectations are self-fulfilling—he compared it to herd mentality and thinking makes it so. It's certainly true in the stock market—reality isn't nearly as important as expectation and speculation.

But Phyllis hadn't been sure Lincoln did understand how important a role the ability to think ahead has always played in the fortunes of mankind. However, she hesitated to pursue it further. Lincoln had absorbed a lot today and still had his own belief list to work out. Nevertheless, and before she could stop herself, she was offering Isaac's sons as an example, telling Lincoln the inability of Esau to anticipate his hunger had led him to sell his legacy to his brother Jacob. It was the story related in the Old Testament—the Torah—the five books of Moses. Today, commodity traders anticipate that bad weather will mean fewer crops and lead to food shortages, or that political upheavals will drive up the price of precious metals. To live each day as it comes, trusting in other entities—divine, government, friends or family—to provide for you, is tolerated by some, while others go so far as to glorify it as a virtue.

Phyllis personally considered shortsighted people to be weak and deluded, but she didn't say so. Instead, she silently filed this thought under the What I Think Today category to examine again at a future date.

Time Out

Lincoln would work out his beliefs. He needed to be alone to rest and get his bearings. Everything was moving too fast. It was only five months ago that the 3rd Center opened in Bloomfield and they had that fateful conversation in the back of Margie's. It seemed like he'd been campaigning for years. He needed to clarify his game plan—to understand the goal with his heart as well as his mind. It wasn't a strategy, it wasn't his platform, and it wasn't just winning. It was never just winning for him. He was not ruthless like some players. In every aspect of his life he had a code of conduct. It was natural to him. Maybe that was what Phyllis meant by creed. He was sure he didn't like to order people around any more than he liked to take orders. He was just as sure that to accomplish anything you need to have a plan, and the other players need to know the plan and play by the same rules. Everyone could see that was the problem in DC in 2011.

There would always be small factions—differences are healthy—but in the 112th Congress there was polarization. The U.S. Constitution was the original game plan, but too many in Washington, DC believed it irrelevant—outdated. Instead of taking advantage of the provision for amendment, these players had chosen to shortcut the process and reinterpret the Constitution, giving new meaning to plain words à la Lewis Carroll's examples in Alice in Wonderland.

What could he do? He hated to waste time and had spent many hours identifying that as the cause of his impatience and exasperation. He had traced the time problem to his love for life and his recognition that life is short; something he understood even as a young child.

As he mused, he realized that he could write down his beliefs in no time; and he would. It was his goals that he needed to work on. He wasn't one to let anyone down. Although he and the Thirteen had put in a lot of time and done a lot of work, it was not too late to turn back. He did not believe in fruitless efforts. Did that mean winning? If so, what was winning? Just as the federal government needed to figure out what winning meant in the Middle East, he had to figure out what accomplishment would satisfy his basic need to use time wisely.

Lincoln called Mario and told him to extend the Christmas holidays and take an extra week off and to tell everyone else to do the same.

"Call it quits for 2011. Everyone needs to refresh."

Mario looked around the room. He had called a meeting of the Thirteen after speaking with Lincoln yesterday. Everyone had shown up except Raeann. She had responded to a call for technical service at Mapleton's community center and found it more challenging than she had anticipated. Paul agreed to bring her up to speed later.

Mario began. "Lincoln called me yesterday. I could tell he was exhausted although he didn't admit it. What he did say was tell the Thirteen to take an extra week off. I agreed it was time to take a breather. An extra week at Christmas wouldn't hurt anyone. I thought it was perfect timing."

"Fine. The trouble is *we* have to work anyway. The city doesn't care how bushed we are."

Janet knew Amanda wasn't serious, but for the benefit of the others she thought she'd better defend their employers. "They don't expect us to be working *two* jobs. You can't blame them for your being worn out—not completely. After all, they're giving us most of the week after Christmas and a huge party."

"Party? How's that?"

"It's traditional," Lisa said. You're going to love it."

There were some good natured jabs and requests for invitations and then Mario signaled for quiet. "We're wasting vacation time. Unless you hear differently, we'll meet back here January 9th. I'm sure Lincoln will have some news for us. In the meantime, have a great holiday and try to relax and enjoy yourself. Forget about the campaign; I'm going to. I'll be leaving for Berkeley to be with family tomorrow, so ask any questions you have now and don't try to get me unless you want to get together for some relaxation and fun in the bay area. In that case, leave a message on my cell. Otherwise I won't guarantee I'll answer."

Janet did call Mario later that night. "I've been worried about Lincoln lately. Can you level with me; I'll keep it to myself, but my intuition tells me he is still not committed to running for Congress."

"Don't be silly. He's just tired."

"Okay; if that's the way you want it."

Mario hesitated. He didn't want to confide his fears to Janet or anyone. On the other hand she and Paul had chosen him for the manager role and had a right to know. They all did. He just didn't want to worry anyone. He wanted them to relax and come back refreshed to whatever news they would get in January. Obviously Janet was already worried.

"You must have a sixth sense, Janet. Lincoln always gives his all to any task, but I think he's not sure he can pull this off and doesn't want you guys to have done all this work for nothing. He's tired, just like everyone else. I really think he'll come back with good news and raring to go in January."

"Well, I hope you're right. If we're going to gather signatures to get him on the ballot the sooner the better. As it is we've got an exhausting eleven months ahead of us. Raeann and I were hoping to get a head start. At least get the petitions ready to go and do some volunteer recruiting over the holidays when we'll have more time."

"Remember, this will be the first election using the new rules. Proposition 14 was passed here in California sometime in 2010 when you weren't here."

"June 8th; I followed Prop 14. But you're right I didn't read the fine print in the document that finally passed. I'll request detailed information for the new rules but I'm almost positive we don't have to declare Lincoln as an independent, which is great. If I remember correctly, there will be no Democrat, Republican or any other party designated for any of the candidates on the primary ballot."

Mario didn't believe that Janet ever forgot anything. She and Lincoln both had minds like steel traps. That would be some match, he thought but said, "That's right—all potential candidates are now *voter-nominated*—the new term. Lincoln will be on a par with every other candidate."

"And I'm pretty sure we have a choice of paying a fee in lieu of gathering signatures to put him on the primary ballot; a pretty reasonable fee."

"If that's the case I think we should pay the fee—I'll pay it—forget gathering signatures and relax and come back refreshed. I think that'll work better in the long run."

"Okay. If that's how you want it. I'll convey that to Raeann, if you don't mind"

"Sure; that's fine. If either of you need to talk more about this, feel free to give me a call. Ignore what I said in the meeting. But that only applies to you and Raeann. Okay?"

"Thanks Mario. If we want to discuss this further we'll combine it with some fun and come up to the big city and take you out on the town. How's that?"

"Sounds good. Happy holidays and convey my greetings to Raeann too. Do you think I should call her to put her mind at ease?"

"Don't worry about it. Just let us know if you have any solid news to convey from Lincoln, otherwise we'll play it be ear as you suggested. Have a wonderful time with your family and make sure you get some good rest while you're at it."

"Thanks. You have a good time too. Enjoy yourself and have some fun. You've been working hard and deserve it. Raeann too. Tell her I said so."

Mario Vacations in Berkeley

"Hey. How would you like to meet Jeff Fullerton and his family tonight? They've invited us to dinner. He's a big fan of Lincoln's; teaches economics at Cal."

Lincoln had been in Berkeley three days. Phillip was still working regular hours and Mario's mother—grandma—was either busy baking or shopping. Of course they had enjoyed good conversation in the evenings but their schedules had allowed Mario to get some extra sleep and peace and quiet during the day. He was ready for some stimulation and Phillip had some pretty cool and intelligent friends.

"Is he a co-worker?"

"No. Jeff is one of my clients. I think you'll get a kick out of him."

"Any basketball fan is a friend of mine."

"I'm not sure about that. He said he heard Lincoln give a speech on campus and talked to him for awhile afterwards. I think he wants to volunteer for Lincoln's campaign."

"He's not in Lincoln's district."

"I mentioned that but it doesn't matter to Jeff. He has libertarian leanings and says Lincoln does too. Our incumbent congressman doesn't need help. Anyway, if he did, I know Jeff would not be interested. Jeff is pretty much a fish out of water when it comes to political choices here in Berkeley. The incumbent wins every time."

"That's why my mom and dad moved to Bloomfield. They met in Berkeley and at that time Ron Dellums was their congressman. No one could defeat him. He was in the House for twenty-seven years."

Mario thought it was fortunate that the Fullerton's lived in one of Berkeley's old Victorians that had a large dinning room with a high ceiling. Luckily the bay area climate was usually mild; otherwise it would be costly to heat the place.

The Lees—Phillip, and wife Emily, their two daughters, Kathy eleven and Elizabeth eight, together with grandma and Mario were a family of six as were the Fullertons; Jeff and wife Evelyn, and children, Kevin seventeen, George sixteen, Alex fourteen and Elaine eight..

After a good meal the children and grandma went downstairs to the playroom where there was something for everyone; ping pong, board games, MP3 Box with electronic games and a huge screen television .

Emily and Evelyn chatted away in the kitchen as they cleaned up and served desert and cordials in the living room where the men were talking politics, sports and investments. Mario wasn't really interested but he asked how their investments were doing; to be polite more than anything. Phillip was speechless for a moment or two. Phillip always made certain Mario received monthly reports but suspected they went directly into Mario's wastebasket As far as he could remember Mario had simply

235

deposited the checks he was sent every month and returned the signed tax returns with no questions asked.

Phillip tried to mask his surprise as he replied, "Well, you know with the global economy being so bad we had to sell quite a few stocks last year."

"That's too bad. At a loss I suppose."

"No, no—we were on top of the situation. We anticipated a lot of fluctuation so we culled and condensed the portfolio and avoided any losses. In fact the *China World* stock we took in during the sale of the restaurant leads the winners. *China World* is in a dozen countries now and keeps expanding."

Phillip was beaming, not only because he had good news to report but because he thought Mario was finally taking an interest in the family business. Unfortunately the look on Mario's face showed displeasure despite the now obviously polite "That's good news. Congratulations," that escaped from Mario's contorted lips.

In the car on the way home, Emily remarked on how everyone got along so well. Grandma added that even the kids enjoyed each other's company. There wasn't a whiner or spoiled sport in the bunch. She also asked Phillip what had happened to Uncle George. Phillip explained to Mario that Elaine had been adopted as a baby and Uncle George was actually her grandfather. He lived a couple hours away somewhere in the valley and used to visit frequently. To grandma, Phillip admitted he hadn't seen Uncle George for quite some time and would ask Jeff about that next time he saw him.

Alone with Emily in the bedroom, Phillip wondered if he had just imagined the look on Mario's face. After all, hadn't Mario asked about the business for the first time ever? Mario was able to convince himself that he had misread the look and his brother might come into the business after all; given a little more time. Phillip went to sleep with a smile on his face.

2012
Let My People Go

Lincoln had come back full of energy and determination. He had reverted to the soul searching he had engaged in when first asked to run. He had reluctantly agreed to the trial but as the representative of others. That was well and good, and of course what a representative was supposed to do, but it didn't give him the fire in the belly that he needed.

Lincoln certainly hadn't avoided an analysis of his position; he was an analytical person by nature and habit. He had analyzed with Phyllis, with Mario, with his supporters and by himself. He had been partially right—the goal was not *just* to win but the goal *was* to win. He had analyzed what it meant to win after his last session with Phyllis and had immediately ruled out power. This last analysis revealed that he wanted freedom first and foremost. Freedom for himself and other people—*all* people. That was the uniqueness of America as embodied in the U.S. Constitution. It was the promise of freedom that made the United States exceptional. *American Exceptionalism* was the phrase peppered throughout the 2012 campaign for the presidency. He had thought about his own campaign slogan—*Let My People Go*. He knew the Thirteen would think it corny and not definitive but it defined his message and reason for running for office far better than Another Way did. Another Way would only be given a chance if enough people yearned to be released from the dictates of a huge and distant government as much as he did.

This release was what he would be pleading for; it excited the passion he was lacking earlier. He would promote the freedom to do whatever he and every other citizen decided they wanted to do as long as it was within the law. No; that wouldn't do. There were already far too many oppressive and unnecessarily intrusive laws. He substituted "as long as it didn't harm anyone else" and harm would have to be proven in court.

He remembered a teammate telling him how his father, Ben, had tried to rent a storage room that had a toilet and wash basin just outside the door. The room was located inside a large basement area in Berkeley in the seventies. The ceilings weren't as high as demanded by code for legitimate rentals. It hadn't been listed for rent but Ben couldn't afford the room he had come to see on an upper floor. He tried to talk the owner into renting the basement area room to him for just a few months. He countered every objection. He didn't mind roughing it. He was engaged to be married and the rent he saved would go toward the down payment he was accumulating to buy his own place before the wedding. He would take showers in the gym next to where he worked in San Francisco where the rents were high. The bridge toll was a small fraction of what it is today. He pleaded for the opportunity to get ahead while the owner fought with his fear of the building inspectors. Two people were willing to enter into a contract where both would benefit but government regulations stood in the way. Somebody knew better what was best for both men.

Lincoln laughed when he heard pundits talk about the do-nothing Congress; denigrating it because it had passed fewer laws than its predecessors. His father had told him about, Jim Eason a talk show host in the eighties who had an afternoon show on KGO in San Francisco. Eason had urged his audience to vote *all* incumbents out and pay them according to how many days they were absent from DC. Obviously his listeners didn't get the job done,

Lincoln had concluded that winning for him was the opportunity to persuade on a platform where he would be listened to; not as a journalist, a commentator or an academic and certainly not because he was a sports celebrity. He wanted the chance to persuade voters as a candidate—to convince them, among other things, that fewer and concise laws would be a big step toward regaining freedom.

Now he was eager to represent himself as well as others and he was on fire.

The Snowbird Trip

Lisa had called Amanda immediately upon her return from what she called the snowbirds' trip. She was eager to tell Amanda the relationship between Janet and Bill was accelerating. Lisa credited the seating arrangements she had maneuvered so that Janet and Bill rode in the same car. There had been a lot of driving. Amanda chuckled to herself when she realized Lisa had driven the same distance with John Hoffer.

Amanda felt like a member of the audience in a Shakespeare play; able to see what was going on but unable to warn or reveal these secrets to anyone. She considered sharing the progress of the two proposed matches with Raeann. After all, Raeann had inadvertently benefitted from the seating arrangements since she had been separated from Paul. Instead, Amanda had sighed and prepared herself for Janet's report which was yet to come.

Because she didn't think it significant, Lisa had failed to mention that Janet and Raeann traded places when it came to grouping the skiers and non-skiers when they reached their destinations. She didn't know that when Bill and Raeann took off together on the expert slope one day, Paul's jealousy got the best of him. To keep him from getting seriously hurt they had to tell him that Raeann was only counseling Bill; helping him to realize that his own jealous feelings toward John Hoffer might be attributed to romantic feelings toward Janet.

※

Amanda entered the almost full room of Lincoln supporters and plopped down, tailor fashion, on one of the last empty chairs. "So how was Yosemite? Was there any snow?"

Paul, Bill, John, Raeann, Lisa, and Janet had taken advantage of the long vacation by piling themselves and equipment into two cars and gone searching for snow.

Raeann was the first to answer. "Despite the dry autumn we thought we'd surely find some snow at Tioga Pass; but we didn't. Instead we ended up at Badger Pass which had four feet of snow the day before we arrived."

"The runs were too tame for Bill," John Hoffer added.

"Bill, Paul and Raeann were the skiers in the group," Lisa was quick to explain. "Badger was not so great for them but there were a lot of other snow activities. We had a lot of fun although we didn't stay very long."

"That's too bad," Amanda said. "Where did you go?"

Paul took over. "After a day of snow activities we drove north to Tahoe and divided our time between Heavenly and Squaw Valley."

"Tell her why, Paul." Paul made a face at Bill before explaining..

"There were no overnight accommodations at Badger Pass. We had to drive quite a ways to sleep and get a good meal. That, and not enough snow, is why we decided to drive north to Tahoe the next day."

"And," Lisa took over, "there was terrific night life at Stateline with loads of great and inexpensive places to stay, see shows…"

"And gamble," Janet volunteered. "You've got to admit gambling was an attraction. And we didn't have to learn any hard lessons because nobody lost much. Paul and John even came away winners."

"That *was* fun," Lisa smiled.

"And in the daytime," Janet added, "While the others skied, John, Lisa and I tried ice skating, tobogganing, even snow boarding ..."

"Don't forget the snow ball fights," John laughed.

Raeann joined in the conversation. "Yosemite Valley, where we stayed before Tahoe, was absolutely beautiful. Heavenly Valley was gorgeous too, with its views of the lake from the top of the lifts although I'd say Squaw Valley had the best trails."

"She should know. Raeann's a connoisseur of ski runs. She challenged the toughest ones."

"That's some praise coming from Bill Adams, and I thank you." Janet noted the slight blush creeping over Raeann's face as she continued speaking. "But you and Paul had me beat on a couple of the steepest runs. I haven't skied much since we moved to California."

"Oh yeah. You have a *lot* of ski resorts in Texas," Amanda teased.

"She's right." Bill pursued that line of reasoning. "How did you learn to ski so well Raeann, living in Texas?"

"My dad was from Colorado and an avid skier. Our family belonged to a couple ski clubs that got good deals on group trips every year to resorts mostly in Idaho, Colorado and California. I spent time on the slopes of Heavenly and Squaw when I was very young. Most of my family are adamant skiers."

John turned to Amanda and asked, "Do you ski?" She shook her head and he persisted, "Have you been to Tahoe ?"

"Yosemite, sure—all the time, but never to Tahoe. I'll have to go some time. I've seen photos of the lake and of Squaw Valley and they're both beautiful, just as Raeann said."

"Now that you've heard all about our adventure," Lisa said, "Tell us what you did over the holidays Amanda?"

"Oh we got together with my aunt and her family a couple times and I had some good conversations with my parents. We went into San Francisco to see the Nut Cracker Suite, a family tradition, and I took Mario's extra week off to get in good with my boss."

"Oh no," Lisa exclaimed. "You worked! Don't let Mario hear that one. He expects you to be refreshed, as he put it."

"I am refreshed. I loved what I was doing and I get to continue with the project which in truth will give me more time for the campaign for a few months because I can set my own hours."

John Hoffer was curious. "What are you doing?"

"Research. Research on gangs." Before she could say more Mario entered.

"Sorry I'm late. Lincoln and Phyllis should be here any minute. Lincoln has come back full of energy and determination and with a more focused goal—just what we wanted."

Everyone gave a sigh of relief and the women freely admitted how badly they would have felt about all the work that might have been done for nothing if Lincoln had decided not to go ahead. They speculated about his probable choices—what else could he do—what would they do in his shoes?

When Phyllis and Lincoln finally entered a respectful hush fell over the room. As a group, they wanted to spring up and hug Lincoln and congratulate him for the decision they were about to hear.

Instead that sat quietly while Lincoln, never suspecting the group knew of his former doubts, laid out his goals for the next eleven months. He spoke from his heart. He intended to focus on promoting his top three priorities.

"First, getting to a smaller government will require a constitutional amendment. There are dangers inherent in such a proposition and I'm aware this pursuit could cost us the election.

"Second, to achieve our other goals California needs to be divided into three separate states. California's two United States

Senators represent constituents exceeding the entire population in twenty-two states. Those twenty-two states have forty-four votes in the Senate. We have only two.

"Third the only way to bring people into harmonious relationships again is to allow them to keep and control more of their assets. The one sure way I know to achieve this is to implement the *Another Way* project."

When Lincoln was finished the room exploded with pent up hugs. No one believed they had ever doubted the outcome of Lincoln's trial run. Even Mario was convinced he had never doubted there could be an outcome other than continuing the campaign. They may have been fooling themselves in that instance, but it *was true* that no one other than Phyllis knew how close they had all been to losing their candidate.

John Hoffer and Mario were the last to leave the room, though not intentionally.

"So how did your vacation go? You didn't go on the trip with the others," Mr. Hoffer began.

"No. It sounded like fun though. Maybe I should have."

"Didn't you have fun?"

"Oh, sure. I had a good time. I went home to visit with the family."

"That's good. Family is always good. How's your mother doing?"

"My mother never seems to age. I doubt that she's seen sick a day in her life. I think her granddaughters help to keep her young. She's crazy about those kids."

"If I remember, she lives in the same house with your brother and his family."

"Yeah, that's right. The kids love her and she gets along with Emily, Phillip's wife."

"You don't see that very often anymore—three generations in one home."

"You don't, do you? I guess parents don't want to impose and adult children want their privacy. I don't know how I or my wife will feel about that when—*if*—I get married, but I can sure see the benefits at Phillip's house. They have a built in baby sitter, cook and housekeeper and my mother is really surrounded by love."

"She's an important member of the family."

"Plus she gets out to the zoo, picnics, amusement parks; all activities most seniors would never think of doing on their own."

"And you don't have to worry or feel guilty when you don't have as much time as you'd like to visit. You know she's well taken care of. I'm glad it's working out for you."

"What do you mean, *working* out?"

"I'm glad you've forgotten. There was a time in high school when you were pretty down on your family. You thought you didn't belong. Remember?"

"No; well, maybe. I was just a kid—but I got over it."

"So it no longer bothers you that Phillip sold the restaurant and your mother went to live with him?:"

"The restaurant? I've got a story to tell you about that. But *my* mother wasn't Phillip's mother."

"I know; he's your half brother. You've got an important role in that family too. Besides brother and son you're an uncle."

"Phillip took over my role the moment he arrived. I. never had a clue he existed"

"Well, I guess you realize now that you and your mother were lucky to have him. You were too young to handle the affairs connected with your father' s death and the publicity. You and your mother were both too shaken by your unexpected loss."

"I guess you're right. I'm not sure what we would have done if Phillip hadn't shown up. I guess mom would still be cooking and I wouldn't have gone to college. Hey; it's getting late. You and I've got to get going."

"Just a minute. What about the story you were going to tell me about the restaurant?"

"Oh yeah. It'll be quick. Do you happen to recall how that first day in Mapleton when I ragged on about franchise restaurants? I was saying how my dad was offered a China World franchise and turned it down because he wanted more flexibility. Well, Phillip traded our old restaurant for China World stock. Since then China World has expanded into several countries and it's gone up in price faster and farther than any stock in the family portfolio. I just thought it was a little ironic."

"Well I'll be. You never know."

Matchmaking Continues

The first week back everyone was so busy catching up at their respective jobs that nobody met for lunch. Amanda was dying of curiosity and finally called Janet and was told that Lisa would be at a conference all day but Janet would manage to slip out for a short lunch.

"Well how did it go?" Amanda demanded as Janet slid into her seat.

"I think we have a real romance going," Janet replied with a grin. "Raeann and Bill skied together the entire trip and I think they are crazy about one another. You know how Paul would do anything for Raeann—well get this—he traded seats with her to let her be with Bill."

An alarm went off in Amanda's head although she didn't quite know what it meant. The women figured they could only keep Paul from riding with Raeann by assigning seats. Something didn't feel right.

"I tried to stay in the back seat as much as I could on the pretense of wanting to stretch out and sleep; which I actually did sometimes. You know they are both excellent skiers and were together the whole time. Even Paul wasn't up to some of the expert runs so sometimes it was just the two of them for hours alone. Bill loved driving and drove all the time—which was fine with me. You know how I feel about driving after living in New York City so long. I'm really not used to it—Easterners don't love their cars the way people in the west do. And Raeann was okay with driving but certainly didn't mind giving it up."

"Probably because of the accident that killed her dad."

Janet was taken back. "How did you know about that?"

"She told me one time. I can't remember when; it just came up somehow. Anyway go on."

"Well they talked—sometimes deep conversations and they laughed a lot just kidding around."

"When you were supposed to be sleeping? That wasn't very considerate."

"Oh c'mon. They're one of the most considerate couples around. The laughing was usually when I was in the front seat too, otherwise it was very hushed." Amanda thought she noted a bit of sadness in Janet as she added, "They were perfect together."

"Well, that was a set back," is what Amanda thought, but what she actually said was "How about your mission? The Lisa-John romance. How'd *that* go?"

"Nothing seems to be cooking although I think Lisa is warming up to John. You know I was with them while Paul, Raeann and Bill were skiing. Every time I tried to get away to leave them alone, John almost panicked and I relented. I think the idea that he was her teacher is holding him back somehow. I can't figure it and I don't think Lisa has admitted to herself yet that she's sweet on him."

Amanda barely stopped herself from saying aloud the words that immediately rose to her lips, "And neither have you when it comes to Bill."

Janet was good at almost everything but she was no yenta and Lisa's report was fantasy. After Janet hurried away Amanda sat thoughtfully with a second cup of coffee. She took consolation in remembering that matchmaking didn't go smoothly in *Fiddler on the Roof* either. It worked in that story because the lovers *knew* they were in love. What do you do when everyone but the lovers see it? I wonder if I'm in love with anybody and don't realize it. She got up slowly and went back to work.

Ironically, neither Janet nor Amanda knew that when Bill was alone with Raeann she was helping him get in touch with the seat of his jealousy. Before they returned to Bloomfield Bill was ready to admit he was in love with Janet. Once convinced that was true Bill wanted to do something about it immediately. Raeann had cautioned him to let the relationship develop slowly. On the other hand, Raeann knew nothing about the plans hatched by Lisa and Amanda.

⁂

Amanda had told Lisa what Janet assumed about Raeann and Bill and asked Lisa for her observation of what had occurred on the ski trip. Lisa had confirmed the driving and ski arrangements and did recall Raeann and Bill sitting together a lot at meals; but then Janet was usually on the other side of Bill. It didn't seem planned. The six of them were all together laughing and just joking around and having a good time. As far as she could recall nobody coupled up. Of course she had been focusing on getting Janet and Bill together. The fact that Janet didn't ski didn't help matters. Lisa kept suggesting that Bill give Janet some lessons but Janet showed absolutely no interest.

Amanda and Lisa had been too busy to check out what they hoped was only a rumor about Bill and Raeann. It had been over a month and Amanda could wait no longer. It took a couple weeks but she managed to get Lisa and Raeann to meet with her in the back of Margie's. They didn't think Janet had been there since the day she arrived. It hadn't been her high school haunt so she had no inclination to go back. The three women felt safe there.

After hugs, greetings and exchange of news Amanda launched the conversation.

"I'll get right to the point. I don't know if this is a rumor that has reached you, but Janet came back from the ski trip believing there is a romance brewing between you and Bill Adams. Of course it should be none of our business and we apologize at the start for bringing it up but we thought our reason was good enough."

Raeann was usually so obliging and friendly that they were taken back by the sudden change in her appearance. Lisa didn't want Amanda to be the lone recipient of Raeann's wrath, if that was about to happen, so she took up the mission.

"We certainly don't want to pry—just either confirm or deny the rumor because..." she paused. "We believe Janet has a crush on Bill and won't admit it."

Instead of an angry explosion, the women were greeted by uncontrolled laughter as Raeann released her pent up anxiety. She realized in a moment that not only did she not have to keep this secret to herself, but she now had co-conspirators working for the some cause; a cause that now promised to end with a swift happy solution. The women, all now in good humor, made plans without caution, never suspecting that their laughter and the rising volume of their voices had attracted the attention of Mario who was working in his favorite booth at the other end of the restaurant.

When Mario overheard the women plotting at Margie's he had first been concerned. He had convinced himself that Bill loved Dorothy because Bill used to date her and always had such admirable things to say about Dorothy whenever her name came up. Hadn't Bill been looking for her for years? At first he considered approaching the players; but which ones? The conspirators? How could he stop them without proof? The fact that no one could find Dorothy didn't help his case. Mario tried several times but just couldn't bring himself to ask Bill directly. On the other hand, Janet might be right; maybe Bill does favor

Raeann; after all they both love skiing. Raeann might be the one in denial rather than Janet.

Mario wanted to protect Janet from disappointment but what if he was barking up the wrong tree? What if there was no tree. He had to make sure his concern didn't mean he was attracted to Janet himself. After some self-analysis Mario was able to answer in the negative. Although he liked and admired her, there was no romantic incentive. In the end, the best Mario could do with his knowledge was to work against the conspirators.

Over the last few months Mario had asked Janet to meet with him or John Hoffer whenever he got wind of a plot to get Janet together with Bill. After three such occasions, Bill became showing signs of depression. Bill was sure Janet was purposely avoiding him and that he had no chance to win her over. Raeann tried to lift Bill's spirits which only increased Mario's suspicions that Raeann, not Dorothy, was the attraction for Bill. Finally, with Janet's well being foremost, Mario asked Raeann to meet him for lunch. Like Amanda, once Raeann sat down his plan was to plunge right in. Instead he made small talk. The meal was coming to an end and Mario kept repeating to himself, *It's now or never, It's now or never.*

"Mario, I have a request and a confidence to share with you. You may have noticed that Bill hasn't been himself lately." Mario told himself she was giving him the opening he needed. He opened his mouth to interrupt but nothing came out. Raeann didn't seem to notice and went right on.

"Bill is madly in love with Janet and he thinks she doesn't care for him because she keeps breaking their appointments to be with you. I presume it's business, but if I can get you to let up a bit on her, at least until Bill can be convinced those missed appointment don't mean she is trying to avoid him—"

This time Mario didn't let Raeann get to the end of her sentence. With great relief he blurted, "I thought Bill was in love with *you.*"

"Why didn't you ask me sooner?"

"Embarrassment. I sure wish I had mustered the courage earlier."

"Well, it wasn't until last week that Janet acknowledged it. Janet told me she finally realized she had loved Bill from the first day she met him at the Mapleton meeting in 1996. Somehow she found out about the tragedy he had just gone through with the murder of his parents. She thinks she was the only one who knew about it. I guess it kinda melted her heart at the time. You know what's weird? She hadn't thought of it until recently. I think it's a memory of the heart. Heart memory. Funny how things work out. Isn't life absolutely awesome?"

Once Bill got the facts straight and saw that most of his friends, whose judgment he trusted, were convinced that Janet was also in love with him, he literally swept her off her feet. They eloped; but not before Bill, at Janet's urging, had a talk with John Hoffer concerning Lisa. Unfortunately, those who suspected John was hung up on being Lisa's teacher were correct. It was going to take some time.

By now Lisa realized she was in love with John Hoffer. The other women tried, but were not successful in their attempts to encourage John. All they could do after that was console Lisa.

On the other hand, once Janet began to realize she loved Bill and had taken them into her confidence the women secretly began planning a wedding. The planning took place in their heads only because the campaign was in full swing and they were sure Bill and Janet would wait until the election was over.

Bill had chosen a weekend to elope. The newlyweds agreed they would have an extended honeymoon after the election, and who knows—maybe a proper wedding then too. None of the Thirteen were aware the elopement had taken place; not even John Hoffer.

Campaign Update

Lincoln had been on the campaign trial for several months, often on his own. He was now a voter-nominated candidate for a seat in the U.S. House of Representatives. Mario tried to get away to critique Lincoln's performance at least once a week, but he was needed in the office now more than ever. Luckily Mario accepted the free services of a professional video producer who traveled with Lincoln and taped all presentations. When he couldn't go, he sent an assistant in his place.

The Thirteen were doing a good job attracting donations of money, services and time. The new volunteers were recruiting even more supporters and the office was bustling. Mario had identified several good administrators among the new volunteers and had disbursed those who weren't needed at the Bloomfield office to other areas in the wake of Lincoln's campaign. Some volunteers were sent ahead of the campaign to find and set up the location for the presentation and drum up enthusiasm before Lincoln arrived.

In April, Kirk Jamison and Arthur Harris had defeated their challengers for the nomination and were now officially the nominees of the Democrat and Republican parties respectively. But due to Proposition 14, like Lincoln Williams, no party affiliation would appear after their names on the official ballot.

Lincoln hadn't been able to get either Arthur or Kirk to support the need for a constitutional amendment so he had to argue that issue on his own against two opponents. However he had come close to convincing Arthur of the need to divide California into at least three states. Although he couldn't count on Arthur as an ally, he only had Kirk arguing against him on this second issue. As for his third focus; keeping more tax dollars close to home—closer to the taxpayer—both Kirk and Arthur were firm in their belief that because of the economy and huge federal debt DC needed those dollars more than ever.

Lincoln tried explaining how the enactment of Another Way in local communities would relieve the federal government of its largest expense. Besides relieving DC of providing safety nets, incentives/disincentives and opportunities having these things provided by a central government two thousand miles away not only made the taxpayers dependent but deprived them of the resources to take care of themselves, their families and neighbors.

Lincoln often used the United States Constitution as his reference. In those debates Kirk would answer questions regarding the scope of the federal government with either Article I Section 8 Clauses 1 or 18; the *general welfare clause* or the *necessary and proper clause* also referred to as the *elastic clause*.

Despite what Lincoln's opponents referred to as his *radical ideas*, all three candidates were holding their own. It was still too early for the pollsters to hold court. They were busy forecasting the presidential nominees. But when the polls began Lincoln's supporters were sure he would be in the lead. Enthusiasm was high.

The summer was coming to an end. Polls had been showing Kirk pulling ahead of his two opponents. Lincoln and Arthur agreed to what both sensed would be one of the most important meetings in their life. They chose to meet at the Ahwhanee Hotel only a couple hours drive. There were big things to discuss and there was nothing as grand and inspirational as the view looking up from Yosemite Valley.

"Be realistic, Lincoln; the handwriting is on the wall—or in this case," Arthur smiled as he tilted his head upwards, "on the cliffs. If we both continue as candidates we'll split the non-Kirk vote and Kirk will win even though he is running in one of the few conservative districts in California. He's got the Democrat's war chest behind him. Just look at the number of ads he has running already."

"And you've got access to the Republican war chest. What do you want from me?"

"Isn't it obvious? One of us has to step down or agree to let a Democrat represent this district. Do you want that?"

"Of course not; but why me? I've been polling ahead of you pretty consistently; not by much I admit, but why must I step aside?"

"Look at it objectively. I know it's hard, but you've got to be practical. I admire the amount of money and supporters you've been able to attract but you don't have the dough to purchase the number of ads you would need to counter Kirk's attacks the month before the election"

"Is this coming from you or are you a messenger for the Republican Party?"

"The Party has authorized me to negotiate a deal with you. A deal that I believe I have tweaked so that we both benefit and by that I mean the county benefits. I know you're not in politics because you want fame, fortune or even power and I also know that's rare. I should know; I've been in this business far longer than you. I honestly care about this country and the Americans that want to live in a land of freedom and opportunity. But, although I don't expect you to believe we're alike, I do hope you'll trust me. There's only you and me here—I'm not grandstanding. We agree on the big issues and even a lot of the smaller ones.

"While trying to convince the Party that I needed to offer you my support for both the constitutional amendment and the division of California, I actually convinced myself." He grinned. "I'm not a bad salesman, if I do say so."

Arthur sat there expectantly with an ever so slight smile on his lips. It was clear he thought he had conveyed good, not bad news.

Lincoln was stunned. So many thoughts flashed through his mind all at once. He could never get a constitutional amendment and the division of California through Congress as an independent—he knew that—but he had hoped to awaken other powerful people who could. He could relate to Arthur calling himself a salesman—after all, isn't that what he saw as his own role? Wasn't it Bill's role—selling Another Way? Wasn't everyone a salesman, selling themselves and their ideas?

With the establishment of the Republican Party behind a constitutional amendment and dividing the state it had a great chance of happening. A part of him was exhilarated beyond belief but there was another part. How would he know if they would keep their promises? No; he didn't trust the Party. What about Arthur? Could he trust Arthur? Maybe Arthur was making this proposal up and the Party knew nothing about it. Just because Arthur insists he's not after power and fame can I be sure he isn't out for himself?

What about the Thirteen? How would they feel if he dropped out. They were counting on him. Look at all the work and enthusiasm they had put into the campaign. How could he let them down. He just couldn't do it. It would be a betrayal of their faith in him. What he said was:

"Could you give me some time to let this sink in? I acknowledge neither of us are attorneys but I know you wouldn't take the Party at its word without getting something in writing and some more arguments to convince me. If you give me time to look over these commitments and assurances it will make a discussion later in the day more fruitful."

Arthur was surprised at the poise and control this young man showed. He was as proud of Lincoln as if he were a family member. Lincoln Williams exhibited a confident elegance. He was practical, thoughtful and inspirational; a rarity in the same man. Arthur believed Lincoln had what it takes to be a leader but wondered if he would follow through. He had seen many with potential that couldn't handle it well. He reached into the brief case at his side and handed a manila folder to Lincoln.

Lincoln tried to duplicate the times at the Ahwahnee Hotel when he had sat in front of the magnificent huge fireplace in the Great Hall and thought great thoughts. The last time it had been winter, but after the holiday crowds; only two or three people had sat peacefully reading in their separate spaces. Today it was the end of summer and kids were running around; a large group was talking and joking, their focused merriment causing their voices to rise to a pitch they would not normally allow.

Another time Lincoln would have enjoyed their laughter, but today he needed solitude and inspiration. Reluctantly, but not begrudgingly, he gave up his space and settled outside on a secluded rock where he could view Half Dome in the distance. The granite cliffs eight thousand feet above were what he needed to firm up his decisions before his next meeting with Arthur.

He had found nothing legally binding among the documents; just promises of support and some arguments and advice. He hadn't expected more. The kind words from others high up in the Party who agreed with him, or had been working for the constitutional amendment and fairer representation in the Senate longer than he had, was a welcome surprise.

There was really nothing to decide when it came right down to it. Kirk was sure to win if Lincoln didn't drop out. There was no question but Arthur's resources gave him the better chance against Kirk. Of course the Thirteen would be terribly disappointed but would see the practicality of it. He could convince them that they were the ones that constructed and marketed the torch that Arthur would carry. He would assure the members of the Thirteen that they could rejoice in Arthur's victory, which seemed the certain outcome of combining the vote. Nevertheless, Lincoln felt sad looking up at the mountains. He was used to winning—no that wasn't it—used to *trying* to win—giving up provoked the sad feeling. He wasn't a quitter. It was good to understand it for what it was. But if he wasn't a quitter neither were the Thirteen. Nevertheless, he had to drop out of the race to win. By understanding the sadness for what it was he could be happy returning to promoting Another Way. The politicians would need such a program if they were going to argue for less taxes and retiring social programs. After all, Another Way allows the money and personal problems to remain at the local level where people can better control graft, waste and identify who needs what better than a huge well meaning bureaucracy far removed from the personal problems. Another Way would let Americans keep more of what is theirs while addressing their unique local problems.

The Thirteen Receive the News

Lincoln briefed Mario when he got back from Yosemite. He asked Mario to call a meeting of the Thirteen but to make sure it was set for a time everyone could attend. After hearing what Lincoln had to say and what he was planning to say to the Thirteen, Mario suggested he spend a few minutes preparing Lincoln's audience. Lincoln understood and agreed to arrive fifteen minutes late.

Mario took pains to break the news to the group as gently as he could. Still it was a shock to most of them. Paul and Amanda seemed bitter, although they didn't say much. Janet and Bill exchanged looks that were hard to interpret. Lincoln was due any minute.

"Well, I guess Mario brought you up to speed," Lincoln began as he took a seat next to Mario at the large desk facing the group. "I want to thank you for all the time and effort you put into my candidacy and assure you it wasn't in vain. This was only our first step at fighting for the kind of country we want to live in. We could have stuck it out, but unless something unforeseen was to occur it's almost guaranteed that with Arthur and I splitting the conservative vote, Kirk would win the election. The polls show our combined votes—Arthur's and mine—are much larger than Kirk's so this way Arthur will be the probable winner."

Paul broke in. "But who wants Arthur as a representative? And how do you know Kirk *won't* win?"

"You would have beat Arthur and Kirk," Raeann said. "We were just getting started."

"And something unforeseen might have happened besides. Why did we just give up?" Lisa couldn't understand why this was happening. "There are three months before the election and Paul and Raeann had all kinds of rallies planned and promotional material ready to go."

"Arthur Harris is known as a moderate. That is something we don't want or need to represent us again. Are you sure about quitting?" Lincoln winced as Mr. Hoffer emphasized quitting, or so it seemed to Lincoln.

Mario stepped in. "It's not a matter of quitting. You of all people know Lincoln is no quitter. You've worked with him on campus and know his spirit. He's being practical—facing reality." Then, turning to Lincoln he continued. "You can explain it better than I can, Lincoln. Go ahead."

"I'll give you the choices and let you decide. Do you want me to compromise my ideals?"

"That's a stupid question." This was voiced by someone, but since it expressed the collective thought in the room, nobody noted or cared who spoke.

"Why would you have to do that?"

"Because my ideas aren't as popular with the voters in this district as Kirk's are."

To Mario's surprise, he countered Lincoln with, "You've been polling about even—all three candidates. Arthur may be working on you with this fear of splitting the conservative vote. You might just beat them both of you stayed in. It's close now and we think we can help you pull ahead."

"Of course you can. Everything you do will push me ahead, but the reality is there are two wealthy national Parties behind the other two candidates and no matter how hard we work we are not going to be able to do what it takes to squeak by in a tight race. A tight race is what it becomes if there are three candidates. Those are the facts."

"Okay. Let's get back on track." Janet took charge. "You asked if we want you to compromise your ideals and the answer would be a unanimous NO. But even if you did, the facts, as you stated them, remain the same. You can't compete with one or two national Parties. If that's reality why didn't we face it six months ago?"

Mario spared Lincoln. "We believed in our platform and still do. We thought if we put it out there we could convince enough voters that it was superior to the status quo and it wouldn't be a tight race. If anyone could inspire them it was Lincoln. The reality that I see is the voters aren't ready—we have to keep campaigning. All of us have to start selling these ideas. It's too big a job for one person. We won't win until we convince enough people that we have a workable plan to bring government closer to the people and keep most of our tax dollars here where we can spend them more wisely on what our community decides it needs."

"Mario may be right. In the meantime," Phyllis said. "We have to decide if Lincoln's winning is worth the risk of giving the election to the Democrats when this is a district that has historically leaned toward the Republicans. As usual, we are being asked to choose the lesser of two evils." This was the first the group had heard from Phyllis in a long time.

Lincoln turned to Mario. "Did you tell them about Arthur's compromise?"

"No. I was leaving that for you."

Lincoln told them about the meetings in Yosemite and his analysis of Arthur's offer. "This is not the election that will get us all that we have been working for; but if the Republicans are willing to support a constitutional amendment and more representation for California in the United States Senate then the next election may be the one. I say we compromise with the

Republicans by helping them win this election. If we stay the course, with the help of Arthur and his friends we may have our own state and a chance to be heard on the national stage."

"But how can you trust the Republicans to keep their promises? You told us there were no guarantees; nothing in writing," Paul cautioned.

"A chance is far better than the alternative. Why must we doubt everyone one and everything these day? What have we been saying? Something about what you do depends on whether you think people are basically good or basically evil? I say take Arthur and his Party at its word and keep advocating our agenda. We don't need an election to spread the word."

This time Phyllis took charge. "Let's take a vote. By secret ballot or a show of hands?

How many prefer the ballot?" No hands were raised. "Okay, it's a show of hands. How many want Lincoln to resign and take Arthur at his word?" Everyone raised their hands. Phyllis announced, "It's unanimous. Lincoln resigns. Does anyone disagree?"

There was some muttering to signify some yes votes were cast reluctantly, but again, no hands went up. Lincoln said with the first grin of the night, "Thanks for saying resigns rather than quitting. As long as we're voting, I'd like to know what you think on a few other matters. Hands okay again?" There were a few audible assents and others nodded their heads.

"First: Should I, as a candidate, endorse Arthur?"

Only a few hands went up Phyllis suggested they should hear all the questions first in case some required discussion. Lincoln obliged.

"Second: Should the Thirteen throw their support to Arthur?"
"Third: Should the group disband?"

Amanda voiced what everyone was thinking. "The first two are unthinkable choices. We don't want to support Arthur or want you to endorse him, so we can dispense with discussing the downside. Let's hear the benefits. Without benefits you wouldn't be considering either action anymore than we would."

"Go Amanda!" That came from Paul who couldn't keep his feelings bottled up much longer.

"All right. Since we've decided to bet the Republicans will keep their end of the bargain, if we're in for a dime we might as well be in for a dollar. It's in our interest to make the Republicans want to keep their promises. That covers the first two. As for the last one, I guess it's a bit of nostalgia on my part as I'd miss you guys, and if we do get a new state it may be during the next session of Congress, so we may need to do this all over again for the 2014 election."

"I buy it and am ready to vote," Paul announced.

Mario took over. "How 'bout the rest of you? Is everybody ready to vote or do we need more discussion?"

They looked at one another and seeing no enthusiasm for debate Raeann said, "If Paul is satisfied then it's likely everyone else is too. I say let's have a show of hands."

"Any other ideas?" Mario looked around the room. "Any objections? Then let's take the issues one at a time." Mario read them off and all hands went up on the first two and no hands were raised for the third. "Okay. That means we need to decide how we want to continue the Thirteen, so be thinking about that. A social club, a political forum, speakers circle, marketing group—some combination maybe? Since I've been calling the meetings I'll get in touch with you all for the next one where we can formalize ideas."

Lincoln's Speech

The Thirteen met a week later. It took that long for everyone to adjust their schedules to an exact date. In the past they had come together with a day's notice. Phyllis had confirmation that her analysis of the situation was correct. If the battle for the kind of future these young people wanted for themselves and their children was to continue, there had to be a sense of urgency, purpose and excitement. They had proven they had the energy and commitment. She felt confident that she had given the right advice to Lincoln when she encouraged him to prepare the best speech of his life and deliver it to his team tonight.

When everyone had exchanged greetings and all were comfortably seated, Lincoln stood and began speaking:

"I think it's fair to say that everyone in this room understands that people are going to do what they want to do no matter how many obstacles are placed in their path. Sure, there are laws and restrictions against using drugs and driving fast, but it's obvious they don't stop behavior; they only punish it.

"You're the only parent in the room, Phyllis, so correct me if I'm wrong, but I'd say excessive regulation makes for a poor parent-child relationship." Phyllis nodded. "I assume excessive regulation would have the same affect on government-citizen relationships. Incentives for this and taxes and fees for that are, in effect, an effort to control citizens." Again Phyllis nodded, and Lincoln turned to the others and continued.

"Americans may be over-regulated but they're not stupid. There were fifty warnings displayed in one public bathroom. Honestly, would people be so stupid as to drink paint, undercook chicken and use electric hair dryers while sleeping? Would manufacturers really put less than ten ounces in a cereal box marked ten ounces if there were no government controls? Would neighbors have such little concern for one another that they would build imposing offensive structures if there weren't zoning laws? Would people act dishonestly, selfishly, irresponsibly if Big Brother weren't there?" Lincoln noted some skepticism from a couple of his friends in the audience.

"Okay. Some people no doubt would—but a minority. And that's what our courts are for—to redress the occasional wrongs rather than oppress the entire population with excessive regulation in order to keep the few in check. We've got to remind ourselves that we're not the only ones today that believe there is too much regulation. In order to discourage a police state, parents and mentors need to emphasize character.

"I think we're missing that special feeling that comes from people working together toward a common mission. They sure had that during the Second World War when everyone was asked to pitch in and do his or her part. That spirit was missing in our recent undeclared wars. The elitist attitude is entrenched; *let us take care of you* has been instilled in the psyche of too many Americans. The Tea Party may be the Rescue Party.

"You and I weren't much of a force in the twentieth century and weren't around in the nineteenth century—even Phyllis," he added with a wink and a grin. "But I've read enough to know in the past Americans were a more open and honest people; not so adept at pretending. Integrity was reinforced in churches, schools, homes and even in business.

"I don't know if I could ever run for political office representing one of the two major parties. I'm probably most like a Libertarian. I suspect most of you are too; at least in spirit. Our Constitution gives us the right to pursue our own version of happiness and to live in liberty. Are there more beautiful words than *liberty* and *freedom*?" Lincoln paused for the clapping and hoots that ensued.

"More and more people understand that morality is not achieved by forcing people to be responsible. In fact they are beginning to see that *forcing* robs an individual of the opportunity to be moral.

"I really think most Americans understand that many people are not responsible for their own misfortunes. Nevertheless, it's a mistake to excuse irresponsibility and to force those who have managed to overcome the same temptations, to support those who have succumbed. Many Americans don't care whether a person is in distress because of his own weakness and lack of effort or because of circumstances which would have been beyond anyone's control. The mere fact that a need exists, is reason enough for these Americans to take action. It used to be that citizens in America, in larger percentages than anywhere else in the world, helped their neighbors. The expansion of the federal government—government on *all* levels—has robbed us of time and money that rightfully belonged to family members and neighbors so that *they*, not a distant government, had the ability to care for one another.

"I honestly believe this unprecedented generosity was meant to be part and parcel of our political system. I'd sure appreciate it if each of you would let me know over the next few weeks if you share this belief or if it's my own personal idea. I need to know from those who do share it, just how pervasive you think it might be." Lincoln noticed that a few of his friends hunched their shoulders as their eyes met as if to say *What is this guy talking about?* This encouraged Lincoln to stand straighter. It renewed his resolve.

"For me, the American ideal ignites, not in oxygen but in a peculiar brand of freedom; a freedom that entails risk. From the start the American political system anticipated citizens living with uncertainty. The political structure was planned, but not the economy. Because no security was offered in exchange for regulation, ordinary Americans often found themselves living on the brink of disaster. This bred empathy for one's fellows; an empathy unparalleled in the history of mankind. But that was before the emergence of the now co-existent welfare state and its 'goodwill by mandate'. Originally goodwill was not mandated; it was the natural outpouring of sympathy by those who had themselves lived with insecurity and could appreciate life's normal peaks and valleys.

"You know as well as I do that leaders have given in over the years to the temptation to buy votes with promises of security. Some of you have heard my favorite de Tocqueville quote; 'A government that provides total security for its people, foresees and supplies their necessities, manages their principal concerns, directs their industry, regulates the descent of property and subdivides their inheritance—what remains but to spare them all the care of thinking, and all the trouble of living.'

"We've got to do a better job of explaining the effects of government programs. Government programs require government spending and more government spending means more taxes and two-earner families. Government spending throws supply and demand out of whack; the overhead goes up and the effective use of human energy goes down and so does the nation's standard of living. The important role of homemaker was diminished as women assumed several roles at a time instead of having a series of careers one at a time.

"I'm not sure that the majority of Americans understand that people cannot be supported by the government; government must derive its support from the people. Socialist countries have proven this beyond a shadow of a doubt. The swing away from socialism and toward capitalism that took place after the Cold War in Western and Eastern Europe and throughout the old Soviet empire, attests to the inferiority of state-run institutions.

"Wouldn't you think if more Americans understood this, the United States wouldn't keep expanding the role of government? Why have they elected legislators that have made government a provider of housing, health-care, child-care, education and retirement security?

"I've come to agree with those who believe that the educational system in the twentieth century indoctrinated Americans so that many subconsciously became dependent on government. I don't know the percentage, but I hear a large number of callers to C-span's *Washington Journal* claim every morning that government's role is to take care of the people. They accuse large corporations and wealthy individuals of stealing power from them. They believe they have no input—no power to make a difference—even in their own lives. They see themselves slipping back and begin to imagine that others are getting their share of everything. That percentage is what we're up against. Once we know the extent of the indoctrination, we will know how large a job it will be to educate these people. They need to understand the odds against government supplying all their needs, let alone wants, so they came make informed choices.

"Socialists could not make socialism work and neither can Capitalists. No central planners—not even members of our own Congress and all the commissions they can muster—can anticipate the reactions of more than three hundred million individuals to changes in the economy and the environment.

"Americans sense they've lost something; but most can't put a name to it. I've come to the conclusion that what we are missing is something that has taken mankind thousands of years to attain; the idea that man is self-controlling and capable of influencing his own existence; the idea that his acts have consequences; the idea that what he does matters; the idea that he has control over his own destiny. I believe this idea marks the highest evolution of mankind.

"People from other nations came to this country because of this idea; this idea that later generations of Americans neglected. Over the years descendants of the framers of our Constitution, as well as the descendents of freedom-seeking emigrants, failed to recognize its worth. Those of us who do recognize it, who care, should not let it go without a fight. Together we can inform and persuade others to fight with us. If we succeed in doing just that, then I think we have a chance of winning.

"I believe everyone in this room agrees that government is trying to do things that should be left to the people. I'm not so sure about the rest of the voting public on this score. However, I did make a list of the things that *I* believe are frustrating the majority of Americans."

Janet and Mario had been taking notes all along and a couple others got out a pad and pen in anticipation of the list. Lincoln paused and took a sip from the glass of water on the desk behind him. He was regretting the length of the speech, especially since he knew better. He was running out of steam just ahead of the climax. He put the glass down and continued, consciously modulating his tone to covey energy and conviction.

"Most Americans are paying more now and getting far less; the harder they work the more their bills pile up; the more tolerant they become, the more violent society becomes; the more jails they build, the more prisoners fill them; the more they pump money into social programs, the more the needs increase; the more they spend on health care, the faster costs rise; the more dollars flow to education, the less educated the children; the more birth control information, the more unwed mothers; the easier they make divorce; the fewer lasting marriages.

"Americans now pay and pay to have social ills taken care of. Unfortunately this allows them to put the less fortunate out of their minds. This often kills the sense of brotherly love they might otherwise feel toward troubled neighbors. They pay and pay and instead of merely being denied the warmth and satisfaction of interacting with the people they intend to help, they see many social institutions they paid for crumbling. So what to do about it?"

"Make a list." Someone suggested this playfully under his/her breath. Lincoln could have been offended, but instead he chuckled.

"You're right; I'm a list maker," he admitted, while unfolding a small piece of paper. "I just happen to have one in my pocket. I hadn't planned to share it with you, but I will. By popular demand! I guess you *might* call it a list," and he began reading.

"I believe the wrong questions are being asked in Washington.

Not how should this be done; but should government do it?

Not larger or smaller government; but is there a different way to govern?

Not how much; but what kind of power should we wield around the world?

Not how to provide cradle to the grave security; but how to boost personal and national potential?

Not how to redistribute the economic pie; but how to increase it?

Not how to make sure results are equal; but how to provide opportunity?

Not government care; but how to encourage citizens to care for themselves and each other?

Not how to use self-sacrifice; but how to use self-control?

"I want more than anything to have you join with me in explaining to our disgruntled, but well intentioned fellow citizens, that they unwittingly exchanged their own power for dependence on government. I want us to show them how they can regain the power that the Constitution guaranteed them as citizens. Don't blame them; simply explain that it is not easy to be an American and that dependency has been the norm since the beginning of mankind.

"I don't know if you guys have really thought about it. Probably those who've gone through Phyllis's classes have; it was unavoidable. But I've done a lot more thinking on the subject since high school. I didn't discover anything really new; I just looked at the old in a new light. I mean it's not news that unlike most animals, humans are extremely helpless in the beginning—dependent for years on others for warmth, food and shelter. New infants are even powerless to turn over without help. They soon realize their nourishment, comfort and happiness come from an all powerful being outside themselves.

"I know some of you studied Joseph Campbell's *Power of Myth*. Remember how our ancestors tried to appease and attract outside control by sacrificing their healthiest infants, their fairest young maidens and their strongest young men for the good of the tribe?" Heads nodded. "For thousands of years men were controlled thus by witch doctors, parades of gods and goddesses and numerous kinds of all-powerful rulers. They were dependent and manipulated through fear and superstition.

"Without awareness of how unique and how precious the idea of responsibility and self-determination really is and without conscious effort to keep it via proper education, it's natural that many Americans have come to see powers outside themselves as their only means to attain security and protection.

"I said it once, and I'll say it again. It's not easy to be an American. The hold of the tribe is still strong. Of course there is a matter of degree, but can't you recognize the same philosophy at work when a family was asked to sacrifice their infant on a burning pyre to placate Molach so that the village would have a good harvest and the many restrictions and demands that are made today on American citizens for the good of the whole?

"I know you well enough to believe you agree with most of what I just said. Many of you are better writers and speakers than I am. I can't do it alone. I need your help. My celebrity opened the doors for our ideas to be heard and now Arthur's candidacy will do the same. Some of you can provide the web sites and marketing material we need to obtain gigs and persuade voters that it is better to be a free and determined risk taker than a slave to an illusive security. Your neighbors, rather than hired bureaucrats thousands of miles away, will have your back. I want all of you to join me in persuading. We can use Arthur's candidacy to advance what we believe in. I believe Arthur, and most people, want to believe in these things too. We have a plan to make it work. Mapleton and Bloomfield are only a start."

e|LIVE

listen|imagine|view|experience

AUDIO BOOK DOWNLOAD INCLUDED WITH THIS BOOK!

In your hands you hold a complete digital entertainment package. In addition to the paper version, you receive a free download of the audio version of this book. Simply use the code listed below when visiting our website. Once downloaded to your computer, you can listen to the book through your computer's speakers, burn it to an audio CD or save the file to your portable music device (such as Apple's popular iPod) and listen on the go!

How to get your free audio book digital download:

1. Visit www.tatepublishing.com and click on the e|LIVE logo on the home page.
2. Enter the following coupon code:
   c445-5cd8-69e9-58f8-9c01-254e-ce49-f3b0
3. Download the audio book from your e|LIVE digital locker and begin enjoying your new digital entertainment package today!